NOW YOU SEE HER

NOW YOU SEE HER

LISA LEIGHTON & LAURA STROPKI

KATHERINE TEGEN BOOKS
An Imprint of HarperCollins Publishers

Katherine Tegen Books is an imprint of HarperCollins Publishers.

Now You See Her
Copyright © 2018 by Lisa Leighton and Laura Stropki
All rights reserved. Printed in the United States of America.

Library of Congress Control Number: 2017954133
ISBN 978-0-06-242863-9

18 19 20 21 22 PC/LSCH 10 9 8 7 6 5 4 3 2 1
❖
First Edition

To all the girls reading by night-light . . .
Just one more chapter.

NOW YOU SEE HER

one

ALL EYES ARE ON OUR COURT NOW. IT'S LIKE SOMEONE'S PRESSED the mute button. Teammates stop talking. Phones are silenced. Random dog walkers linger and little brothers stop banging on the bleachers. Sophie Graham bobs in ready position behind the baseline on the opposite side of the net, spinning her racquet between graceful fingers, waiting for the serve that could finally end this game.

She looks good out there. Always does. Crisp tennis whites in stark contrast to the black braid swinging slightly as she rocks. She's hard not to watch. If I hadn't beaten a million other Sophies over the years, I might feel intimidated in my crappy tennis shoes and secondhand skirt.

I bounce the ball twice.

All the random pickup games on public courts, all the

thousands of forehands and backhands hit off dented garage doors in tiny town after tiny town, all the broken strings on shitty racquets—they've all led me to this moment, on this court, against this girl, with this serve.

Bounce, bounce, toss, swing, hit. The ball catches the line and Sophie drives it back with equal force. A perfect return. I only manage to clip the ball with the head of my racquet. Ad out.

I wish I didn't care. I shouldn't care because it doesn't even matter who gets to play first singles for Morristown when varsity season officially starts. By this time next week, I'll be gone. Again.

You girls knew I'd be transferred eventually. Old people move south. There's a bigger demand for home healthcare down there. It will be another adventure. We're a family. We have one another no matter where we go. My mom could have talked all night. But my sister, Mae, and I didn't need to hear much beyond: we're moving again.

It won't take long. Never does. Mom could be planning to leave tonight for all I know. It will be our eighth move in fifteen years.

We've lived in Morristown the last three—our longest stretch ever. Morristown with its tree-canopied streets and Main Street shops is the kind of town reserved for movie sets. Where you can walk root-cracked sidewalks at night and see historic homes lit up like little dollhouses. Where beyond those manicured lawns and prized gardens, real life is actually happening inside those Easter egg–colored homes. There are happy parents laughing with their kids at the dinner table, new dads pacing across creaky wooden floors with swaddled babies. Sometimes it seems too good to be true. If I didn't know better, I might think everyone was pretending.

But I don't love Morristown for those nightly exhibits and the stories I've made up in my head to go along with them—*Dad just got a promotion. Mom burned the lamb chops. Sarah made varsity soccer as a freshman and Garrett is student of the month. Mexico or the Bahamas for spring break?* I don't even love Morristown for its nationally ranked schools or clay tennis courts. I love Morristown because I thought it was the one place where we might actually stay. I love it because I thought it was home.

But I can't think about any of that now. If I ever want anything to change, it's got to start with me. Isn't that what every counselor at every new school in every new town always says? I need to focus all the frustration, all the confusion and loneliness and anger. I need to channel it. Control it. But mostly, I need to win.

Because I've spent all of high school playing second singles and maybe if I finally make it to first I can change my mom's mind; maybe then we can stay. And I'm fully aware of how stupid that sounds, how unlikely it is that me taking Sophie Graham's first-singles spot might actually convince my mom to stay, but it's all I've got. My last attempt to control an uncontrollable life.

I serve again. Ace her. Back to deuce.

Angry steel-blue clouds are gathering over the trees

behind the courts, and thunder grumbles in the distance like a time bomb. I'm exhausted. My T-shirt is soaked. It's starting to get dark. They'll turn the lights on soon.

My first serve is weaker this time, my muscles screaming. We rally but I'm tired and sweating. Sophie charges the net, drives a volley to a corner of the baseline. Too good.

I take a deep breath. Will myself to focus. I have to win. Winning means playing first singles. First singles means more attention from college recruiters, more opportunities for scholarships, the possibility of a life after high school. A life that I could build myself. A life with roots instead of wheels. A life my mom won't be able to rip me away from.

My guidance counselor, Mrs. Veta, likes to call these options—and according to her, options are good for girls with thick school files and single moms whose job security depends on people who are slowly dying.

But right now this match has become about more than my future, more than my chances at staying in Morristown another year. More than the back and forth, the points and games and sets. Right now, this match is about someone like me, Amelia Fischer, beating someone like her, Sophie Graham. This match isn't about tennis at all. I wonder if they ever are.

"Ad out," I call. I bounce the ball twice. If I win this point, I'll take the game back to deuce. If I take the game back to deuce, there's no reason why I can't win another, take the advantage, come back. It's not over yet. This doesn't have to be over.

But just as I pull my racquet back to serve, out of the corner of my eye, I see something move, a shadowed form in the thick trees beyond Sophie. My arm stiffens in response and I know as soon as the ball strikes the strings that it'll hit the net. Sure enough, it catches the top of the tape and bounces back.

I just wasted my first serve of match point on some kid messing around in the woods. I dig my fingernails into the gummy grip of my racquet because I want to scream.

"Second serve." My voice echoes across the courts, thinner after my first fault. I glance to the stands to see my mom and Mae there watching me. Mae must have told my mom I had challenged Sophie for her spot on the ladder, but I never expected them to come. I can't help but wonder if maybe this match might mean something to them too. Maybe if I win, we really will stay.

My stomach twists, my hands shake. I can feel the nerves start to take over, but I can't let them. *Breathe, Amelia, breathe.* I pull the racquet over my head and stretch my arm. I have to win this point. Two bounces. Another toss.

This time, I manage to send the ball over the net. It bounces sharply in front of Sophie, whose glossy braid swings over her shoulder as she pulls her racquet back. But instead of slamming a return, she stops midstroke and raises one delicate, petal-painted finger into the air.

"Out!" Her voice sings with triumph because that's it. Match point.

The rest of the team gathered on the bleachers lets out

a collective sigh. It's impossible to tell if it's relief or disappointment.

It takes a second for the word to register, to understand what that single syllable means. I've heard it on and off for ten years. I can't be hearing it now. But when I see Sophie bouncing up to the net to shake my hand, it finally sinks in. My serve is out. I just double-faulted my way through another town.

I just lost everything.

two

I FOCUS ON SOPHIE TO STOP THE LUMP IN MY THROAT FROM TURN-
ing into a sob. Thanks to some extensive cyber stalking, I
know Sophie Graham from just about every angle. I know
how she looks when she wakes up in the morning. (Perfect.) I know what she eats for breakfast on a daily basis.
(Avocado toast. Gluten-free bread. Duh.) I know her signa-
ture nail polish color. (Vanity Fairest. Subtle. Classic.) And I
remember the exact expression on her face after Zach Bateman organized a flash mob to invite her to homecoming last
year and she snapped a selfie. (It's the same look she has on
her face right now. Triumph.)

"Nice match!" Sophie sings. She practically glimmers—
dewy, porcelain skin, teeth so white and straight they hurt
to look at. She probably never needed braces—or if she did,

her parents definitely invested in Invisalign so she wouldn't have to suffer through awkward orthodontia.

I'm not sure why I started hating Sophie Graham. Maybe because there's always been a version of her wherever we live. Or maybe it's the way she alternates between looking right through me and examining me with a judgy intensity like she somehow knows I'm wearing dingy granny panties underneath secondhand jeans. Or maybe it's the countless times I've witnessed her post some ridiculous selfie only to watch the likes climb to the hundreds seconds after it's live. Or maybe it's just everything. Her flawless skin, those unnerving eyes—one clear blue, one swirled green. Her quarterback boyfriend. The model-pretty mom and suit-clad dad. Three smiling faces in the *Morristown Gazette* advertising their law practice, the only one in our small town. Their perfect house. Their perfect life.

I really shouldn't be surprised. Sophie Graham isn't exactly a special snowflake. Wherever there's a tennis court, you'll almost always find a Sophie.

I was seven the first time I held a tennis racquet. We had moved into another unremarkable rented house in another unremarkable rented town. There was a sad-looking park practically in our backyard that had a tennis court with a sagging net and cracked asphalt next to a dilapidated playground. Mae and I begged my mom to let us go play there alone, like big kids, and she eventually agreed, but insisted on sitting on a patio chair in our backyard watching us the whole time.

One day there was an older woman on the court with a bucket of balls, just firing serve after serve over the net. I sat outside the chain-link fence that separated the playground from the tennis court and stared, riveted. There was something about the sound of the ball bouncing off the strings of her racquet—to me it sounded better than Mozart, better than whatever ridiculous boy band the girls on the bus would listen to every day. It sounded like winning.

Eventually the woman introduced herself as Mrs. Spring and asked me if I'd like to try to hit a few balls. I hesitated before taking the sweaty grip of the racquet from her hands, but I felt something vibrate through my arm the second my fingers wrapped around it—power. Turned out Mrs. Spring was a retired teacher, and for the next eight months she was my first tennis coach. She taught me everything I know about tennis, the most important thing being that it isn't just for rich kids. Mrs. Spring taught me that you don't need fancy lessons or a country club membership to win. All you need is a can of balls, a racquet, and a wall.

The thing is, I can't compete with the Sophie Grahams of the world at school. I'll never win homecoming queen. I'll never be elected class president. I'll never have a schedule full of AP classes. I'll never have the right hair, the right car, the right boyfriend, or the right family.

The only place I can really compete with the Sophie Grahams of the world is on the court. And I almost always win. Almost.

As I reach across the net to shake Sophie's hand and our

fingers touch, the first strike of lightning explodes in the sky, bathing us in white light and sending a strange shock up my arm. Before I even have time to wonder if she felt it too, Sophie jerks her hand away from mine and runs back to the rest of our waiting team.

One of the doubles players calls out, "Looking good, first singles!" and Sophie does a little twirl. A camera flashes and I notice that the kid from the school paper is snapping shots of Sophie. Did they really think it was necessary to cover our challenge match or did Sophie hire him to follow her around to capture moments for future posts? I'm honestly not sure which would be more depressing, but I have to admit Sophie kills it on film. She has the confidence to move her body into all the right poses—hand on hip, head tilted ever so slightly, chin lowered just so. Sophie would never get caught hunched over in the front row in a group shot. She's in back. Angled. Shoulders back. Striking.

Coach Harvey tries to throw her arm around my shoulder, but I pull away, so it falls to her side instead. "You should be proud, Amelia. It was anyone's game out there and second court is just as important as first." A fat raindrop falls, and she glances to the sky. "Now get home before this really starts to come down, and we'll talk more at practice tomorrow."

Racquet bags are gathered and squeals follow another low rumble of thunder. My mom avoids the eyes of other parents as she makes her way over, but there's no ignoring the familiar good-byes and weekend planning that never include her. She joins Mae under a tree instead.

"You looked really great out there, sweetie." She tries to touch my arm, but I stiffen. All of my anger and frustration at losing suddenly has a new target, a new focus—the woman who's uprooting us from our lives once again.

If she notices, she doesn't let on, only says, "All set?" as though we'll walk out like all the other families, parents hugging kids, towels waiting in cars, some nasty stew simmering in slow cookers at home.

But I'm not all set. I feel angry tears prick my eyes and I'm praying the skies will just open up already to help me pretend. "Well, I hope you're happy. Might as well go home and start packing." This gets Mae's attention. She widens her eyes a bit at my tone. The truth is I know my mom feels awful about having to leave again. It's not her fault there aren't enough old people who need their blood pressure taken and their medicine doled out in Morristown. They send her away and we have to follow. She needs this job. We need this job. I know she hates everything that makes us different. I know it kills her to pack up our lives at the start of my senior year. To leave the first place that's ever felt like home. I know all of it. But right now, I want her to feel it. I want her to hurt.

"Oh," my mom begins. The pity in her eyes and the defensive note in her voice make me hate her. "We don't have to start tonight. . . ."

"Actually, you're right," I say, cutting her off. "I don't have to start packing." Hot anger fuels my words, and they come easily now. Whip fast with sharp edges. "Because I'm not leaving." The mix of panic and disappointment and fear and sadness manipulating my pretty mother's features only presses me onward. "I'm almost eighteen. I have options now."

Out of my peripheral vision, I see Sophie's mom hug her close, beaming with pride. Sophie Graham with her perfect life, never moving, always winning. I want my mom to shoot back with words just as sharp and permanent as mine. I want her to yell and punish me. I need her disappointment. I need a fight.

"Let's go home and get cleaned up and we'll have pizza and eat ice cream out of the carton and watch a movie like we used to. Just us girls." There are bags under her eyes, and I've never noticed how the skin below her cheeks sags a little, like it's given up or something. She left for work when it was dark this morning, but still managed to show up to a challenge match I didn't even realize she knew I was playing. My mom's exhausted face fills me with the strangest mixture of hate and . . . hope. Maybe there's still time to convince her to stay. She can put in a request for another family in the area. She could work at a nursing home, find a new job where people aren't always dying, stop having to transfer so much. Mae and I can talk to her, maybe we can figure something else out. It'd be easy to agree to pizza and ice cream, to apologize and have an actual conversation about our future. But I'm not in the mood for easy.

"I'm not hungry. I'll probably catch up with the team and let them know this was my last match." Truthfully, we've left too many towns for me to bother with good-byes. There's no one who will really care that I'm leaving, anyway. Also, I'm starving, but I'd rather chew on my own arm than continue this conversation.

"I'll go with Amelia," Mae says absently, and I realize she's punishing our mom too.

My mom nods because she's not in the mood for hard. "Okay then," she finally manages. "Wear your seat belts." She lingers for a second and I know she's waiting for me to change my mind. She's worried, maybe considering putting her foot down the way she used to. But it's not going to happen. Not tonight. Another few drops of rain begin to fall, and after a quick glance at the sky, she gives up and jogs to the car.

"I'm not ready yet," I say to Mae just to be difficult.

She wrinkles her forehead and looks up at the churning clouds, just to be sure we're living on the same planet. "Amelia," she groans, dragging out each syllable the way she's done since she learned how to talk. She turns toward the woods where a dirt path cuts through the low brush and leads to an almost-empty parking lot. Lightning streaks in the distance, and her shoulders jerk at the boom that follows. "Ugh. I'll try to catch Mom. If not, I'll just wait for you in the car. Don't take forever, okay?"

I'm too annoyed with her to bother with a response. I just got my ass kicked by Sophie Graham. I'll take as long as I freaking want. But as I watch her walk away, I want nothing more than to follow her. To let go of the match, to move on. I want to find Mae sitting in the front passenger seat ready to

13

dissect every second of her day, her latest texts from her latest crush, her disgusting school lunch, the statistical probability that we'll open the front door to our house to find moving boxes scattered everywhere. We can scroll mindlessly through Sophie Graham and co.'s Instagram feeds, escape for a little bit, get lost. I want this almost as much as I wanted to drive straight home, to eat the pizza and ice cream, to be okay.

But as much as I want to be distracted, as much as I want to talk to her about all that stuff, I'm just not ready to put this loss behind me yet. I need some time to be sad and pissed off. I'm relieved when the sound of the last car engine trails off into the distance, leaving me alone with the roar of the gathering wind and the low moan of tree branches in response.

It's strange to walk back to the tennis courts beneath this angry sky instead of running for shelter. But I bounce the ball and focus on the familiar motion of its release, its loyal return. And then I serve with my eyes shut. Serve from memory. Serve with complete abandon, opening my eyes only to see the ball strike the service line with more force than I've ever been able to muster in an actual match. Instead of rolling to a stop in front of the fence, it gets wedged in one of the links.

"Hey!"

A shout simultaneously snaps me away from the serve of my life and scares the shit out of me. When I turn, I see the guy who was shooting the match earlier for the school paper. I've seen him around, but he always seems to have a camera in front of his face, so I've never really looked at him before.

The sky spits out a few more drops of rain and the wind follows close behind, taking his next words with it. I roll my eyes and jog over to him so I can hear. This better be good.

"You haven't found a lens cap by any chance, have you?"

I'm serving tennis balls in a gathering thunderstorm after losing the single most important tennis match of my life. The odds of me noticing a tiny sliver of black plastic are about a million to one. The odds of me giving a shit about his little piece of plastic are less than zero.

The sky chooses this exact moment to stop spitting and start dumping. Buckets. Sheets. An absolute flood. Rain like I've never felt.

"Um, no. Sorry," I shout over the thundering pelts. We were dry and now we are wet. Just like that.

His hair is plastered to his forehead and his shirt is sticking to his body. The thin fabric is practically transparent, and he just grins this goofy grin in the pouring rain. Now that there's no camera blocking his face, I notice that he's cute. Even in this storm, I can tell. And he's only a little shorter than me, kind of a bonus since I'm used to towering over everyone. I feel a flutter that makes me forget about my mom and moving and Sophie and double faults that ruin everything.

"I'm guessing you don't have an umbrella?" The corner of his mouth lifts and rain runs down his face, a few drops lingering on a fan of dark lashes completely wasted on a boy.

He's funny and cute. I laugh and shake my head, more confident somehow. Apparently my guard washed away with the rain.

"Guess we better make a run for it." He grabs my arm and I'm too surprised to do anything except be dragged along behind him. The canopy of trees above does a pretty good job of blocking the rain, and he lets go of my arm. "You always practice during storms?" The boy wrinkles his forehead. *Only when I lose the single most important game of my life.*

"Oh yeah, I find that the threat of getting struck by lightning takes my serve to the next level. Adrenaline and all that." I feel something shift inside, like when you wake up and could swear it's Sunday but realize too quickly that it's Monday. We're moving. There's no time. "You always trail after Sophie Graham to take her picture?" The words tumble out before I can stop them, laced with misdirected anger.

The smile leaves his face, and I wish I could take them back. "I don't follow . . . I mean, I work for the school paper and they're doing a profile on Sophie next month." He runs his fingers through his sopping hair and looks like he wants to say something more. I'm annoyed with myself for ruining the moment, but I also feel like I've somehow dodged a bullet. I learned a long time ago that my life is a lot easier without attachments.

"Got it. Well, see you around, I guess." I pull my hood over my soaking hair even though it's pointless. It might be kind of nice to stay in these woods with this boy, protected from the mess out there. But Mae's waiting and I've already said too much.

"Good game, by the way." His hand accidentally brushes against mine as he reaches up to push his hair out of his eyes, and my stomach does a little flip at the contact. "I totally think you nailed that last serve." He raises his eyebrows, smiles, and jogs back into the storm.

For a split second, all I can do is stare at my hand and wonder if he meant the ball I just served or the one Sophie called out during the match, but before I can ask, he's already been swallowed up by the rain.

I'm tempted to go after him, to ask what his name is, to forget, for a second, all the things that are holding me back. But thunder cracks and the spell is broken. My life in Morristown is officially over. Might as well go home and start packing.

three

BY THE TIME I GET TO MY CAR I'M SOAKED—THE KIND OF WET THAT finds its way into every last pore. Suddenly I can't wait to see Mae. I can't wait to tell her about the random photographer. I can't wait to hear her dissect Sophie's inevitable post-victory selfie. Maybe we can pretend for a second that we don't have to leave. Or not.

The best thing about sisters is that they don't hold grudges the way friends do. Mae always seems to have a sixth sense about when I'll need space and when I'll need her the most— somehow she's just always there.

It's been a while since we've gone through what Mae and I dubbed "the stages of moving," like the stages of grief only with more crying. I'm rusty, so I guess it makes sense that I lingered for too long in denial and bargaining. We learned a long time ago not to fight our mom when it's time to go. I was stupid to think, even for a second, that winning this ridiculous match would change a thing. It just doesn't work that way.

I swing open the door to my fantastically shitty car. "You're never going to believe. . . ."

My voice trails off when I flop into the seat and realize the car is completely empty. My whole body deflates. So much for our sisterly sixth sense.

To keep from crying, I close my eyes and wrap my fingers around the steering wheel. Something about the slightly musty smell of the interior and the sound of the driving rain on the windshield brings me a weird sense of peace.

This piece-of-shit car is the one thing in this world that's purely mine. I bought her with a wad of small bills from some shady guy on Craigslist a few months after passing my driver's test. Mae nicknamed it the Crimson Wave because she claimed all the babysitting I'd done to earn the money had put me in a state of permanent PMS. The name stuck when the car turned out to be a raging bitch. She starts only when coaxed with multiple pumps of the gas pedal and I swear there are some songs on the radio she just refuses to play. She censors boy-band bullshit with static. My kind of car.

I turn the key in the ignition, and my bitchy little car roars to life. Lightning streaks overhead and the thunder is even closer now, the horizon an inky blue. When I make my left out of the parking lot, the sewers are overflowing with runoff and my wipers can barely keep up. I lean forward in my seat, knuckles white as I squint against the wet, blurry world in front of me, barely able to see the road. My pulse quickens.

We rent an old farmhouse five minutes from the school, and normally I can drive the route with my eyes closed. Left, straight, two-way stop, right, right, left onto our long gravel driveway, overgrown on either side with weeds and grass and trees that no one will ever cut back. But the colors outside my windows have all washed away, muddled like something you might rinse a paintbrush in. It's like I'm stuck in an Impressionist painting, too close to see anything clearly.

The music has turned to static and I stab at the radio knob to silence it, even though the rain on my roof is just as distracting. Too late, I notice the streetlights that swing overhead are out, failing to mark my first turn, and I've missed it. The sheets of rain make my car feel even smaller, and the trapped, panicky feeling I get whenever I have to climb into an elevator lands like a punch to my chest. I just want to be home. Now I'll have to take the long way in the middle of a storm when I can barely see a thing.

Lightning erupts in the woods ahead so low it has to have hit something near the ground. I brace myself for the inevitable crack of thunder. I should have left with my mom and Mae. Stupid. Of course there's no side streets on this road, no intersection so I can turn around, not even a rocky shoulder to pull a U-turn, not that I'd try it in this weather. Just overgrown farmland on the outskirts of town. My foot shakes a little from nerves as I creep along the road. I could run faster than this, cut across the field and be home and drying off in five minutes.

As if on cue, a thump, dull and wrong, reverberates under my car like it just broke apart and ran itself over.

"Shit. Shit. Shit." Why wouldn't the worst day of my life to date get even worse? I pull Crimson to the side of the road and stab at the hazard lights. My heart is pumping double time as I consider the storm, my car, what I might find underneath it. With shaky fingers, I dig through my tennis bag in search of my phone, which, naturally, ran out of battery in study hall. The screen is still black, of course. I turn off the engine and pull the hood back over my already-wet head. "Shit."

Thunder rips the sky apart as I open my door, and the force of the wind almost takes the whole thing off. I hold my breath and bend down to peer underneath the car. My passenger-side tire is completely flat, rainwater rushing over the deflated rubber. I duck back into the car and dig my fingernails into my palms, closing my eyes. Of course I have a flat tire in the middle of a violent thunderstorm after losing the most important match of my life. There is no other possible scenario.

Headlights shine behind me, and relief explodes in my chest because there's no way I'm changing the flat in this weather. A truck has pulled over, but I can barely make out its details through the blurry rain. A tiny, irrational voice in my head wonders if maybe it's the hot photographer, and I can't stop myself from straightening my dripping ponytail. My eyes are glued to the rearview mirror as a guy steps out with a hoodie pulled tight over his head.

He's way too tall to be my photographer, and something about the way the dark skies cast a shadow where his face should be makes my breath hitch.

Trust your gut. When we were living in Brighton, Iowa, above a house turned donut shop along the main drag of town, there was a karate studio two doors down. While other little girls at Brighton Elementary perfected first position in light pink tights and ballet slippers, Mae and I learned that we could rip someone's ear off if we pulled hard enough, if we really needed to. I remember thinking how stupid it was that our mom saved parts of her paycheck so we could take that class. I remember wishing that we could spend the extra money on movie tickets or even dinner at an actual restaurant. *It's gross,* we complained. *It's important,* our mom responded.

I open my door a crack and scream over the rain, "I'm okay," waving him away with my arm. "My dad's coming." I raise up my dead phone. I have no idea why I play the dad card, but it just slips out and I'm glad no one else is around to hear it. The man stops halfway between our cars for a second and I frantically turn Crimson's key. The car does its standard groaning, that exhausted broken-sounding turn of the engine when I know it's not going to start right away. *Not now. Not now. Not now.*

And then I hear him shout our names. "Amelia? Mae? Is that you?"

I'm the strangest mixture of confused, relieved, embarrassed, and scared all churning together because I must know him and now I look like an idiot for lying about a dad I do not have and for being stuck on the side of the road in the first place. Someone please put me out of my misery.

I open my car door wider, squinting to see past the blinding sheets of rain, and all of a sudden he's there and his fingers are wrapping around my wrist, too fast, too tight.

And there's no time.

"Is this . . . ?" But before I can finish asking if this is some kind of a joke, before I can even get a glimpse of his face, he yanks me out of the car.

This can't be happening.

I twist back toward my car, but his fingers only grip my forearm tighter. And I'm yanked to his chest so close I can see every carving in his silver necklace, adrenaline heightening my senses and slowing down time. It's surreal to have such focus, to see the silver links woven like a tapestry, the circular medallion at the end etched with a man cradling a baby. It feels important. Blood rushes to my head, panic pounds through my temples. The rain drives against the skin on my lower back, and I realize that my sweatshirt has ridden up and I'm almost completely exposed. I'm going to be one of those stories, the warning parents tell their teenage daughters about because if it happened to that Fischer girl it could happen to you.

You get in the car, you never get out of the car, our self-defense teacher said. Big white kidnapper vans had haunted Mae's

23

dreams for weeks, but our mom made no apologies. We needed to know how to protect ourselves. Through wild eyes I see the safety of Crimson retreating behind me as this monster drags me away. We're coming up closer to his car now, too close, and then I'm thrown like a doll over his shoulder and nothing makes sense anymore.

I have to do something. Anything.

I scissor my legs and dig my nails into his wet sweatshirt but he only squeezes me tighter, stopping for a second to heft my body higher over his shoulder. Crimson is farther now. Too far. I squint through the rain to see something, anything, that I can use to describe him to the police. In self-defense class we were challenged to describe a stranger five minutes after he left the classroom. We didn't realize we were playing a game until we couldn't even remember if he was wearing a baseball cap. This man is tall, taller than me probably, and has a strong, lean body, white skin possibly but it's hard to be sure through the rain and the dark and the fear.

Listen to your program. Apparently we're wired to survive, but I don't have very much time to listen if any instinctual force is coursing through my veins right now. He's slowing. This is it. I can't get into that truck. So instead of listening, instead of fighting, instead of screaming into the pouring rain and empty streets, I stop. I let my body go limp, my arms hang, my legs drag. I play dead. My weight heaves against his grip and his hands slip ever so slightly.

It's an opening.

I pull my leg back and swing it as hard as I can, my tennis

24

shoe making solid contact with his stomach or groin, something soft and vulnerable. He groans as I claw at his neck, my fingers locating the chain, wrapping around the metal so that when he drops me, it follows. For a second I'm free and off-balance and on all fours, the slick road beneath my hands grounding me to the earth, scrambling away from the man with no face. He's behind me within seconds, adjusting the hood that's slipped off just slightly in the struggle. I know I'm fighting a losing battle, my fate sealed as a cautionary tale whispered over coffee, in school pickup lines, during mommy groups.

But I push to my feet and fling my body into the flooded street, away from his truck, away from the shadowed stranger, his necklace gripped between my fingers. Headlights creep over a crest in the road. It's fight or flight, and I choose to fly.

My throat constricts. I wave my arms in the air, but the dazzling white light advances too fast. And then there's nothing but the piercing scream of a horn and I know this is it.

The last thought I have before whatever comes next is that I should have at least asked the boy with the camera his name. I want to laugh at the absurdity of it. But before I can laugh or even scream, it's over.

four

MEMORIES BUBBLE TO THE SURFACE, IN RHYTHM WITH A STEADY beeping slightly out of my reach. I lost my chance to play first singles. Rain. Rain so heavy it washed away the world. A boy with a camera. My stupid car. Thunder. Lightning. Panic.

The plink of the beep continues, but the memories come faster now, flooding in like too much rain. A man. No face. Wrong. My arm. My body.

A man.

A man.

A man.

Mae.

I gasp for air as I force my eyes open, away from this nightmare. But the beeping continues. And I'm not in my room, my shabby floral wallpaper replaced by vanilla-colored walls. The beeps come from machines and there are metal rails on the side of a bed that is not mine and a tray table with a plastic-covered plate, applesauce, and a glass of water. I'm not at home because I'm in the hospital. I'm in the hospital because someone tried to take me. He knew our names. He knew our names.

"Mom?" I intend to scream the word, but instead choke on it as though I haven't spoken in days. I need my mom to wrap her arms around me and rock me back and forth like she used to when I was small enough to hold. To make all of this go away. To tell me everything is going to be all right.

"Oh, sweet girl, welcome back!" I know right away that it's not my mom's voice, but it takes a few seconds for my eyes to adjust to the light for visual confirmation. "I'm Mandy. Your parents just went to make a call. They'll be right back, and my goodness, they're going to be happy to see you up and at 'em."

I try to sit up, mostly to explain that I don't have parents, I have a mom. There is nothing more annoying than when people assume there must be two. For whatever reason, everyone prefers to wrap my single-parent family into a nice, nuclear bow. But I'm too scared, too exhausted to think of words sharp enough to slice through the ribbon.

"The man . . . my car . . . Mae?" My voice sounds strange and wrong but that's the least of my worries. I have so many questions to ask. But the memory of what happened already seems blurred, like it happened to someone else, and I can't quite get the words out.

"Shh, not so fast." The nurse gently pushes me back into the bed. "You've got quite a bump on that head of yours and I don't want you passing out on us again." She pulls out a tablet and swipes her finger across the screen. "Let's check your vitals and then we'll see about sitting you up."

I close my eyes as she pokes, prods, listens, and nods her way through all of my body parts, but I don't need her cheery affirmations to know that I'm just fine. My neck is a little sore, my head hurts, and my brain seems a bit fuzzy, but aside from that, everything feels surprisingly functional. I should feel relieved to be alive, I should be talking a mile a minute. Asking questions. Finding out if they caught the man who was trying to kidnap me. I need to know who he was and how he knew our names, to make sure Mae is safe. But I'm completely numb and somehow unable to string the words together to find out what truly happened.

"They tell me you're a tennis player."

I manage a polite smile and mumble something that sounds vaguely like an agreement.

"Well, you're lucky. No broken bones. You'll be playing first court again in no time." She gives a little wink.

If she didn't sound so genuinely happy for me and I didn't think the sudden movement would make me pass out again, I honestly might have punched her in the boob. Instead I manage, "I'm not first singles."

But good old Mandy just clicks her tongue and runs a thermometer across my forehead. "Shh, you're going to be just fine. Your parents will be back in just a minute and then

Dr. Langstaff is going to want to take a look at you."

I close my eyes again and inhale deeply. Clearly this woman is useless.

"Hi, Dad!" She affects a singsong voice, like a character on a tinkly kids' show reminding children not to bite their friends. "Our tennis star is finally awake and doing great."

My eyes are already rolling before I even open them. "My dad died when . . ." But before I can finish my sentence, I open my eyes to see a man rushing toward me. His lips are moving but I can't hear anything he's saying. I'm completely paralyzed until his hand grips my arm and I know. Something about the way he moves toward me, too purposeful. Too fast. It's him.

And then I'm screaming and kicking and punching. The man with no face is here and he's pretending to be my dad and oh my God this is so freaking messed up.

As it turns out, Nurse Mandy is part ninja. Before I can blink, she's in between us and saying something in what I can only assume to be calm and soothing tones, but I can't actually hear her because I'm still screaming. Another nurse rushes into the room and tries to pull the strange man toward the doorway.

"What's wrong with her? Why doesn't she recognize me?" The man is yelling and trying to brush the woman off him. "Honey, it's me, Dad."

I shake my head and keep screaming. My dad died when Mae and I were babies. There was an accident. This man is not my father and I have no idea why he's here and pretending to know me unless I've been kidnapped or something.

"Shh, shh, don't get yourself all worked up now, honey. Everything is fine; you're going to be just fine." Mandy's plump fingers are smoothing back my damp hair, desperately trying to calm me down. When they finally manage to get the stranger out of the room, the wave of panic recedes just enough so I can stop screaming.

I want to tell her that I'm pretty sure I've been kidnapped and that we should probably call 911 or the FBI or whoever the hell you call when a strange man takes you to the hospital and tries to pass you off as his daughter. That I can prove it because I remember something . . . something important bobbing just below the surface of my memory, something silver. My mouth can't seem to form the words that could articulate any of this, so I settle for, "Want . . . Mom."

But before she can respond, the door to my room flies open and a tiny blond woman flings herself at me.

"Sophie, thank God. We've been worried sick, but you're awake now. It's going to be okay."

Sophie?

"I know it was just a concussion, but it's all been so horrible, so, so horrible." She's hiccupping words, and tears are swimming in front of crystal-blue eyes. "I thought I lost you." She claps her hand over her mouth even though there's nothing more to say.

The woman who is not my mom keeps mumbling, straightening the bedsheets to occupy her hands. But I don't hear a word she's saying because I'm stuck on her very first word. It plays on a crackled-sounding loop: *Sophie. Sophie. Sophie.* I'm cold all of a sudden, but sweating and shaking, and my skull feels like it might possibly explode with the weight of her name. I know this woman. I recognize her. How could I not? She's tiny and perfect and expensive and always, always there.

A fuzzy blackness threatens to consume my field of vision but I fight back, blinking it away because I have to see. I rip the covers off like they're on fire and the woman startles, clutching her heart with her hand and scanning the room for help. Rubbing at my eyes doesn't make anything come into focus the way it needs to. I see creamy white legs instead of familiar tan ones. It's okay though, it's a trick of the light, the hospital room, medicine. I rub my thighs too hard, half thinking this unfamiliar skin will peel away to reveal my own legs.

This isn't happening. I'm dreaming. I slap at my cheeks and now the woman is up and screaming at the nurse to get help but I can't hear the sound because I'm pinching at my arms, which I've always thought seemed like such a stupid way to see if you're dreaming, but there's nothing else to do.

And there it is. Delicate strands of silky black hair woven into a braid that has fallen over a shoulder that, looking down at it, is much too narrow. No auburn split ends, no frizz, not even a rubber band, but a Morristown blue-and-gold ribbon tied at the end in a bow. I don't have much time because the woman is now standing with the man, pointing and crying and explaining, so I yank away cords without a thought and scramble out of the bed, dizzy and unsteady as blood rushes away from where it needs to be. But I need to see my dark eyes fringed with thick lashes that I'm secretly so proud of because I always get asked if they're fake. I need my messy bun, the scatter of freckles, those two stupid zits I couldn't cover up this morning, my one crooked tooth on the bottom.

Eyes clenched shut, I grip the cool porcelain sink and it already makes me feel better, more aware and alive and present. I'll laugh about this later. Maybe I'll tell Mae if she promises not to make fun of me. I'll tell my mom that they need to reduce the painkillers, that I'm having side effects. We'll figure this out. We'll go home. There are more voices outside. *Be brave, Amelia,* I think. *You are strong, you are you.* I lift my chin and open my eyes, staring levelly in the mirror.

One blue eye. Navy around the edges and icy in the middle. The other green. Perfectly clear, pale skin, almost yellow on account of the lights or the shock. Probably both. Rosy lips. Straight teeth. Raven-colored hair.

Not me. Not Amelia.

I squeeze my eyes shut again and try to block out the deafening noise, the thunder of voices flooding under the crack in the door. And in that familiar darkness, I'm me again.

Open. Sophie.

Close. Amelia.

Open. Sophie.

I'm in the midst of some sort of hurricane, a war of hair

whipping in a swirl over the curve of a cheek, across a delicate, sloped nose, hiding wild eyes.

When I open my mouth to scream, I watch in horror as the girl in the mirror opens her mouth.

I'm not me. I'm not Amelia Fischer. Somehow, I'm the girl in the mirror.

I'm Sophie fucking Graham.

five

MY VISION CREEPS GRAY ALONG THE EDGES, AND THIS TIME I FALL
until I'm swallowed completely by blackness. I feel myself
crumple downward, the only familiar thing that's happened
since I woke up, strong arms carrying me back to bed, words
floating in and out. *Car accident. Head trauma. Hallucinations.
Short-term memory loss.*

I want to sit up; I want to try to explain to them that
there's been some kind of terrible mistake. But then I remember the face in the mirror that isn't mine, and I let myself sink
back into the darkness. That place seems safer.

I have no sense of time, but when I open my eyes again
there's light streaming in from the window and I'm alone in
the room. Beside me, a clear bag hangs from a metal stand
and tubes are attached to my body. Everything is punctuated

by a slow and steady beep from a large machine opposite the bed.

My mind flashes back to eighth grade, when we were living in a tiny two-bedroom bungalow in Kentucky. My tennis coach at the time, Mr. Grant, forced all of us to do yoga. I spent the entire ninety-minute session discovering that I was the least-flexible human being on the planet and trying to calculate how much longer we had in our current school before my mom got out the old orange suitcase, cue-ing another move. I hoped they'd at least send us somewhere warm.

But then at the end of the session, the instructor told us to focus in on every single part of our body, to relax every toe and then our feet and then legs, until we felt, actually felt, every square inch of ourselves. And for the first time ever I felt a real connection with my body and it was kind of amazing. Not amazing enough to convince me to suffer through another ninety minutes of stretching, but amazing just the same.

And now I find myself clenching and unclenching, furl-ing and unfurling, lifting and lowering until I'm sure that I'm really here, present and in control of my body. You are you, I think. The stress of losing that stupid match and the thunderstorm and the man with no face created some kind of crazy hallucination, or maybe it was some kind of hyper-realistic dream—either way it's over now and you are you. You are Amelia Fischer.

I need to open my eyes. I need to look down and see

my hands, my legs, my chipped blue toenail polish. But that hallucination, that moment I stared at someone else's face in the mirror, still feels too real and I can't bring myself to do it. Because with my eyes shut against the world, I'm still me.

I want Mae. I need her to make the nightmare go away the way she used to when we were little and slept curled up in the same bed every night. I want my mom. Fear has replaced any anger I have ever felt toward her, and I need her to pull me close and promise this will go away, that she will make this better the way only a mom can. I want to smell our laundry detergent, eat takeout off mismatched plates, and fight over the remote. Moving doesn't matter anymore. I can't believe it ever did. I'll go anywhere. I'll smile and study and make friends and volunteer. I'll be good.

So I take a deep breath. I open my eyes and kick the blanket off.

I notice the petal-pink toenails first. Wrong. And then I see the creamy white skin, soft and smooth, and under the hospital gown, lacy underwear with polka dots. So wrong.

I fight tears as I run unfamiliar fingers up my body. The skin on the inside of a forearm is so white it's almost translucent, like the shimmery powder Mae and I always swipe across our collarbones at Victoria's Secret.

I need to block out this new storm and try to remember what makes me *me*. My birthday. November 14. The day of my birth. Red and orange and brown leaves, sweater weather, Thanksgiving around the corner. It's mine. Tears manage to slip down my cheeks despite my clenched eyes because I know when I open them, I know with a sickening certainty, that every mark or bruise or baby-fine hair will belong to someone else and remembering some stupid day won't change any of that.

The tears come fast now, followed by a low, keening wail that sounds nothing like any noise I've ever made before. Is it because I have Sophie's vocal cords, her mouth? Or is this just the kind of sound you make when every rule you've ever understood to be true has suddenly changed?

The room fills up with people. Two nurses and a doctor appear as quickly as if I'd pushed the little red call button on my bed.

"Sophie, I'm Dr. Langstaff. You're in a safe place and I'm here to help you." The doctor holds a syringe and a container, measuring out a clear liquid. "I'm going to give you some medicine to calm you down and help you sleep." He inserts the syringe so the medicine flows into my IV. It drains the screams right out of me, like he's pulled the plug on my lungs.

I lie back down on the bed and look up at the doctor, praying that he'll understand me.

"I need help," I say. My throat is raw and sore. "Something's happening to me. My name is Amelia Fischer and I live at 6528 Mayberry Drive. My mom is Carol Fischer and my little sister is Mae. I'm not who they say I am." But even as I speak the words, I know he won't believe me. I think of my birthday again, try to recall the date, but can only come up with May and I know it's not right but my head is pounding and my body is weak. I'm not sure *I* believe me.

"Sophie, you were in an accident." Dr. Langstaff lifts the IV bag and types something into his computer. "You hit your head and you're a little disoriented. I promise you'll feel better soon, but you need to rest."

"I can tell you anything," I say, desperate now. Even the medication can't stop my tears, which pour from these unfamiliar eyes in rivers. "My birthday is May 23. My middle name is . . ." My mind is fuzzy again, and I curse the medication because I can't remember my own middle name and it makes me cry harder. "My name is Amelia, um . . ."

But the doctor doesn't even give me a chance to try.

"Yes, Sophie, you were born May 23. Now dream of your birthday and I promise everything will get better." He pulls more liquid from the vial and pushes it into the IV, nodding as my eyelids grow heavy. "Let yourself sleep, Sophie. We're taking excellent care of you."

My last thought before I fall asleep again is that I'll be stuck in this hospital forever if I try to make them believe the unbelievable. Because the last thing I remember is a man trying to take me and a car barreling toward me, and now I've somehow woken up in Sophie Graham's body.

But if I'm Sophie, then what the hell happened to Amelia?

six

THE DRUGS DON'T LEAVE ROOM FOR DREAMS, JUST A SLEEP SO black it feels like dying. But there's another nightmare just waiting to take the place of that blackness and it just so happens to be my current reality. I keep my eyes shut against it for a little while longer.

"I thought they said she'd be awake by now. We should call the nurse." The voice is deep and rings with an authority that makes it very clear he never calls anyone himself. It must be Sophie's dad. I can't believe I didn't recognize him earlier. After I've watched the Graham family celebrate countless birthdays, vacations, and Father's Days via Instagram, he's way more familiar to me than the one blurry picture I've unearthed of my own dad.

"Let's not rush her. They said she needed her rest. We're

going to have to be patient." A defensive note sharpens Mrs. Graham's voice. She doesn't call the nurse.

I try to keep my breathing even and stop my eyelids from fluttering too much. I need time to get my bearings and it's pretty clear that I'm not going to figure out what happened to me all drugged up in some hospital bed. I need answers and the only way to get answers is to act like being stuck in someone else's body is a totally normal thing. And to pretend to sleep. At least with my eyes closed it's easier to believe I'm still me.

"We've been sitting here for hours. Where's the doctor?"

"She was in a terrible accident, Robert. This type of trauma is expected." Their voices are hushed, volleyed back and forth with practiced control. I have no idea who these people are but the tone doesn't seem to match the beautiful faces imprinted in my memory. I always pictured families like the Grahams coming together in a tragedy, not whisper-fighting.

"There's nothing normal about her not recognizing me, Hillary," Mr. Graham throws back.

"No, what's not normal is what happened to that poor Amelia Fischer."

And there it is. All sound is vacuumed up out of the stuffy room after the words leave Mrs. Graham's mouth. I'm only left with the thump of someone else's heart pounding through a skull that is not mine. I'm dead. Amelia is dead and I'm stuck and I'll never go home, hug Mae, say sorry to my mom, or be me again.

"She's in intensive care, Robert." Mrs. Graham's voice shakes. "At least Sophie isn't in a coma. Kathy Lenore was telling me that every hour that poor girl doesn't wake up makes it more unlikely that she ever will."

I feel a scream roiling in the deepest part of Sophie or me or whoever the hell I am. But I manage to keep it in because I'm not dead. I'm not dead yet.

"What in the hell was she doing in the middle of the road anyway?"

And just like that Mr. Graham expertly shifts the blame. Like it's my fault that my car broke down and some terrifying man tried to abduct me. It takes every ounce of willpower I have not to shoot up in bed and launch the truth like a dagger. I was being chased, abducted. Why isn't anyone talking about the stranger from the night of the accident? Did the police catch him? Are they even looking for him? Do they know he was driving a black truck? Or was it an SUV? A black car? I squeeze my eyes shut harder and hope no one notices.

The rest of me is torn somewhere between relief and agony. Relief that Amelia is—that *I* am—a real person, a real person who is still alive. And then agony slices through that fleeting hope. My real body is lying unconscious in the intensive care unit. Does that mean Sophie's in there? Trapped somewhere between life and death? And what the hell does any of this mean for me, in this body, in this life?

"Will she even know me?" For the first time Mr. Graham sounds like the man I remember from the videos Sophie is always posting on her feed.

"She will. I know she will. Eventually. They just don't know how long this amnesia will last. But there's nothing on the MRI, no permanent damage. Dr. Langstaff said it's most likely shock."

The scream comes crawling up my esophagus again. I want to cry and yell and try to explain that something has gone terribly wrong. I want to ask them about the man who tried to take me. I want to explain that he somehow knew my name, that he's after us. I need to ask them about what I took from the man, what was gripped in my fist. I need them to help me remember. Because if I can remember, we can find whatever it is—maybe it's downstairs with my body in the ICU. It will prove that this whole insane out-of-body experience is actually happening because how could I have known about whatever it is I can't remember. Needles of pain scratch up the back of my neck and spread to my skull in response to this impossible situation. I can't afford to spend any more time in that black, terrifying sleep with the mixed-up dreams. In order to understand what's happening to me, I have to be awake. In order to stay awake, I have to get the doctors to stop drugging me. In order to avoid said drugs, I'll need to pretend like it's totally normal that Mrs. Graham's tears are splashing on my arm right now.

I flutter my eyes a bit and blink them open.

Sophie's parents bolt upright, pasting smiles across their beautiful faces. That's more like it. "Hi, honey." Mrs. Graham's blond head bobs behind Mr. Graham as though she's photobombing him. "Your dad's here, isn't that nice?"

42

Something about the way she says it, the tension in her voice, makes it feel like she's willing me to act normal. To pretend to remember in spite of the sympathy that's shining in her eyes.

"I've been so worried about you, Bumblebee. We all have. Do you remember . . ." He stops himself and clears his throat. "I mean, are you feeling any better?"

"I feel good, actually. Much better." I sit up in bed a little to prove it, swallowing back a gasp when Sophie's dark hair tumbles over my shoulder. "What happened exactly? I guess I'm still a little hazy on the details."

Mrs. Graham hovers closer to me, her face just inches from mine. "There was a car accident," she begins.

"Jesus, Hillary." Mr. Graham's words are more of a hiss. But if it weren't for the pink rising on Sophie's mom's cheeks, I'd have wondered if she even noticed the interruption.

"But everyone's fine. Everyone's going to be just fine. Just some bumps and bruises." Mrs. Graham pastes on another shaky smile and I wonder if it's because of her husband's insult or the lie. Maybe both.

"Car accident?" As much as I don't want to know, don't want it to be more real than it is now, I need to hear what happened. I need to know if my memories of the man and my escape and the car barreling toward me actually happened.

"Never mind that right now." Mrs. Graham waves her hand to dismiss the details. "How do you feel? Thirsty? Hungry?" She grabs a glass of water sitting on a table near the bed, sliced cucumber floating among the cubes. I have to admit it looks amazing. Especially since it feels like I've been sleeping with a cotton rag shoved in my mouth.

But given that I'm fighting for my life inside a near-stranger's body, thirst isn't exactly my highest priority. I ignore the water and focus on my biggest, scariest question. "Is she . . . Is Amelia okay?" I lean forward now. I have to know. I have to hear.

"That's right, you're remembering. That's a good sign, honey." Mrs. Graham claps excitedly and looks like a deranged preschool teacher. "Dr. Langstaff is going to be so pleased. I told him you were a fighter!" She shoots Mr. Graham a triumphant look, but he's staring at me too intently to notice.

"The only person you need to be worrying about right now is yourself," Mr. Graham snaps. The words come out sharp, angry almost.

Mrs. Graham's hands freeze between claps and I can actually feel my jaw drop. What kind of a person says this after an accident? I remember the way the man's fingers dug into my flesh when he grabbed my wrist. I remember the sickening sense of vertigo when he carried me to my car. And for one horrible moment it feels like Mr. Graham can see it all playing in my eyes like some kind of TV show he's choosing to turn off because it's too violent, too scary, too real.

"Robert! The girls have been on the same tennis team for the past three years. Of course she cares about Amelia." Mrs. Graham pushes her husband out of the way and grabs my hand. "Sweetheart, she's going to be just fine." The lie never reaches her eyes. I wonder if it's more for me or for her.

"Did they, I mean, was there anyone else there? When I hit her, I mean." My voice catches on the word *hit*. I have no memory of the impact, but it doesn't stop me from wondering what it sounds like when steel pounds flesh.

Mr. Graham clears his throat and pushes up from the chair. "Replaying the accident over and over isn't going to help anyone." He's agitated as he walks to the window, pushing his fingers through his hair and making it stick out a little on the side. I wish I knew if he were always like this. I expect the conversation to end; I imagine he's used to guttural sounds and brisk movements getting him what he wants. But it doesn't work this time.

"You mean Janie? You had just dropped her off, sweetheart. She's just fine." Mrs. Graham's voice trembles. Fine. Fine. Fine.

"No, I mean a man. Someone else. Another car." Tears gather in my eyes and tremble along my lashes. "I remember . . ."

"That's enough, Sophie." My shoulders jerk in response to the volume of his words. Even Mrs. Graham is startled, her hand at her neck. "Where the hell is the doctor? She's clearly confused." Mr. Graham closes the space between us and jabs angrily at the call button next to my bed. It's almost like he doesn't want me to remember.

"She's fine, Robert. She just needs some more rest."

Bile rises in my throat, but I swallow it back. Getting sick certainly won't get me out of this bed and neither will Dr. Langstaff. I need a better plan.

"I'm fine, I'm fine." I use their favorite word and smile to show them how calm I can be. "You're right." After I say the words, I can actually feel the tension in the room melt away like magic. The Grahams clearly want to brush this whole horrible accident under the rug, but I can't afford to let that happen. Not when I was almost abducted and killed. Not when the person trying to take me knew my name and Mae's. The details will have to wait. I have to make sure Mae is okay. I have to figure out a way back to being me.

All at once, with more certainty than I ever can remember feeling, I know I have to visit Amelia. My body. Whatever it is now. I'll get back or at least find whatever I took from the man.

"I just need to go see Amelia," I say.

The forced smile drips off Mrs. Graham's face, bringing her color along with it. She stands, leans over the bed, and pulls the thin blanket closer to my face. "We've worn you out, sweet girl. Time to rest."

I stare at them then. The two vaguely familiar strangers sitting next to my bed, fear etched into the lines around their eyes, worry turning down the corners of their mouths. Part of me wants to argue, to explain that I'm not their daughter and if they want their precious girl back they have to let me go.

But instead I just nod along because I'm guessing that's what they expect Sophie to do, and if I want to save myself, I'm going to have to save Sophie first.

seven

TURNS OUT SOPHIE GRAHAM IS ADORED. I'M PRETTY SURE I ALWAYS
knew this. You don't have thousands of mostly random people following your life via social media if you aren't. But
witnessing firsthand the genuine concern Sophie's mom has
for her well-being is something else entirely. I'd like to blame
it on the accident, or on the hospital stay, or on their tenuous hope that whatever crazy their daughter demonstrated in
hours past will stay far, far away. But I know better. This is
the Grahams' version of normal.

Mrs. Graham is a machine. She hasn't left my side for a
minute, which is wildly inconvenient considering my escape
plan or lack thereof. She also looks like she's moonlighting as
a commercial actress for laundry detergent. I've never heard
her mention anything about working or showering or even

eating. Sophie is her business, her work, her hobby. When-ever I stir or need absolutely anything, she's there, ready and willing.

Unless what I need are details about the accident or access to a phone, my phone, her phone, a random stranger's phone. I'd kill for a quick Google search, key words like *concussion body swap coma* bobbing around in my mixed-up brain. It's almost like now she's trying to pretend the accident never happened. Every time I bring it up or ask for my phone, she just smiles and wonders if we should ring Dr. Langstaff for something to help me sleep or mumbles about hospital rules against cell phone use.

My throat burns when I imagine my own mom down-stairs in the ICU. Is she holding my hand? My real hand? Is she saying anything? Has she slept? Has she left? How is she paying our bills? The accident obviously delayed the transfer and if she's not working for a new family, she's not getting paid. Colors swim in front of my eyes and it feels like I can't breathe in enough air. Maybe Sophie's lungs are too small for these problems.

Mrs. Graham pulls the curtains open to let in sunshine that has finally broken through relentless clouds as if on cue. She turns and smiles and I can barely swallow now, the lump in my throat jagged and suffocating. And bitter. Will I never have the chance to hug my mom again? To apologize for being such a bitch about our move? To eat pizza and ice cream straight from the carton? To forget all the crap that went wrong, to grow up, to appreciate all the stuff that went even a little bit right?

In the summers, when Mae and I were out of school, she'd bring us to work with a few toys scattered in the back of our messy car. It was my job to make sure Mae stayed out of trouble even though I was barely a year older. We never knew what she did in those houses all day, but to distract Mae, I'd make up stories. Our mom was a fortune-teller, a spy, or even a witch. The good kind that saved people. Even when I was old enough to understand that she sorted weekly medication, changed dressings on papery skin, and washed soiled bed linens, it was easier to play in some random person's yard all day if we thought our mom was concocting some sort of potion inside.

Often I'd catch a look of pure exhaustion etched into the angles of her drawn face in the evenings when she slipped out of the house, but before she opened the car door, she always saved a smile for us. And sometimes chocolate for being such good girls. I didn't understand why she had to work so hard. I didn't get it yesterday. I probably don't even now. Knowing I might never have the chance to truly understand, to thank her, makes it hard to breathe.

"Daddy's tied up with paperwork this morning but said he'll try to come down as soon as he's finished." Oh. My. God. *Daddy?* A sense of dread worms its way in at the memory of the strange man rushing into the room, at the idea of a dad in general. As bizarre and neurotic as Mrs. Graham appears, she is a mom. I have experience with moms. But dads? I've never had one, and it feels way too late to get stuck with one now. Especially someone else's *Daddy*.

Mrs. Graham fusses with some daisies in a vase. There are bunches of flowers and cards everywhere. "Just remember how much your dad loves you and how hard he works for our family." Mrs. Graham says this as though she's trying to convince herself. Maybe she's mad he's not here every second like she is. Maybe she's tired. Maybe they fought about it.

It actually surprises me that he's not here. The guy barreling toward my bed the first day in the hospital, while traumatizing at the time, felt more in line with the idea of Mr. Graham I always had in my head. Through Sophie's lens he seemed omnipresent. I hadn't imagined him working, let alone fighting with Mrs. Graham and avoiding his daughter. Seeing him through Sophie's eyes feels like emotional vertigo.

I realize Mrs. Graham is staring at me, waiting for some sort of response. I have no idea how I should be acting. How would Sophie act?

"Um, okay?" is all I can manage. "I'm actually feeling a lot better today. Can you tell the doctors I'm ready to see Amelia now?"

Mrs. Graham's smile falters. "Sweetheart." She sits on the edge of the bed. "Amelia Fischer is very, very hurt. Patients in the ICU can only be visited by family members. Plus"—Mrs. Graham's eyes brighten—"if all goes well when Dr. Langstaff checks you out, we'll be able to go home this morning.

Aren't you ready to start getting back to normal?"

My throat tightens again and I feel like I can't get a full breath in. It feels like such a loaded question. As though everyone's impatient for the weakness I've displayed to pass, as though this injury, this incredibly fucked-up situation that no one even knows about, is just an inconvenience that can be remedied with a change of scenery. I can't go home to Sophie Graham's house, to her life. There is no normal I can get back to. I can't leave this hospital. I need to go downstairs and find my body and hold hands with myself or something until the universe decides to switch us back.

I imagine Sophie's tiny fingers gripping my lifeless ones and an electric current rushing through us, zapping me back into my rightful place. But then what? Would I wake up? Or would I find myself trapped in a hospital bed, stuck in some limbo between life and death? I want to believe that if I'm able to switch back, I'll wake up, alive and whole, but there are obviously no guarantees. I want to believe I'm okay with that.

And then there's the man from the side of the road. Someone tried to kidnap me. Someone who knew my name. But who? Why? Am I still in danger lying helpless in a hospital bed? What about my mom and Mae? Are they okay? The familiar rush of panic comes hard and fast now and I have to fight for each shaky breath. The only thing that scares me more than these questions are the potential answers.

Mrs. Graham tucks a stray strand of hair behind my ear. I recoil at her touch. I'm not much of a hugger or a toucher.

My mom has always called me a prickly little thing and while *little* isn't a word I ever would have used to describe myself, *prickly* is about right. When you've always got one foot out the door, you stop trying to make friends, you get used to sitting alone at lunch, and you learn to travel light. You don't move seven times in fifteen years without developing some thorns.

It's the thought of my mom. My real mom. My sister. Being bound to these strangers. Trapped. The man with no face who knew my name, who knew Mae. It's all too much, and I know what comes next. I'm hot now and Sophie's body feels too small. I might not have appreciated my height when I was in my body, but it was nice having that weight behind me, the knowledge that I could create more space for myself in the world if I needed it. I feel claustrophobic in Sophie's child-like frame, like my soul is too big for this body. My breath quickens and I sit up in bed, squeezing my eyes shut against the constriction in my chest even though it is not my chest.

Mrs. Graham's voice is faint in the background. "Breathe through it, Sophie, deep breaths, baby girl." The sound of her voice only fuels the panic. My mom and Mae understand that the silence makes it easier to breathe, they know when to give me space.

I've been dealing with panic attacks my whole life. I know the drill and I've learned how to turn the tides of panic and regain control. I block out Mrs. Graham's voice and slowly blink away the blurriness of the room, let the woman's fuzzy form come back into focus.

"Good girl. That wasn't such a bad one." Mrs. Graham rubs my back and I can't stop myself from jerking away.

Apparently, the Sophie Grahams of the world aren't strangers to panic attacks themselves, but somehow I can't imagine anything ever making perfect Sophie Graham anxious. She always seemed so confident, so sure of herself when she glided through the hallways, arm linked with Janie McLaughlin's or wearing her Zach Bateman jersey to the homecoming game. Her Instagram posts are instantaneously liked by dozens of people and she has an entourage of fans at every single tennis meet. What could someone as perfect as Sophie Graham possibly have to feel anxious about?

"Knock, knock!"

The simple words are almost enough to bring back the suffocating waves. It's Dr. Langstaff. He's going to say I'm fine and release me and I'm going to be stuck in Sophie Graham's life forever. Or he'll know that I just had a panic attack and medicate me. I have no idea which is the lesser of two evils anymore. I manage to ward off further panic by focusing on staying. Staying present, staying unmedicated, staying at the hospital. When the door opens, it's Sophie's dad who walks through.

I should feel relief, but something about the efficiency in his gait makes me uneasy. I can't be sure if it's him specifically or if it's just because I'm not really used to being around grown men when I'm stuck in a hospital gown, but I'm uncomfortable and I'm supposed to be his daughter. He strides over to Mrs. Graham and kisses her chastely on the cheek.

The gesture feels forced and strange, causes heat to rush to my cheeks, and I curse Sophie for blushing so freaking easily. I never had that problem. Thankfully Mr. Graham kills the moment, his deep voice ringing with false cheer.

"I ran into Dr. Langstaff in the hallway and he says we're going home today, Soph. We're so proud of you. Always such a fighter." His teeth are too white and too big for his face and he seems to be forcing everything, from the kiss down to the smile. Alarm bells sound in my head, but I hit my mental snooze button and remind myself that this is Sophie's father. Not all men are kidnappers.

"I actually think I need to stay, I mean, I don't know if I'm one hundred percent," I mumble. I can't go home with them. I can't leave. Not without switching back to my real body.

Mr. and Mrs. Graham exchange a look. "Honey, you can't feel guilty," Mr. Graham says. He makes a move to come closer to the bed but reconsiders, hovering awkwardly near his wife instead. I wonder if he's always hesitant around Sophie or if my reaction when I woke up has spooked him. "That's what this is about, isn't it? This is no one's fault and your friend will be just fine."

It's like he can't even say my name. Or doesn't bother.

"How about you take a shower and get cleaned up for Dr. Langstaff? Then we'll be all ready to go," Mrs. Graham says. I don't have to be her real daughter to know I don't have a choice in the matter. She pats a neatly folded pile of clothes.

"I brought your things from home so you can get back to being you."

I would laugh at the irony of her statement if I wasn't so completely desperate to figure out a way to stay.

Mrs. Graham helps me out of bed and I don't know whether to push her away or grab hold of her tighter. Physically I'm fine. A little sore and trapped in someone else's life, but beyond that I'm aces. Still, she turns the shower on and hangs a towel on the back of the door, lingering in the tiny space as though she's going to help me lather my hair or something. I don't care whose body I have, I'm not about to let Mrs. Graham scrub me down.

"I've got it," I snap, the way I would at my own mom. She seems unfazed, so I make a mental note just in case I'm stuck as Sophie for another night. I lock the door behind her.

It doesn't take long for the small bathroom to fill with steam, the mirror fogged over. And it's a good thing. I don't know if I could stand to look into Sophie's different-colored eyes again. Instead, I let the hospital gown drop to my pale-pink toes and look down at a body that isn't mine. I assess Sophie's muscular legs, her taut stomach, her perfect boobs, up to the gentle curve of her collarbone. Looking at her body makes me feel like a voyeur. It's creepy and wrong and I feel my head begin to swim. Sophie is so much smaller than me. My five foot eight inches of muscle and bone and size ten feet have been replaced with a body made of tiny pieces and soft edges. I consider throwing this new body into the shower and closing my eyes, never looking again, but I can't resist taking a towel and swiping across the glass to find Sophie's intense eyes and porcelain skin, gripping the edge of the sink to brace myself against the shock.

My hand instinctively reaches to my midsection, feeling for the slightly raised birthmarks that line my back like a constellation. But now there's nothing there and as my fingers worry against Sophie's soft, unblemished skin, I realize the beauty marks were a few of the trillion tiny things that made me Amelia.

My throat burns as I watch tears gather in Sophie's eyes, trembling as they fight to hold on. I'm spellbound by the intimacy of watching a stranger cry. A single tear slips across Sophie's lower lashes, racing down her cheek, and I smash it with the back of my hand harder than I intended. These strange eyes water even more, silent tears racing to catch up. Enough is enough. I shut off the shower and get dressed. I need to get down to the ICU. I understand what Mrs. Graham said about the likelihood of me waking up the longer I'm asleep. I need to get back into my own body. I'd rather be stuck in a coma than in Sophie Graham's life.

eight

I EMERGE FROM THE BATHROOM IN A PINK-AND-KELLY-GREEN TROPICAL-flower-print dress complete with matching flip-flops. Even my pink underwear and bra coordinate. I look like cruise-ship Barbie, but Sophie's tragic fashion sense is the least of my worries.

The room is empty except for Mr. Graham sitting on the edge of the bed checking something on his phone. I wonder if it'd be too obvious if I slipped back into the bathroom. I don't know how to be alone with someone else's dad and I especially don't know how to be alone with a dad who thinks I'm his daughter. I have no idea what to say. Luckily, he speaks first.

"It's now or never." He nods to a wheelchair in the hallway.

Pure panic washes over me. The wheelchair can only mean one thing. I've been released from the hospital. But I can't leave with this man. I can't go to Sophie Graham's house and pretend to live her life. I need to get back to myself. I need to see my mom. I need to escape.

"I can't." It's the only thing I can think to say. The only words that come to my foggy brain.

A look of annoyance flashes across his face. "Mom said you mentioned going to the ICU before we leave. She thinks it's a terrible idea but I've spoken with a nurse and she's cleared it with your friend's mom. And I'll take you on one condition."

I know I'll agree to anything he says. Anything. I just have to get downstairs. I can feel it.

"We move forward. Nothing good ever comes from dwelling on the past, Sophie. You are strong and healthy and none of this is your fault. We focus on getting you better. Bottom line."

It's not the individual words that shock me. They all sound reasonable enough, like something I'd have imagined Sophie's dad saying to her in a situation like this. It's the layer of fear hovering just below the surface, making his eye twitch ever so slightly, that gives me pause. I've scared him. I've upset some sort of balance and he's over it. There's a note of accusation there too, the-jig-is-up sort of thing.

This isn't really the kind of deal I expected Mr. Graham would make with his beloved daughter. He always seemed so doting when he came to watch her play tennis, like the perfect father or something. His ultimatum catches me off guard because it's almost completely devoid of concern and pretty much the exact opposite of the calm, sensitive, this-will-take-time approach the doctors and nurses have been advocating. But I nod my head anyway and it's settled. Because I'm not her. I'm not Sophie. She can worry about all this crap when we switch back.

We roll through hallways and down two different elevators and are greeted by a nurse who checks Mr. Graham's ID and instructs us to wash our hands. We finally push through a set of big red doors and enter a room full of hospital beds and humming, beeping, living, breathing machines. The room is divided by curtains, I guess to give everyone at least a little bit of privacy. In some of the makeshift rooms, people sit on chairs next to the hospital beds reading books, talking quietly, or even sleeping. Many patients are alone or being attended to by nurses and doctors. Despite the underlying mechanical hum and antiseptic smell, the space is dim and peaceful.

Sophie's dad stops to talk to one of the nurses and guides me toward the back of the room. He pauses in front of a curtain and plants a kiss on the top of my head. Before I can remember to flinch away from his touch, I remember something else. A gurgle of nerves coursing through my stomach, a steady stream of tears, a kiss for courage from my dad before I say good-bye to Grandma Hazel. And for a second, I forget that I've never had a grandma, that I've never had a dad.

For one millionth of a second, I am Sophie. I did not remember and now I do.

Grandma before called to mind a wrinkled woman pulling a chicken potpie out of the oven on some lame commercial. Grandma now has a name and a sepia-toned memory of faint cigarette smoke and jelly beans. I wonder if I'll get to keep her when I go back, if I'll be some sort of mixed-up version of Sophie and Amelia. If I'll remember.

Before I push up from the chair, before I struggle to my feet and face whatever is on the other side of that curtain, I let myself wonder what it would be like to go home with the Grahams. For another one millionth of a second, I wonder how long it would take before the strange nuances of this new family felt familiar. Before my old life hovered just slightly out of reach and then drifted away altogether. Does it still hurt if you can't remember what you lost?

I think of all the Father's Days we ignored. I remember how much I hated being the kid with a mom sitting across from her at Donuts for Dads. I remember the countless nights Mae and I spent making up stories about our dad. Sometimes he was a famous actor. Other times he was the author of our favorite picture book about a girl who makes a spaceship out of garbage in her garage with her dog and flies to the moon, because it seemed like the kind of story our fantasy dad would tell us every night when he tucked us into bed. But most days he was just a regular guy. A man with a decent job who would make our mom laugh and rub our backs so we could fall back asleep if we had bad dreams.

I wonder what kind of person I would have been if my

dad hadn't died right after Mae was born. I wonder what it would have been like to have a dad who sat at the dinner table with us every night. I wonder what kind of life we might have lived together as a family without the shadow of another move, another city, another life always looming over us.

All of the wondering and questioning swirls and I feel like the chair beneath me is no longer grounded on tile but rather sinking into quicksand. I can't stay here. I've never had a grandma or a dad or anything else that Sophie has. If losing my real birthday and gaining a Grandma Hazel is any indication as to how easy it is to forget, I have to get back. Every hour I stay, every minute, every second, maybe I'm losing more of myself.

Maybe I'm not even aware of what I've lost.

I stand, pull the curtain, and make good on my promise to Mr. Graham. I move forward.

At first I think it's just another patient, another victim of some unknown tragedy that ended with the ICU. But then I realize it's me. It's *my* hair that has been partly shaved, *my* neck that is braced, *my* arms attached to a million different machines, *my* life seemingly slipping away with every beep and artificial breath.

Fresh stitches slash across one eyebrow and a large bandage is covering the area of my skull that has been shaved. My lips pull down from the weight of a tube keeping me alive, and instead of my sun-kissed cheeks, I see yellow and blue and a sickly green color. A death palette. My eyes are closed and unmoving beneath the lids. Is Sophie—the real Sophie—stuck in this body?

The thought makes me feel like a ghost haunting my own funeral and I'm sinking again, my vision fuzzy along the edges. I haven't drowned yet, I can't drown now. I breathe deeply, fighting off the dizziness as I inch toward the bed, Mr. Graham's voice trailing behind me like a spirit.

"Her car broke down. They're not sure if she hit her head and got disoriented, but this isn't your fault, Sophie."

Someone shifts in the shadowy corner. "Mom." Her name comes as easily as Sophie's sepia-toned grandma. I'm still me.

I hadn't noticed her sitting there before and for a one dizzy second I don't recognize her. Is it because I'm seeing her through Sophie's eyes or has she really transformed in a matter of hours? She looks like a rag doll someone left out in the rain too long. If it didn't feel like a dream before, it does now.

I want to wrap my arms around her. I want to tell her that Mr. Graham is wrong, I wasn't disoriented or crazy when I ran into the road. I want to tell her how scared I was when the shadow man grabbed me and how terrifying it felt to have someone try to take me away from her, from my life. I want to tell her that I never would have stayed behind, that the only option was to remain a family. I want to tell her that I love her.

Instead, I whisper, "I'm so sorry. . . ." and she doesn't even flinch. I hear her whispering under her breath. It takes me a second to place the words of a song she used to sing to Mae and me.

"Amelia, Mae, give me your answer true.
I'm half-crazy all for the love of you.
It won't be a stylish marriage, I can't afford a carriage.
But you'll look sweet upon the seat of a bicycle built for two."

It was the song she'd sing when Mae and I would wake up in a new place, scared and sure there were monsters in our closet. My mom would pull back her blanket, letting us crawl inside her bed where it was soft and warm and safe. She'd sing to us until we finally fell back to sleep.

My mom squeezes her eyes shut, and I can feel the pain radiating from her body, the song whispered over and over to her broken daughter. And I hate myself for ending up here. I hate myself for fighting with my mom, for accusing her of ruining our lives.

But I hate myself the most for the secret part of me who's scared to go back.

Mr. Graham clears his throat and I know my time is almost up. Before I can let in any more fear, I reach out and grab my own hand, interlocking Sophie's fingers with my clammy, limp ones. Fully ready or not.

I close my eyes and wait a beat, sure that I'll feel a spark. As I open my eyes, I pray that I'll be lying on my back in the bed, but there's no flicker of energy, no shifting of the world on its axis.

I'm still Sophie and my body is still lifeless on the bed.

I lunge forward and grip my frail shoulders—whose are they now? Mine? Sophie's? Maybe I need to get closer; maybe

I need to whisper magic words to reverse whatever spell put me in the wrong body. Maybe if I just click my heels together three times, I'll find myself back home.

A steely arm shoots out and pushes me back, almost knocking me to the floor. My mom's eyes are blazing.

"Take your hands off her." Each word is hissed in an angry staccato as she grips Sophie's forearm. "I figured you were here to say sorry, not cause more damage."

I can't hear what she says next, something about a mistake, because suddenly the machines connected to my body start beeping. My mom presses the staff-assist button and springs into action, running her fingers over the printed scribble of my heartbeat, pulling open my hospital gown and checking the electrodes, repositioning the finger probe. It's second nature the way she moves. When a nurse pulls back the curtain and knocks me farther out of the way, my mom says, "Respiratory distress. Using accessory muscles to breathe."

Before I can even be impressed or confused by a side of my mom I've never seen, or had the chance to respect, a sharp pain explodes in my skull. I fumble with items on a narrow table, squinting through the pain, searching for the silver thing in my memory. If nothing else, I need to know what I took. But the pressure bleeding into my vision is too much. I have to shut my eyes against it.

I can't remember why I'm here. I can't remember who the person is on the bed. I don't recognize the woman running her fingers along cords checking connection points on machines that are keeping me alive. For a moment, I only recognize my dad's voice, excusing us from the ICU. I feel his fingers dig into my shoulders as he presses me back into the wheelchair, trying to comfort and reassure but squeezing just a little too hard. For a moment I'm relieved to be leaving and ready to get back to my bedroom at home, to my crisp white sheets and the patterned pillows that my mom and I ordered online from Restoration Hardware Teen.

It's not until we're at the door when the beeping stops and I hear a woman say, "She's stabilized. Thank God. She's back," that something in me snaps back into place like I've been defibrillated.

Amelia.

This is how it must feel to be lost in space. To not know which way is up or down as your world spins out from under you. I grasp for stability. A memory, something, anything that makes me uniquely *me*, uniquely Amelia. I file through all of my biggest fights with Mae, the name of my first baby doll, the way a tennis racquet felt in my hands the first time I held one. And surprisingly they're all there. I think.

Except I can't remember the way my bedroom looks. I can't remember if I shared a room with Mae or if I had a room of my own. I can't remember the walls or the bed or the floors. The only room I can picture has a crisp white duvet that looks like a cloud and a mountain of artfully arranged throw pillows.

I hadn't planned for this. Accept a coma, even death? Fine. But continue stuck as Sophie and be forced to watch myself—my Amelia self—slip away? Absolutely not. And what if I forget the shadow man next? What if I forget what happened to me?

Suddenly all I can think is that I have to warn her. I have to warn my mom about the stranger. What if he comes back? What if he's already been here? I'm still in danger. I know this with more certainty than I've ever known anything before. We're still in danger.

"Wait! Mom! You have to be careful! There's someone. . . ." It comes out louder, more frantic than I intended.

Mr. Graham politely presses me back into the wheelchair and rolls me over to a young nurse and asks her to please remove me from the ICU as quickly as possible.

"There's something silver. It's a clue! You have to find it!" I shout over my shoulder as the nurse frantically pushes me away. I watch Mr. Graham grab both of my mom's hands, turning her around so her back is facing the door. He wraps his arms around her and her shoulders begin to shake. It's so unexpected, so intense, that I have to look away.

A few minutes later, Mr. Graham assures the worried nurse that his daughter is "under a great deal of stress" and "still recovering" and releases her with an Instagram-worthy smile. She just seems thankful not to have to call security. Before I can open my mouth to ask him what in the hell he was doing with my mom, he asks me what in the hell I was doing with Amelia.

"What the *hell* was that, Sophie?" Mr. Graham whisper-shouts, eyes blazing. "I know you've been through a lot with the accident, but you can't scream nonsense and climb all over critically injured hospital patients. What in God's name is wrong with you?"

But before I can even begin to formulate an answer I see Mae curled up in one of the waiting room chairs, head collapsed on her forearm. I'm on autopilot now and I've got nothing to lose. I can't go home with these people. I have to warn Mae. I have to save myself.

I jump out of the wheelchair and make a beeline for my sister, screaming, "Mae! Wake up! It's me!" at the same time as Mr. Graham roars Sophie's name. But I completely block out the sound of his voice because I'm Amelia and I'm shattered and my whole entire family is shattered and I need to fix it all.

Mae sits up groggy and confused, her eyes puffy, her chocolate-colored hair greasy and limp. She's swimming in one of my grubby sweatshirts and her tall, lanky body is reduced to a curled-up lump.

Does she look worse through Sophie's eyes? As her sister, I remember her hair being shiny, her eyes brighter, her face prettier. The pale girl standing in front of me looks exhausted and plain.

Her eyes narrow as I approach. I realize my sister has never looked at me with such disgust. "Mae," I whisper, waiting for recognition to soften her features. But she only breathes deeper and faster, her hands gripping the arms of the chair, knuckles white.

"Get away from me." Her voice comes out a growl.

I instinctively take a step back. I know if I look close

enough I'll see the sadness buried beneath her anger and it will break me.

"Sophie," Mr. Graham hisses as he grips my upper arm and yanks me back toward the wheelchair. I stumble a bit walking backward, my eyes never leaving my sister's. But the musky scent of his deodorant brings with it a clash of muted sound and color as my father drags me away.

I'm crying so hard it's almost impossible to breathe. One hand is sticky with cotton candy, the other holds a plastic light-up toy. I'm pointing at a stuffed lion in a glass case, snot running from my nose to my lip, competing with the tears rolling down my cheeks.

"But I want the lion, Daddy. I. Want. The. Lion."

A strong arm drags me away, the same spiced-wood scent filling my nose. The same helpless anger. The same desperate want.

"We don't always get what we want, Sophie."

I squeeze my eyes shut against the barrage of color and sound and intersecting details colliding within Sophie's skull. It's too much.

When I open them again, I'm back in the wheelchair and I can still feel Mae's hard, angry eyes following my exit. There's nothing I can say to make my sister smile or laugh or understand. It's like that day at the fair, only now I need something much bigger, much more important, and completely impossible.

nine

MR. GRAHAM WHEELS ME INTO THE HALLWAY UNTIL HE FINDS A quiet corner. His eyes dart around to make sure that there's no one watching us, and then he bends down to my level, his face inches from my own. "Look at me." I force myself to look at him so he doesn't have to grab my chin, which I know with a sick certainty that he's done before. His eyes bore into mine and I immediately look down, afraid that somehow he'll see through Sophie's face and recognize me for the broken imposter that I am.

"What you did back there was completely inappropriate. This family is in pain and Amelia Fischer is fighting for her life. I'm not sure what's come over you, but this has to stop. Now."

Blood rushes to my cheeks and my eyes burn. I'm a mess.

I need my mom, I need my sister. I want to run to them and explain everything. My throat aches and my lungs burn with the injustice of having them so close yet so completely inaccessible. This is what it must feel like to be trapped under ice with safety in sight but no way to break through to the other side. No way to reach dry land, no way to breathe.

"I'm sorry." My voice rings with truth. I am sorry. Sorry that my body is on life support. Sorry that my family is being torn apart. Sorry that I've somehow ended up in someone else's life. Sorry that I might actually be losing my mind.

Oh God, what if that's it? What if this is just some kind of mental breakdown and I really am Sophie, but the accident has made me somehow feel like Amelia? What if I've completely lost myself and my sanity and I'll never, ever find my way back?

But then again, what if I'm not?

Honestly, I'm not sure which is more terrifying.

For one irrational minute I consider telling Mr. Graham that my sister is sitting in that waiting room, wearing one of my sweatshirts, the sleeves pulled over her hands. Would that be enough to break the spell? To set me free?

Mr. Graham sighs and looks exhausted. He can't hide it as well as Mrs. Graham. "I thought taking you to see that girl would give you some closure. Help you realize that none of this is your fault. But I see now that I was wrong." Mr. Graham stands up and begins pushing me back toward my room. "I've already discussed it with your mother and if things don't improve soon we'll be forced to take serious measures.

I've begun doing research on rehab facilities that specialize in this sort of thing."

God, if only he were right. If only there was a place that could fix me. Doctors that could send me back into my own body, awake and whole, place me right where I belong. But something tells me the kind of place he has in mind would be more likely to pump me full of sedatives and put me back to sleep until I forget Amelia Fischer ever existed.

Mrs. Graham paces like a palace guard in the hallway outside my room. She looks from the wheelchair to her husband and back, sizing up the situation without asking a single question, forgetting in that moment to be perfect. But instead of an argument, she offers a smile and looks ten years younger again. "Ready?"

"Yes," Mr. Graham and I say at the same time. He pats my shoulder and continues. "Hillary, you'd be proud of Sophie. You should have seen how composed she was visiting that poor girl and her mother. She's definitely ready to get back home and into the swing of things."

It feels like mental whiplash. There isn't a single grain of truth in Mr. Graham's words and yet the lies roll off his tongue like gospel. And why lie about something like this? Isn't this the kind of stuff that parents are supposed to share with each other? Aren't these the kinds of problems that families solve together?

Because even though my dad died when I was a baby and we never, ever talk about him or it or anything, we still address all of our other shit together, as a family. Typically over a carton of shared ice cream. Unfortunately, I don't think this is an issue that a carton of mint chocolate chip can solve. And honestly, why lie? This was all my fault, so why pretend like everything went perfectly on our little field trip? Especially when Mrs. Graham didn't want us to go in the first place. Why not force me to take some of the responsibility?

Mrs. Graham purses her lips, and I can't tell if she's mad or worried about me leaving or maybe she can just tell that her husband is lying through his perfect teeth, but before I can figure it out, she forces her lips into a benign smile and says, "That poor, poor family. Her parents must be beside themselves."

I feel the stupid urge again to tell her that there is no such thing as parents-in-the-plural at the Fischer house, but it's not worth it.

"I'll just go get my stuff together," I say, but when I get to the bathroom, the space is cleared out.

"Looks like Mom already gathered your things. Let's go!" Mr. Graham claps his hands. And that's that.

We walk through the hospital slowly, our own twisted sort of parade. Mrs. Graham is waving to people as we pass and Mr. Graham is back to looking like the dad I always admired from afar. Somehow everything looks a little different up close, though, like I'm stuck in the center of a snow globe and instead of a tranquil, sparkling landscape, it's all swirling chaos and violent undertows.

As we get into the car, Mrs. Graham twists around in her seat, worry etching lines into her smooth skin. "Are you sure you're feeling up to going home?"

"She's fine," Mr. Graham says before my brain has even started to form a response. "Aren't you, Bumblebee?"

Mr. Graham peers at me through the rearview mirror and I'm not sure there's anything left to do but agree. "Uh, yeah. Of course. I'm fine."

But I'm not fine. I'm terrified. I'm leaving the hospital in someone else's body, living someone else's life. I used to have this recurring dream where I wasn't able to see. I've never needed glasses, I've always had twenty-twenty vision, so I'd inevitably wake up in a cold sweat after watching the world pass me by in lumps and colored blobs, blindly grabbing for glasses that were never there.

That's what this feels like. The real Mr. Graham isn't anything like the jovial person he seemed from far away, and something in Mrs. Graham's sagging posture in the front seat oddly reminds me of my mother.

Although their car looks perfect from the outside, all chrome and luxury, the reality of the car is hellish. The leather seats are hot and sticky and there's a weird smell, like something is rotting in the trunk. My stomach heaves when the car lurches into gear, and I scramble to lower the window.

As we pull out of the parking lot, I catch the eye of a girl waiting at the bus stop just outside the hospital. She stares in blatant admiration of the pretty people in the expensive car. I sense her jealousy and remember how easy this all looked to me as an outsider. One big, happy family; wide smiles on pretty faces.

That girl at the bus stop has no idea that the beautiful raven-haired girl sitting in the back seat is quietly losing her mind. She'll never know and I can't tell, so there's nothing left for me to do except buckle my seat belt and go along for the ride.

ten

I'M NOT SURE IF IT'S THE CAR, THE PASSENGERS, OR THESE UNFAMIL-
iar eyes, but as soon as we drive into Morristown, everything
looks different. We pass the bridal boutique on Main Street
and I remember twirling on a platform in front of angled
mirrors, a tiny ballerina in a music box. As we turn the corner onto First, I remember the creamy taste of vanilla ice
cream at Mia Moo's, but could swear I love chocolate. And
when I see the sign for Kate's Corner Bookstore, I remember the way it feels to run my fingers down the spines of the
newly stocked hardcovers. I'm pretty sure that last memory is
mine. Or did Sophie lean her back against the farthest shelf
to read away afternoons too?

   The rows of historic homes are somehow even more
charming through this car window. I wonder if our

dilapidated farmhouse would look any different. Doubtful. It needs to be painted in the worst way, but suddenly I can't remember what color.

I picture the synapses and connections in Sophie's brain flashing and linking with every passing moment. I picture pieces of me, Amelia, mixing with Sophie like cream into coffee, swirling and separate and then together. Changed. Now you see her. Now you don't.

Mr. Graham takes a left into Kensington Estates, the most exclusive neighborhood in Morristown, and I'm not surprised at all. I can't be sure whether I knew Sophie lived back here or if I know because I'm currently occupying her body, and the uncertainty makes me a little sweaty. Most of the homes are gated and set so far back they're hard to see. All were built to resemble the historic homes in town. The architect was even featured in some design magazine. The houses in this neighborhood are the best of both worlds. They look like oversized Victorians or sprawling Tudors, but the floors don't creak and the moldings are freshly painted and smooth. History is highly overrated, particularly when its roof is leaking.

Mr. Graham pulls into an enormous garage and I linger, trying to remember Morristown as I know it. Digging for treasures in Hattie's Consignment, the green velvet chair in Angela's Tea Room, the upstairs, far-right corner of the library where it feels like I'm the only person left on the planet. I squeeze my eyes shut, trying to hold the details close, somehow lock them into place. I stay there for a minute, too terrified to open the car door because I can't help but worry that the more I smell and see and feel of Sophie's world, the more diluted I'll become.

"Sophie?" Mrs. Graham's eyes are worried, but Mr. Graham has already disappeared inside the house.

"I'm coming." I get out of the car because there's nowhere else to go.

When I walk through the door into Sophie's home, instead of the barrage of recognition I expected I don't feel a thing. Balloons, plants, flowers, cards, stuffed animals, and other random Get Well paraphernalia overwhelm the gigantic mudroom. It's like nothing I've ever seen. Some monster tried to kidnap me, I was run over by a car that cost more than five years' rent and am currently fighting for my life in the ICU. Pretty sure I don't even have a wilted bunch of carnations waiting for me at home. We moved so much that I got tired of having to say good-bye, so I stopped making friends, and by the time I figured out that we might stay in Morristown long enough for me to actually have real friends, I'd forgotten how to make them. Turns out I was pretty good at the whole sarcastic-loner thing.

Mrs. Graham sees me eying the gifts. "The entire butler's pantry is full as well. I've already put Zach's beside your bed. They're just stunning. Don't worry . . . I didn't open the note." Her face is flushed with pleasure and she gives me a little wink. "Plus, Daddy hasn't even emptied the trunk yet. You are loved, sweet girl."

Can anyone really be loved this much? This feels like

a classic case of quantity over quality. Unless it's different for Sophie. Unless she truly is adored by fifty of her closest friends and relatives. Based on Mrs. Graham's watery eyes and over-bright smile I can tell she needs this; she feeds on having a butler's pantry full of proof that her daughter is important and beloved. Maybe it makes her feel important and beloved too.

The doorbell rings in the distance and I'm thankful for the distraction. All these flowers smell like a funeral home. Way too close to home for me. I wind toward what I hope is the front door and figure when I don't recognize the person on the other side I can just blame the accident.

"Oh, honey, are you sure you're up to it?" Mrs. Graham's worried voice trails after me. But now that I'm actually out of that hospital bed, I'm feeling pretty good. A little sore, but the kind of soreness you get after a tough tennis match. Plus, I need to get this woman off my back if I ever want to go home.

"Positive." I try to put a little pep in my step because Sophie strikes me as one of those obnoxious, naturally bouncy people. That seems to work because Mrs. Graham hangs back.

On my way down the hall, I marvel at the sheer number of family photographs that line the wall and compete for space on every available flat surface in the Graham house. There are photos of an elaborate wedding. Photos of Mrs. Graham pregnant, delicate fingers cradling a tiny bump. Photos of Mr. Graham holding Sophie's hand on her first day of kindergarten. Grandparents, dogs, sun-kissed children lumped together on the beach, forced smiles under the gazebo on the green.

It's fascinating to glimpse the evolution of a family. Mr. and Mrs. Graham are standing in that gazebo with his hands on her pregnant belly and then all of a sudden he's holding a bundled baby and then the hand of a toddler. Sophie's body might grow but there's the shadow of that baby in her face, different and yet all the same. It's abundantly clear where Sophie gets her obsessive Instagram habit. I guess maybe if my mom had that many pictures of me all over our house, I might think everyone was interested in knowing what I ate for dinner, too.

Until this moment it never really occurred to me how strange it is that we don't have any real family photographs around our house. When you move around as much as we do, it doesn't make sense to make friends or put holes in walls when you'll just have to fill them in a few months anyway. We are professional movers, can fit a house into suitcases. This doesn't leave room for a lot of extras.

The only decorative item we own is our house angel, a tiny porcelain house that my mom always said made every new place a real home because it was magic. It was the best game for Mae and me growing up. The morning we woke up in another new, strange, shabby-looking rental, we'd search for the small painted house our mom would hide somewhere in the new space. It would distract us from yet another move. It seems ridiculous now, but it was enough then.

Seeing this house, these pictures, makes my old house feel empty. It never felt that way before. Where are the snapshots documenting our first steps? The obligatory first-day-of-school pictures? Mae and me growing increasingly awkward as the years go by? I try to visualize the walls in our house, the stairwell or entryway, the mantle. Surely we must have had some toothy baby pictures or a faded snapshot of us in those dopey matching overalls I vaguely remember wearing, but I can't think of any. Are my memories being replaced by Sophie's, or is it possible that we never had any pictures? Somehow neither rings true.

The doorbell rings again.

"Got it!" I call, tugging myself away from the smiles. I pull open the heavy door at the same time as the doorbell ringer has turned to go and am met with the fairly impressive backside of the tallest guy I've ever seen. Granted, I'm now roughly the size of a six-year-old, but still. The back of his hair flips up a little at the ends, in desperate need of a cut, and he's wearing jeans even though it's pushing eighty degrees outside. He's wearing a vintage T-shirt that's so thin, a hole is starting at the seam. In a matter of seconds, I've expertly sized him up, which feels much more Sophie than Amelia. I try to access some part of Sophie's brain to place him, but if it were that easy, I wouldn't have taken the scenic route to the front door.

He turns around, probably because he can feel the heat of Sophie's gaze on his ass.

"It's you," I whisper before I remember not to.

80

And it's him. The boy from the tennis courts.

"Oh, hey?" he responds. It doesn't take more than those two little words to tell me he doesn't want to be here. "My mom baked these for you. She wasn't sure if you were back yet." He offers the basket, lifting a corner of the towel to reveal the most perfect scones I've ever seen. They smell like heaven. But there's something else there too. Something that gives me that tight, butterfly feeling I wish I could stretch away. Something that feels a little like shame.

You can practically taste the warm air, that's how incredible it smells in this perfectly cramped kitchen. I'm so hungry. My mom never lets me have anything that smells like this. If I go up onto my tiptoes I can just barely reach the top of the counter. I grab blindly, groping for the source of that amazing scent. My fingers land on something so hot that I almost surrender. Instead, I stuff the lump into my mouth without a second thought. Flakey, buttery pastry practically melts on my tongue. It's even better than I imagined. And then I hear laughter and his singsongy voice. "Sophie stole a scone! Sophie stole a scone!"

I know him now. His name is Landon Crane. He's a neighbor. He's the photographer for the school paper. There's a history there I can't quite reach, but it's clear Sophie doesn't get his dry sense of humor and punishes him for it. Naturally. My curiosity collides with Sophie's distaste, and I jerk backward, almost dropping the basket of scones all over the ground because now when I look at him, my stomach pulls.

He's less golden and there's nothing I can do about it.

"Sophie! Who is it?" Mrs. Graham comes to the door holding a dish towel. I wonder if it's a prop or if she's managed to wash something after being home for five minutes. She makes me tired. "Oh! Landon, so nice of you to drop by." She takes the basket from my hand and smiles without showing her teeth. "Please thank your mother for me. So thoughtful. Any chance you know if they're gluten-free? Not to be a bother, it's just Sophie's sensitive stomach."

Oh super, we don't eat wheat and are total assholes about it. I can't resist messing with her a little. "Huh. I ate a bagel before I left the hospital today. My concussion must have cured me because it was delicious and I feel great. A real miracle."

Landon choke-laughs and stops when he figures out I'm not joking.

Mrs. Graham, meanwhile, is trying to translate my words into a language she understands. "Well, okay then. I'm sure someone will enjoy them! You know, we're just getting back into the swing of things around here."

Translation: I will be giving your beautiful scones to the cleaning ladies tomorrow. Please leave now.

"Well, I'm sure the cleaning ladies will enjoy them." Landon smiles broadly at Mrs. Graham.

Holy shit, he actually read my mind. I can't help but honk out an Amelia-style snort. My eyes lock with Landon's. He smirks at me and I smile back at him. We're stuck in the moment together for a few beats until he shakes his head, almost like he's annoyed with me somehow. "Yeah . . . okay . . . glad you're feeling better."

Meanwhile Mrs. Graham is taking the whole scene in with a look on her face that can only be described as visceral horror. "Landon, please tell your mother I'll return her basket." She retreats into the house and closes the door an inch, but Landon doesn't need a cue to leave. He's already halfway down the brick path. I push the door back open to watch him go and catch him shaking his head just slightly.

"Sophie, I know you don't like Landon, but he's our neighbor and I did not raise my daughter to . . . snort." She can barely form her lips around the dirty word.

Huh. Apparently, sarcasm is frowned upon in the Graham house, but kindness is a blood sport. No wonder everyone is in such good shape. Passive aggression probably burns more calories than a spin class. Also, what could Sophie possibly not like about Landon? Being thoroughly annoyed by this fact would be a priority if I weren't stuck in someone else's body. Sophie's mom turns on her heel and carries the basket back to the kitchen. I make a move to leave, to finally escape to a quiet room. To plan.

But as I start for the stairs, Mrs. Graham pauses in the hallway to straighten a frame. "Lovey, I know you're still healing and might not be feeling back to normal, but let's not forget how important the start of the school year is for you. You'll have states and ACTs and college essays . . . and . . ."

I cut her off. I'm not Sophie, I'm in a coma, I'm in the wrong body, and her words stress *me* out. "Um, okay? I'll just go get some rest then." It's probably easiest just to agree with everything she says and let the real Sophie figure things out once we switch back. A dull buzz sounds from Mrs. Graham's pocket. Her phone. How could I have forgotten Sophie's phone? Now that we're home, maybe they'll let me have it back. I can Google and research and learn. I can figure this out.

"Oh, um, can I have my phone now?"

Mrs. Graham is only half listening to me, absorbed by her own screen. She mumbles, her eyes downcast. "Oh sure, just needs to charge, let's not worry about that just now." It's beyond annoying that this woman refuses to hand over my phone, her face illuminated by the comforting glow of her own. I feel the overwhelming urge to grab her phone and run, but they probably have a prescription for that. Too risky.

Sophie must have a computer in her room, anyway. I walk up the stairs and pretend like I know where I'm going—or *do* I know where I'm going? I can't even tell anymore. A huge grandfather clock at the end of the upstairs hallway begins to sound. The noise startles me into motion. Do we even have a clock in our house? I try to picture our kitchen or the dining room. I try to remember the color of the walls or how we got to the front door if the doorbell rang, the exact shade of my mom's eyes, but I can't remember any of it. The ceiling height that at first had seemed palatial now feels comfortably lofty, like anything lower might suffocate me, might pound me right down into the ground. I could touch the ceilings in my house. I think.

In the hospital, I was two floors away from my previous life. Here, I might as well be a universe away. Sophie's world bears no resemblance to my own. We couldn't be more different. Why me? Why her? Why us? Why this? Am I crazy or dead or the subject of some weird psychological experiment?

The final chime rings out to mark the hour and then silence. The details of my life that I always took for granted are being drowned out by the ominous drone of the Grahams' grandfather clock, replaced only by the soft ticks and tocks of time slipping away.

eleven

THE STAIRCASE IS WIDE AND FLANKED BY THE KIND OF HUGE BANIS-
ter that orphans and servants slide down when they're
exploring the houses of rich people in Disney movies. Gallery-
framed photographs march up the wall like rungs on a ladder,
a timeline of Graham family perfection. From Mrs. Graham's
tiny baby bump all the way up to some stunning black-and-
white photographs taken of Sophie on a beach somewhere
recently. The only ones missing are of Sophie's future wedding, the train of her dress spilling like a waterfall down
these very stairs. This must be what it feels like to have your
life flash before your eyes right before you die.

I try to remember if any memories rushed in like a wave,
if time hung in the air for a second, if life hit rewind before

the accident. Is everyone's history documented by flawless snapshots? Is mine? But those memories, that life, it feels hazy and distant compared to the sharp contrast and crisp lines of the Grahams' photos.

Upstairs, there's nothing standing between me and the relative privacy of Sophie's room except four closed doors. Since I have no idea which room belongs to Sophie, I figure my best bet is to try them out one by one in order of appearance, Goldilocks-style. When I open the first door there's a huge white table and the walls are lined with pristine shelves holding paints, fabrics, and rows and rows of wrapping paper. This one's way too crafty.

The second door I open features a room painted a tasteful shade of greige with a canvas proclaiming "Be Our Guest" hanging over the bed. The window treatments tie into expensive rugs over hand-scraped floors that coordinate with linens and throw pillows. So many throw pillows. A cozy blanket is draped so naturally it's unnatural near the footboard. This one's way too impersonal.

When I open a set of double doors at the end of the hallway, a flash of fur barrels toward me and I barely have time to think, let alone react. The dog is approximately the size of a large rat. Yapping and jumping and scratching, its paws tracking tiny paw prints of pee on the hardwood floors.

"Oh my God," I can't help but yell, horrified. I push at the thing with my foot and it yelps, backs up, and plops into a puddle of urine, offended.

"Sophie?" I hear my name called from downstairs. "Is everything all right? What's gotten into Banks? Don't let him out of our room."

"I'm fine," I scream down the hall. Banks is cocking his head at me as I back out of the room and pull the door shut. When it clicks, I let the air out of my lungs. Of course Mrs. Graham has a rat-sized dog squirreled away in her master suite. He probably lives in one of her many, many pillows. This room is way too gross.

And then, finally, I open the fourth door to a room that's *just right*. Well, just right for Sophie, I guess. There are no clothes on the floor or nail polish lining the dresser, no hastily made bed or closet door left open. But the tennis trophies that stand proudly on a shelf near her bed and yet another gallery wall featuring artsy black-and-white snapshots of Sophie and her perfect boyfriend and all of her friends indicate that this is, in fact, Sophie's room.

I snoop around a little, pull open the cabinets in her bathroom, unzip cosmetic bags tucked in the back of a linen closet, rifle through the contents of her bedside table, through photographs of smiling friends, proof of a happy life. Zach's flowers are pretty impressive, a cheerful blend of roses and lilies. I pluck the envelope from between the blooms and pull out the tiny note card inside.

Zach Bateman.

Jesus. He didn't even include a "get well." And thank God he added his last name. How else would I have known that it was Zach my boyfriend versus Zach the TV star? This looks more like the card my mom would get from her company on her birthday than a get-well bouquet from a boyfriend.

I feel something looking at me and turn toward a chair near the window. There's an American Girl doll that looks exactly like a miniature Sophie with black hair so fine it must have been taken from her own head and eyes so bright that for one horrible second I'm sure they're going to blink at me.

I can't help but think about how jealous six-year-old me would be over that stupid doll. It was on my Christmas list every single year until when I was eight my mom finally bought me a generic version with eyes that didn't shut. I stopped asking for dolls after that. There's something a little satisfying about seeing that the authentic version is even creepier than the one my mom bought me all those years ago. I can't resist picking her up from the rocking chair. One blue eye, one green. They must have had it custom-made. This fact makes the doll even more depressing. As I grip her around the middle, I feel something beneath her dress. There, tucked beneath her mini doll camisole, is a half-empty packet of birth control pills.

I snort at the hiding spot and can't help but feel a little surprised. It's not that Sophie is some kind of prude, but I can't exactly picture her having sex either.

When Mae and I were bored at night we'd play a game we dubbed Virgin, Slut, or Everything But. Mae came up with the game to keep my mind off the rejection after Jake Radcliff stood me up for homecoming. I tried to protest the "slut" category, but the name stuck because sometimes when you're locked in your bedroom with your sister and your heart is broken, rhyming trumps feminism. Anyway, the rules of the game were pretty simple. One of us would randomly say the name of someone we went to school with and the other had three seconds to categorize them using absolutely zero evidence whatsoever. It was the equivalent to the endless game of Would You Rather? whispered in borrowed bedrooms over the course of our childhood. *Would you rather lose an arm or a leg? Arm. Duh.* Mae and I had pegged Sophie as an "everything but" girl, and as I run my fingers over the rows of plastic-encased pills I can't help but imagine the look on Mae's face when I share this little trinket of gossip with her. My second thought is that I'll definitely have to leave Sophie a note telling her to use back-up protection before I switch back. It's only fair.

But the grandfather clock in the hallway marks another half hour gone. I'm wasting time. I pull open Sophie's desk drawer. Jackpot. Her razor-thin laptop shines like a beacon and I say a silent prayer of thanks that Sophie has her own computer. We had to go to the library for that.

I force myself to think back to lessons teachers taught about doing thorough research on the internet. Nothing terribly helpful or specific comes to mind aside from the fact that we're never supposed to use Wikipedia as a source, so I pull up Google, plug in some key words that describe my current predicament, and hope for the best.

Thunderstorm kidnapping concussion body switch truck

The first thing that comes up is related to brain-injury awareness. Super.

I decide to refine my search a little.

Body switch coma

Aside from a list of the twenty best body-swap movies there are lists of different kinds of comas, each one more depressing than the next. The worst is something called locked-in syndrome, where a person's entire body is paralyzed except their eyes and they're completely aware of everything happening around them. I think back to my body in the hospital. My eyes were shut tight and I can't help but hope that Sophie isn't aware of what's happened to us. For one horrible second I feel something like relief that I'm here in Sophie's life instead of trapped in a hospital bed. I shake my head to clear it. I can't afford to lose focus. I have to believe that if I'm able to get back into my body, I'll wake up.

Clearly it's time for a new research tactic. I type *Amelia Fischer, Morristown* and the moment I click enter, articles flood the screen.

I do this thing when I'm scared to read something where I squint because somehow it's easier to read bad news when you can only make out a third of the words. Mae caught me doing it with my report card once and almost peed her pants laughing. She accused me of trying to use the power of my mind to transform a C+ into an A—and she wasn't exactly wrong.

I feel my eyes instinctively slit as the headlines flood the computer screen. *Tragic accident, severe head trauma, critical condition*. Even through my blurred vision I can see the impossible facts.

It's completely surreal to see the same pixelated photo in every article. It's old, the same one they ran in the Haven, Kentucky, local paper of me in eighth grade playing on the varsity tennis team. I remember the flash of the camera and the way my cheeks hurt from smiling, my stomach in knots with every click. The spotlight never looked good on me.

I close my eyes to preserve the memory so it doesn't get muddled by any of Sophie's. There was a reporter who came to school during lunch to ask me questions and I was so proud of my thoughtful responses. I didn't tell my mom because I wanted it to be a surprise. The day the paper came, my mom looked . . .

The memory is getting harder to feel and I squeeze my eyes shut tighter. She looked worried. I remember wondering why. Did she think I'd mess it up somehow? Shortly after the article ran, we moved again. I'm not surprised that it's the only picture anyone could dig up because for as long as we've been in school, my mom sent notes opting us out on picture day. When you can't afford the photos, what's the point of even taking them?

Looking at the photo makes me wish the papers at least had my senior picture to run, which I saved months of babysitting money to pay for in the beginning of the summer. The photographer insisted on shooting me in the park, positioning me on a rickety old bridge spanning a river tumbling over smooth rocks. The poses were forced and uncomfortable and my long hair, usually pulled back, kept getting stuck in my lip gloss.

When they arrived in a thick envelope, Mae poured over them, said I should always wear my hair down. I waved off the pictures as cheesy and lame. Deep down, though, I loved how grown up I looked, how much I resembled my mom. The sun bounced off my auburn hair that day, spinning it gold, and my skin practically glowed. More than anything, though, I loved the moment I unwrapped the prints. I loved holding a physical picture of myself in my hands. It felt real in a way that a digital image never could.

I caught my mom in her closet a few nights later long after I was supposed to be asleep. A metal lockbox was open beside her and her eyes were fixed on the photographs. It took me a minute to notice that her shoulders were shaking and tears were streaming down her cheeks. I slipped back to my room before she could see me.

The memory looks a little different somehow and I wonder if it's because I'm seeing it through Sophie's eyes. I was so embarrassed to catch my mom staring at my pictures. It was so awkward to see her so unguarded, so emotional, that it never occurred to me to question why. Or maybe I was just scared of how she might answer. Maybe a girl like Sophie would have asked more questions.

I hope I still get the chance.

I shake my head. All of this worrying and wondering

won't do me any good; I need answers. I click on the first article.

> The September 19 storm, which caused widespread power outages across Ohio, also left a local teen in critical condition. Amelia Fischer, seventeen, varsity tennis player for Morristown High School, was struck by a vehicle along State Route 9 shortly after five p.m. The teenager's car had become disabled, and authorities believe she was waving for help. Police blame flooded streets and driving rain, making it near impossible for the seventeen-year-old driver of the other vehicle to see Fischer. No charges have been filed.

No mention of a black truck. No mention of the man who tried to abduct me. A shiver of doubt worms its way into my head. What if I'm wrong? What if I really did imagine him? What if I jumped in front of Sophie's car on purpose? Was I hallucinating? I click another article.

> No charges have been filed after the accident that left Morristown senior Amelia Fischer, seventeen, in critical condition. The seventeen-year-old driver of the other vehicle is listed in stable condition at Marymount Hospital.

As I reread the words, I feel someone's eyes on me. For a second I fully expect to turn around and see the real Sophie standing in the doorway, jaw set, eyes wide at the stranger in her room, sitting in her chair, typing on her computer, living her life. It's like I'm waiting for that moment when I'll pull the hair in front of my face and no longer see black but my familiar reddish brown.

But when I shift around in my seat I see Mr. Graham at the bedroom door—face tense, eyes unblinking.

"Dinner's ready." I think of Banks behind the master bedroom door, cocking his head, sensing that something is different. Can Mr. Graham see through me too?

"I saw someone. The night of the accident. I think someone was trying to take Amelia."

The words are out of my mouth before I can stop them. I have no idea why or how, only that I need someone to know. I need someone to help.

Mr. Graham stays perfectly still, listening. I take it as a cue.

"He was driving a black truck. We need to call the police. I didn't get a good look at him, but Amelia, her family, they're in danger."

"Stop." He barely speaks above a whisper, but somehow the command still registers as yelling. "I have no idea what's come over you, but we will not be involving the police any further. Do you have any idea how hard my team is working to make sure that this family can't press charges against you? You've almost killed someone, Sophie. The storm doesn't matter, her car doesn't matter, whatever you think you saw on that road doesn't matter."

"But . . ."

It takes him two strides to close the distance between the door and my computer. He snaps the screen shut and rips it off my desk.

"This conversation is over." He leaves just as quickly and quietly as he entered, the sound of Mrs. Graham's voice calling us for dinner punctuating his footsteps down the stairs.

twelve

I SHOOT UP IN BED AS SOON AS HIS FINGERS TOUCH MY CHEEK. HE'S found me. He's come back. Scrambling back against the headboard, I use the blanket as armor and wait for my eyes to adjust to the dim room.

"Oh lovey, I startled you. I'm sorry." My heart hammers against every inch of my body as I connect Mrs. Graham's voice with the touch that tore me out of an already-restless sleep. The last thing I remember was being afraid to lose myself overnight, to fall asleep as Amelia but wake as Sophie. The good news is I'm still me. The bad news is I'm not sure how long the mom who is not my mom has been watching me sleep.

Also, by the look of her made-up face, it's time to wake up. I couldn't have slept more than an hour all night. Her eyes are wide as they flick back and forth, taking in my huddled form.

She takes a deep breath and sits on the edge of the bed. I'm worried she's going to try to touch me again, so I stay frozen just to be safe. "I know we've been pushing you to get back to normal, but if you're not ready . . ."

"No." I bark the word by accident and attempt to peddle back with a smile. "I mean, I'm fine." Weak. I can do better. I let the blanket drop for good measure. "I'm one hundred percent, truly." She holds my gaze, still searching. "I just don't want to get any more behind." Understanding makes her face go soft. That's the stuff.

She considers this for a beat and pats the bed, ready for normal just as much as everyone else. Accidents that leave your daughter all mixed-up inside are very inconvenient. She stands to go but pauses at the door. "I love you, baby."

There's something about the sound of her voice; it's like when I hear the terrible nineties ballad that Scott Matthews and I slow danced to at my first school dance. The opening chords begin and I automatically bend my legs and hunch over in an effort to shrink myself to the size of an average seventh-grade boy. Only this time, the singsong of Mrs. Graham's voice rips me back to a trippy memory montage featuring "I love you, baby" on a loop. First I feel the cold metal railing as I walk up the steps of the school bus, her familiar words nudging me forward. And then she's checking my ears for signs of infection. Next I'm terrified, yielding to make a left on green. And then I'm trying on a new shirt in a dressing room, showing her my report card, lying on the beach. I could go on and on and on. The memories don't wash over me so much as click back into place.

And suddenly I can't remember the sound of my mom's voice. I can't remember if she told me she loved me all the time or if she held back. I don't remember my first day of school or learning how to drive. All those memories are just gone. And it's becoming clear that I'm running out of time, because the longer I stay, the more goes. Tit for tat.

The door clicks shut behind her and I notice the time. 5:15. At first I'm disoriented by the possibility that this might be p.m., but realize with horror that I've been ripped out of the only sleep I'd managed to get all night long while it's still dark in the *morning*. The room is fuzzy and a dull pain is beginning to throb at the base of Sophie's skull. Now that I'm confident I'll still be here when I wake, I lie back down and close my eyes. I have to sleep.

By the time I reawaken, I only have time for one of my patented five-minute showers. I sift through Sophie's expensive closet to find skinny jeans, a white T-shirt, and camel ballet flats that probably cost more than all the clothes in my closet combined. I also now know that I wasn't the only one to find the tropical-print dress from the hospital horrendous. The small sliver of closet devoted to the same brand is shoved in the back, tags still on every gaudy piece. They have Mrs. Graham written all over them, and I can feel her pulling them out for picture day after picture day after picture day. I mentally apologize to Sophie for underestimating her fashion sense.

I can't help but feel a little pleased with myself when I catch her reflection in the full-length mirror. Five fifteen a.m. my ass. Sophie has never looked better, even if I feel like I'm wearing the world's most elaborate Halloween costume dressed in Sophie's expensive jeans and tissue-light T-shirt complete with a different body and a bunch of her unwanted memories high-jacking my brain. More trick than treat.

When I finally get downstairs, Mrs. Graham is focused on preparing something on the stove and Mr. Graham's face is buried behind the newspaper. I feel like I've waltzed into a cereal ad from the 1950s. Breakfast in my house consists of Pop-Tarts and fights over whose turn it is to use the bathroom.

Mrs. Graham turns from the stove, takes one look at me, and blinks hard. Twice. "Sophie?" Eggs pop in the pan below her raised spatula and for one amazing moment I wonder if I've somehow changed back into Amelia. But one quick glance in the enormous mirror hanging above their table dashes that fantasy. Sophie's hair does look effortlessly chic all tied up on top of her head though.

"Is there any coffee left?" I ask. I tried my best to cover up the bags beneath Sophie's tired eyes, but maybe I should have used more concealer. Coffee couldn't hurt.

"Coffee?" Mrs. Graham practically chokes on the word.

Shit. Wow. "Er . . . tea?" I sputter.

Mr. Graham lowers his paper, and I follow his eyes to the messy bun sitting atop my head. It's not my best work. Styling somebody else's hair is surprisingly challenging, but

I never knew dads made it a point to care. Not a selling point, if you ask me. "Trying . . ." Mr. Graham takes a sip of his not coffee and clears his throat. "Trying something new, Sophie?"

I pat the knot of hair on top of my head self-consciously. "Oh, yeah, I guess so. I'm just so . . ." I try to think of something, anything that will divert their attention away from the fact that their daughter is a victim on *Invasion of the Body Snatchers: The Millennial Edition*. "I'm just really excited to go back to school. You know, see my friends, er, Zach, whatever." I try to sound convincing. I just need to get out of here.

"Of course, but maybe it's too soon. You just don't really seem like yourself, Soph. . . ." Mrs. Graham looks desperately to her husband.

"Hillary!" Mr. Graham's tone is sharp. "She's up and ready to go. I think we all just need to get back in our normal routine after . . . well, after everything." I guess that includes not talking about the fact that he refused to listen to my concerns about a freaking attempted abduction and viciously stole my computer out from under my fingertips last night.

Mrs. Graham looks like she wants to argue, but she stops herself short. "Honey, I can skip yoga and we can go get mani/pedis. You could even get a blowout? I just don't want you wearing yourself out."

"I'm fine! Really!" I try to sound peppy. Based on my limited interactions with Sophie during tennis, she always seemed to be talking in exclamation points. I just need them to think I'm okay. I need to figure out a way to warn Mae about the man who tried to take me. I need to see her and make sure she's okay. I need to figure out why the hell I'm stuck here and how to get back into my old life. I have no idea how to make that happen, but I'm pretty sure I won't get any closer if I'm stuck being Mrs. Graham's prisoner all day.

A horn honks out front and I wrinkle my forehead. I hadn't considered how I'd get to school, only how I'd get out the front door.

"Oh, that must be Janie. She said she'd come get you today since your car . . ." Mrs. Graham stops short, her eyes flicking to her husband's.

"Your car is being taken care of," he finishes smoothly. Dude has an answer for everything. "Now, don't make your friend late, Sophie." Mr. Graham smiles broadly and folds up the newspaper. End of discussion.

Mrs. Graham looks like she wants to say something more and Mr. Graham looks like he just wants everyone to play the role of the perfect family that he's so carefully crafted for all of us.

"Okay! Well, see ya!" I cheer the words in an effort to appease Sophie's poor mother and grab a banana.

Sophie's mom practically chases me into the mudroom and I worry that I've forgotten to do some sort of secret handshake or, God forbid, hug her. But instead she pulls a drawer open and hands me Sophie's phone conspiratorially. It reminds me of a trunk stuffed full of bags after a trip to the mall, us sneaking them upstairs as though we're on some sort of team, and I hate it. The whole exchange makes me feel dirty, but I play along and feign appreciation because it's easier. At this point I'm actually thankful for Mr. Graham's potentially destructive insistence that his daughter return to school immediately following a hospital stay.

Mrs. Graham whispers, "Text me if you aren't feeling up to a full day, okay?" I nod even though I don't understand this strange language—their weird nicknames, passive-aggressive fights, and forced optimism. The Monet beauty of Sophie's life has given way to a Picasso reality. My family is missing so many of the pieces that seemed to make the Grahams the perfect, glossy puzzle, but maybe the Grahams are missing pieces too. Just different ones. Maybe we're all mismatched and cobbling our lives together with puzzle pieces that never seem to fit quite right. Maybe everyone's pretending.

I kiss her cheek because she looks like she needs it. Desperate times call for desperate measures. At least now I have the internet back.

Unfortunately not even the internet can help me deal with Janie McLaughlin, who is currently laying on the horn in Sophie's driveway. I know that Janie and Sophie have been best friends since pretty much forever. They walk the hallways through school with linked arms, perpetually sit shotgun in each other's cars, and pretty much constantly have their heads bowed toward each other, sharing inside jokes that leave the rest of the world firmly on the outside. Janie's the runner-up to Sophie's prom queen and she was the second singles to Sophie's first until I moved to Morristown.

Honestly, I can't remember ever having an actual conversation with her. She and Sophie are always huddled together, laughing and whispering during tennis practice. When they miss balls or accidentally hit them into the woods during practice, they wolf whistle and call each other dumb bitches. It's like they speak an entirely different language that no one bothered to teach me. When I see Janie waiting in the driveway in her sparkling white Range Rover, I suddenly realize I'm supposed to be fluent.

Shit.

"It's about time. I was worried you were gonna make me ring the doorbell." She looks me up and down slowly, apparently a patented move in this crowd. "Sleep in?"

When I don't answer, she backpedals. "I mean, I love you no matter what, thank God you're feeling better, but we need to go. Like now. I have a calc test first period and Mr. Jones locks the door after second bell."

I just nod and climb into the passenger's seat. I've barely shut the door when she starts flying down the driveway, hardly slowing enough to let the gate open all the way or check for traffic. I grip my seat, digging my nails into the soft leather as Janie accelerates from ten to forty in seconds, panic tensing every muscle in my body. While adjusting the volume of the sound system, she glances over when all I really wish she'd do is keep her eyes on the road. "Shit," she says, yanking the wheel to the right without checking her blind spot and pulling the car over with a jerk.

"Oh my God, I'm such an ass. You're freaking out in this

car. Are you okay? Sophie, you're, like, super pale. Everyone knows it wasn't your fault, so you don't have to worry about that, okay?" Her fingers graze my forehead as though she's checking for a fever, a movement so automatic, so intimate and true. The Amelia in me flinches, the Sophie in me remembers.

I press one of my hands against the wall, but the trick doesn't work and the world still spins. Vodka sloshes like a pool of fire in my belly. Oh God, I'm going to be sick. Janie's hand is cool against my forehead as she holds the glass of water to my lips. When she tells me everything is going to be all right, I believe her.

I try to remember if I've ever tasted vodka, if Mae ever had to hold my hair back after a night out. But I can't remember any drinks or any parties. Was it because I was never invited or has another part of Amelia slipped away?

It's impossible to know for sure anymore.

"I . . ." *Jesus, Sophie, Amelia, anyone, say something.*

Her brown eyes flick back and forth between mine. "You're scaring me, Soph."

"No, oh my God, no. I'm fine. We're fine. Let's just get to school before we're late." I look down because I have no idea how not to. She continues staring, her eyes practically burning me, until she finally sighs. Janie pulls back onto the road after checking behind her twice, the speedometer hovering at twenty-five the remainder of the ride. I'm caught off guard by their friendship. I guess it never occurred to me that behind their pretty faces and all that exclusivity and popularity there was a genuine connection between them. God, I miss Mae. I try to pull up a mental image of her, but I can't quite remember the color of her eyes or the exact pitch of her voice.

Mae is fading. My sister, my best friend, is slipping from my memories. I have to figure out a way back before I lose her altogether. I have to find her at school. Mae is the missing piece. She has to be.

thirteen

SOPHIE'S NAME IS SHOUTED FROM MULTIPLE DIRECTIONS AS WE walk into the building. The memories trail directly behind the chorus of "welcome back" and "are you okay" and "we've missed you." Mingling colognes bring a sharp memory of crowded bodies in a dark basement, random guys rubbing up against me to the thrum of too-loud music. The mixture of chemical perfume and a history filled with way too many hard ciders leaves me gasping for fresh air, a familiar burn clawing up to the back of my throat before we even enter the building.

With the gentle squeeze of a girl's fingers on my waist, I'm playing Light as a Feather, Stiff as a Board, unseen hands lifting my tiny body practically to the ceiling. Fear hovers along the ragged edges of the memory, fear that I'll be dropped on purpose because Vivien Novack told everyone that I'd lied about meeting all the members of our favorite boy band. My cheeks blush at the memory, at the fresh pang of embarrassment.

The sound of a shrill laugh brings a stab of anxiety so sharp it almost takes my breath away. I'm twelve. It's the first week of seventh grade and the first time everyone's expected to change for gym class. My uniform is neatly pressed and the scent of detergent brings with it a wave of homesickness. A huddle of the tallest girls in the class snicker and stare as I pull skinny arms into the T-shirt and yank it over my stomach. And that's when I notice a rainbow of sports bras around the locker room, the safety of summer a distant dream since apparently everyone's grown up without me.

The memories roll over me and I'm dizzy with them, terrified that the flood of Sophie is going to drown out what's left of Amelia. I must have had the same memories, minor flashes of the life I've lived, all taken for granted. Remembered and dismissed because they belonged to me. I knew they'd always be there if I needed them.

But now my memories are systematically being replaced by Sophie's. And yet, they all somehow feel familiar. Is it possible that perfect Sophie Graham experienced some of the same feelings as completely imperfect Amelia? Maybe Sophie isn't anything like the person she pretends to be. Or maybe it's that she isn't anything like the person I assumed she was.

I can feel Janie looking at me out of the corner of her eye and it makes me uncomfortable. I instinctively grab for my phone, the movement so effortlessly automatic that by the time I'm in, by the time it's registered my fingerprint, I've forgotten it's not my phone at all. It's as if my thumb has a mind of its own as I bypass the onslaught of messages to scroll through a seemingly endless feed of perfect, tiny moments. Snapshots of lattes with foam-swirled hearts, group selfies where Sophie's dimpled smile and easy confidence tugs you closer like a magnet.

The images give me whiplash. Sophie's inner monologue butted up against all these perfect moments makes me feel like I'm facing the wrong way in a car, my brain unable to sort out whether I'm going forward or back. I lower my chin and do my best to ignore everyone in hopes that rumors of Sophie's newfound social awkwardness will spread quickly and the barrage of cracked memories that come with all the smells, sounds, and half hugs will stop.

I try to imagine myself skirting along the edges of all this. What did I look like? Who did I talk to? Kids from class, Mae if I saw her in the halls, Abby Porter and Caitlin Davis at lunch, Payton Crew in art. With three hundred kids in our class, everyone pretty much knows everyone, even if you've only been here for three years. It's still easy to make yourself invisible. Easy to glide through the halls with my eyes trained above everyone's heads, pretending to be busy or preoccupied, anything other than lost.

But it's like Sophie and I go to different schools, orbit completely different planets. People actually see her. They look at her and expect her to look back. The view from

Sophie's place in the universe is already giving me anxiety and first bell hasn't even rung.

"Okay, well, I'll see you at lunch?" Janie's voice shakes a little bit. I wish I could do a better job because her glassy eyes tug at my heart, Sophie's or Amelia's, I have no idea which. I have to get the hell out of this body.

"Yeah, sure . . . Um, thanks for the ride," I respond, but Janie has already rushed away, possibly to cry. I need to find Mae. I have to warn her about the shadow man. I have no idea how I'm going to convince her to trust me, but I have to try. Maybe she knows something and maybe connecting those pieces will help me get my old life back. Because if there's one thing I do know, it's that I can't muscle through lunch in the cafeteria as Sophie.

"Sophie!" Jesus. It never stops. Even worse, it's a shout that's way too loud to ignore. Even for me. The girl has striking green eyes and a head full of wild, unruly hair she somehow manages to pull off. This time I stop walking. Brooke Rydell. I don't know much about her besides the fact that she orbits Sophie like the sun. Brooke links her arm through mine and I see the two of us as kindergarteners, arm in arm, trailing behind our class on a nature walk. Just like that, she's no longer a stranger. "Soph, we've been so worried. Did you get my messages? How are you feeling?" She looks me up and down and barely takes a breath. "OMG, what happened to your hair? Have you seen Zach? I heard he sent you flowers. Adorbs. When you were late this morning I thought maybe you'd be out again, but then Hayden Peterson said she saw you guys pull in. You haven't been responding to any of your texts and you've missed *so* much. . . . Holy shit! Did Tyler and Winnie get back together?"

Her eyes wander toward a couple full-on making out in the middle of the hallway. I think it's pretty clear they did indeed get back together, but I stop myself before I say something Sophie might regret.

I feel like this kid in a picture book Mae made everyone read on repeat when she was four—a kid who was having a terrible, horrible, no good, very bad day. Only I'm pretty sure that little asshole wasn't dealing with the ramifications of an inexplicable body swap.

"Where's Zach?" I manage, mostly because I don't know what else to say.

"He's waiting by your locker. Duh." Brooke takes a step back, still holding my arm. "But are you sure you're okay? You know no one blames you, right? I keep thinking I could have been with you and you know how I never wear my seat belt and omigod it's just hard for me to even think about so I can't imagine what you're going through. I called your house after you didn't answer any of my texts, your mom said you were all better, so you're better, right?" I'm not sure how she's able to breathe through the litany of words and I wonder if she's always like this.

The sun glints off a tiny diamond stud in her ear and I feel another memory slip into its rightful place in Sophie's brain.

Janie's flashlight catches on one of Brooke's earrings.

"Truth," she whispers.

"Borrring . . ." Janie drones, but she's smiling when she says it. "Okay, okay, what's your biggest disappointment?"

"Oh, I don't know, maybe the fact that my dad has been cheating on my mom for years and all she ever does is talk shit about him and my brothers couldn't be more excited at the possibility of two Christmases and parents fighting over us and trying to win our affection with freaking Xboxes or something. So yeah. That, I guess." She tosses a handful of popcorn in her mouth and continues without missing a beat. "Your turn, Sophie."

"Dare," I say, as always. I've never been very good with truths.

Desperately, I try to call up a memory of sharing secrets at a sleepover from my own childhood. Nothing bubbles to the surface. No bright-pink sleeping bags, no microwave popcorn, no donuts for breakfast. There's nothing. I have Mae and my mom, a few tennis teams, some acquaintances at school. It never seemed like a big deal that we didn't do sleepovers, that we weren't invited to birthday parties, that we never kept a toothbrush in a drawer at someone's house. I was desperate to stay in Morristown because I didn't want to leave, to have to be visible and new before I managed to find my way back under the radar. It takes a lot of time and effort to be ignored. But even just the brief glimpse into what I've been missing makes me feel a little sad.

It's too much. This is all just too much.

"I think I need to find a bathroom," I say. Brooke's nose

wrinkles and she says something about our sacred pact to never use school bathrooms, something I don't hang around to hear. Instead I cross the hallway when there's a break in the stream of students and search for the nearest exit. My hands land on cool metal and I'm almost free, away from the Janies and the Brookes and the questions and the narrow hallways overflowing with way too many memories that aren't really mine when . . .

"There you are, babe!"

Zach.

It has been approximately seven minutes since Janie and I walked through the doors and I've already had more contact with people than I've had since moving to Morristown three years ago. Each person brings a new memory, each memory steals another piece of me. I'd like to tell Zach to back the hell off, but it doesn't sound like something Sophie would say to the guy who famously asked her to homecoming by arranging a freaking flash mob at the pep rally.

"Oh, hey . . . you." The words are forced and my smile is tight. Zach leans in for a kiss and I automatically recoil. I've never kissed a complete stranger and I can't risk the ambush, the onslaught of private memories and feelings threatening to extinguish me piece by piece. His lips were aiming for my cheek, pressing against it dryly, so small victories.

"Where are you going?" He falls into step beside me and wraps his clammy fingers around mine and I pull my hand away like a reflex.

"I just need some air." I rush ahead and push on the metal

bar to the courtyard door just as first bell rings. I have to force myself not to react to the sound of that bell like one of Pavlov's dogs. Sorry, Sophie. First period just isn't a priority today. "You should go. I don't want you to be late."

But he reaches across me to hold the door open instead. "You know I have Mr. Morgan first period. The guy barely has a pulse. I'll keep you company." He goes for my hand again, almost awkwardly, as a group of jersey-wearing guys head to class together. They walk backward, calling out, "Yo, Bateman, Kepner's before practice?" or "You hear about Galligan's this weekend?" or "Tateman's DD" and again I'm a foreigner with one foot out the door.

It occurs to me that he hasn't even bothered to ask how I'm doing. We haven't spoken since the accident. And besides the Zach Bateman flowers, there hasn't been any contact. Maybe he sent a text, but I never responded. Why isn't Sophie's perfect, all-American boyfriend playing his perfect, all-American part and at least pretending to care? I let his hand drop away and he doesn't try to hold mine again.

"I actually need some space," I say, stepping outside.

I've accidentally slipped into Amelia and it shows on Zach's face. Clearly he's not used to being rejected. He blinks a few times and lets out a breathy-sounding laugh as though the joke's on me.

"Whatever, Sophie," he grunts more than says. "Oh, and you're welcome for the flowers." Stepping back into the building, he lets the door slam behind him like the seventeen-year-old Casanova he is.

114

Maybe Sophie would go running after him and try to convince him to stay, but I can't stop a triumphant smile from finding its way to my lips.

First, freedom. I head to my favorite spot on campus, a grove of trees off the parking lot on the western side. Mae and I always linger here as long as we can before school starts. She spends the rest of the day hanging out with her friends, but the mornings have always been ours. It's like she knows I need extra time before I face everyone at school. But today the bench is empty and the sight of it creates a lump in my throat.

"Sophie! Wait up!"

I freeze, recognizing the voice. Sure enough, Landon Crane, the boy with the golden eyes, jogs over and falls in step beside me, a smug grin on his face. "You need me to kick Bateman's ass, just say the word." He makes a show of flexing, but it only accentuates his too-skinny arms and the fact that Zach could completely kick his ass in a fight.

I laugh. "I'll keep you posted."

Even though he's treating me like his annoying little sister, I can't stop my heart from swelling the tiniest bit. I wonder if it's because he's the last person I saw as Amelia before the accident.

Who am I kidding? It's more than that—I already like this boy. Maybe it's because he always has his camera looped around his shoulder, like he's worried that life will pass him by if he doesn't capture it. Or maybe it's because he's the only person in Sophie's world who doesn't take himself too seriously.

Landon's friend is waiting for him by the door. "Yo, Landon, second bell."

He shifts to walk backward toward the school. "Hope it has nothing to do with any sensitive stomach flare-ups." He raises his eyebrows, clearly making fun of Sophie and her lame family.

God, I wish I could make fun of them too. I'd do just about anything to let myself in on the joke. I curse Mrs. Graham for referencing bowel issues because there are not a whole lot of witty comments I can make in regards to poop.

"Nope. Everything is moving right along."

Oh my God. Did I really say that? Did I really imply that I'm pooping my brains out after eating those damn scones?

A smile cracks his face, and he snorts out a surprised laugh.

"Shit." The word falls out of my mouth before I can stop it. Seriously, Amelia? Two unintentional poop jokes in under twenty seconds?

Now he's really laughing, and I can't help but join in.

"You're funny, Sophie Graham. I forgot that you used to be funny." He's looking at me like he can't quite believe what he's seeing. "You coming?"

It occurs to me for a second that it might be easy to go. Maybe I should follow, stop holding on so tightly, forget. That might be the key to getting back. Once that final sliver of Amelia is gone, I'll shoot up in the hospital bed, save my family, and we'll be safe again. But the possibility doesn't ring true. The risk of letting Amelia slip away is too great, like some rare side effect to an experimental drug that could cure your cancer or cause a blood clot to travel up your leg only to explode when it finally gets to your heart. What would happen to Mae and my mom if I forgot to try to save them? What would happen to me? I shake my head and mumble something about study hall first period.

"Okay, well . . . good luck then." Landon runs his fingers through his shaggy hair as he turns around and pushes back into the school. I watch as he's absorbed into his group of friends, consider his wide smile after he wished me luck. If only all of it were that easy.

fourteen

I SPEND ALL PERIOD OUTSIDE AT THE PICNIC TABLE WRITING DOWN A list of things I know, details I can't forget, trying to make sense of them. Maybe if I write the words down, they will magically form into some type of plan.

september 19 storm
black truck
something silver. key chain? necklace? bracelet? do guys even wear jewelry?
man, fit, strong
sophie's memories replace amelia's?

There's no real rhyme or reason to the memories as they come, but the longer I'm Sophie, the faster they seem to come.

kidnapper the key
kidnapper knows our names

I run Sophie's delicate fingers over unfamiliar handwriting. It's so strange to see the loopy, graceful letters flow from my brain onto a page. I have to admit, her handwriting is better than mine. If only the words on the page weren't so scary. The bell for second period is about to ring and I'm still not anywhere closer to where I need to be—somehow there are more questions than answers. And then there's Mae. He said both of our names. I have to warn her.

I close the notebook and shove it back into Sophie's bag beside her wallet. At first I'm just curious; it never even occurred to me to wonder how much cash Princess Sophie carried at any given time. But nothing could have prepared me for what I found. I count the twenties slowly, then the ones, and zip open the pocket to count her change. $103.72.

It's not like it's the most money I've ever seen in my life or anything stupid like that. I worked hard. I bought my own car. In cash. But still, the thought of Sophie walking around with $103.72 in her wallet on a random Wednesday while Mae and I scrounged around for loose change to fill up my gas tank on a weekly basis feels like the biggest divide so far.

But it might also be my biggest break.

First bell rings for second period just as I pull open the door. The dull hum of students rushing off to class punctuates each step. I block out the noise. I have four minutes to get to Mae's locker before she heads into her next class, so I have to hurry. I channel my normal self, eyes down, walk the edges, avoid any and all human interaction. It's the most Amelia I've felt since I woke up this morning, and I'm loving every second of it.

I see the beat-up shoes too late and collide with a body. The memory that comes with it is a burst of heat and vibration and energy that almost knocks me over. I remember unbuttoning his shirt, the feel of his chest.

I expect Zach Bateman when I look up.

I see Jake Radcliff.

I check my fingers, still pure white and narrow, still Sophie. That's weird. That can't possibly be right. I had a huge crush on Jake as Amelia, despite his reputation. We shared study hall, and he surprised me with his hilarious portraits of the teacher, Mr. Ninny. When he asked me to homecoming, I think I was so surprised I forgot to say no. It was the first time I felt like anyone had ever noticed me and the first time I ever wanted to be noticed. Too bad it all ended like a terrible nineties movie with him bailing at the last minute via text while I was all dressed up in a second-hand dress with nowhere to go. My forehead wrinkles with the feeling of whiplash and I prepare to shove him out of the way. But before I can react, his eyes soften and his lips curve into a smile. What the hell?

"I heard you were back."

I narrow my eyes. Jake and Sophie move in completely different social circles—hell, they're in different hemispheres. Am I missing something? Before I can ask, he slips a note into my book bag and walks away without looking back. I think about reading the note, but there's no time. Jake Radcliff can wait. I have to find Mae. There's no point sitting around the hospital all day, so unless something horrible has happened, she'll be here.

I turn down Junior Row and scan the hallway for my sister's brown hair and freckled cheeks. She's just shut her locker when she spots me in the hall.

"Mae!" I know I have to warn her. I have to make her understand that she's in danger, but somehow when I run to her, all I can think about is all the other stuff. How much I miss her and my mom. How much it hurt to have her look at me in the hospital but not really see me. I need to tell her that we were wrong about so many things. We used to sit up all night and wonder what it would be like to live like the Sophie Grahams of the world. Secure in big houses with alarm codes, a mom who stayed home every day and folded laundry and cooked dinner and a dad who gave her a kiss after work. We fantasized about living in the same place forever, clichéd lives with white picket fences and happily ever afters. We dreamed of closets full of new clothes and perfect lives. We were sure that we'd be happy if we had all those things, all that stuff.

But we were wrong.

I realize it now in this moment, staring at my sister through a stranger's eyes. Sophie's house is big and cold and empty in spite of all the stuff they try to fill it with. There's no one she can crawl into bed with when she can't sleep at night, no one she can match the rhythm of her breathing with in order to banish bad dreams. There's no sister so close they're practically twins. There's just a house. Full of stuff. Inhabited by people who seem more like roommates than a family. My throat aches with every pent-up emotion, all the tears I haven't had the space to shed. I want Mae. I need my sister.

If only it were that easy. Mae's poker face is nonexistent. She blinks through confusion first and then moves quickly into pure, hot anger. Because I'm the five-foot-nothing girl with bird bones and weird eyes who almost killed her sister. How could I forget?

As much as I want to wrap my arms around her and blurt out this whole insane story, I stop myself short. I have to stick to the plan. I need to get Mae to trust me.

"I know I'm the last person you want to see right now. But I'm here to help."

Mae's brown eyes are wild and stragglers who haven't made it to class yet stop to stare. "Help?" I don't even recognize her voice. I tell myself it's because of the anger, not because she sounds different to Sophie's ears. Not because I've forgotten the sound of my own sister's voice. "You don't even know me and now you're here to *help*?"

"Look, you might not know this, but Amelia and I have been getting closer."

Mae snorts, and I almost lose my nerve.

"I mean, not like best friends or anything, but she told me that you guys might be moving and about your mom always getting transferred and all that stuff."

"There's no way she'd ever tell you any of that." But I see a flicker of doubt soften her features just for a second. She couldn't really argue because I did know this stuff. And it's not like it's common knowledge. The only possible way Sophie could know any of this is if Mae's sister had confided in her.

"Well, she did. And I can't even imagine what you guys are going through . . . after everything." I might break in half saying these words, so I continue before I lose my courage. "Some of the girls on the tennis team pooled their money together and we want you to have it." I offer her the bills and loose change with a shaky hand.

Horror twists her features as her eyes flick around the hallway to see if anyone's heard. "We don't need your money," she whispers, the breathy words laced with venom. I feel miniature in front of my lanky sister. We always complained about our height, hated towering over most of the girls and a lot of the boys too. But we were wrong. Being short is awful. I feel like a little gnat that Mae's going to swat away.

I knew she wouldn't want to take it, but I also know how much we need it. Without my mom's salary there's no grocery money. No way to pay the rent. It's not like we have some savings account with money in it. My mom works and Mae and I babysit whenever we can to bring in a little extra money, but we barely make ends meet on a good day. I don't have to be in the right body to know we haven't had a good day since the accident. There was no more work for my mom in Morristown and she was supposed to be starting her new job next week. There's no way we can leave, but no way for us to make ends meet if we stay. Especially now.

"Please. We all wanted to do something and we didn't know what. It's the best I've got for now, but I might have more. Later. Can you meet after school?"

Mae reaches her hand out and for a second I think she's going to take it. I think that this stupid plan might actually work. But then she knocks the money to the floor.

"I don't need your hush money, Sophie. I know it must be hard for you, running over my fucking sister and all." Mae can't control her volume now. "What the hell is wrong with you? Do you have any idea what you've put my family through? And you think you can fix it with a hundred dollars?" Mae takes a step forward and I shrink back. I wonder if the real Sophie would. "It must be so easy for you. Oops, sorry I hit your sister. My bad. Here's some cash." Mae's eyes are glassy but I know she'd rather die than let Sophie Graham see her cry. "Well, I don't want your charity. Sorry." Her voice is shaking and I know she has to look away now or she'll break in half too. The bell rings and my sister turns away from me, her back rising and falling as though she's just run a race.

"I . . . I just . . . I saw someone the night of the accident. A man," I call after her.

Mae holds her breath and I wonder in that moment if maybe there's a reason for all this. Maybe the universe is letting me borrow Sophie's body so I can keep Mae safe. Maybe this will work.

"He was driving a black truck and he tried to . . . he tried to take me . . . I mean, her. He tried to take Amelia. And he knew your name." Shit. That completely came out wrong.

She shakes her head slowly back and forth but doesn't even bother turning around. "Before you start spreading around a bunch of lies, maybe get your story straight, Sophie." Her voice cracks on my name and I want to scream and grab her and hold her and never let go. But all I can think as I watch her walk away with her chin raised with as much confidence as she's probably ever had to muster is that I'm losing. I'm losing her.

I'm losing everything.

fifteen

I AM WAY TOO OBVIOUS LINGERING IN THIS EMPTY HALLWAY, AND IT won't be long before I get in trouble. The concussion card would be easy to play, but I'm not willing to risk the attention that comes with it. Best to keep a low profile. I turn down the art hallway and slip into a bathroom that's pretty much always empty. As a card-carrying introvert, I'm a pro at identifying good hiding spots in public places—and the Junior Row girls' bathroom happens to be one of the best.

Sophie's phone blows up, new messages appearing on her screen every few seconds, pushing the older ones down. I'm at ground zero, two lives in rubble all around me, holding evidence that everything continues on. I can't even feel all bitter because with every ping and vibration comes words of support, hope, and love.

I lean my back against the cool cinder block wall and slide down to the floor, clenching my jaw to bite back tears. Mae doesn't believe a word I said. In fact, she thinks I'm lying, but for what? Attention? Absolution? It doesn't even matter. She didn't listen and I need a plan B.

I dig around for the notebook again and see the crumpled piece of scrap paper Jake threw into my bag. Jake. I wrinkle my forehead.

Smoothing it over my knee, I read the word *tonight* in blocky print. Tonight what? What the hell would Jake Radcliff need to tell Sophie about tonight?

"Sophie?" The voice cuts through my frustration, and I scramble to hide the note.

"Soph? Are you in here?" Another voice. *Am I in here?*

Janie pops her head in the bathroom. "You're here." She lowers her chin a little and approaches me slowly, like I'm a rabid raccoon foaming at the mouth.

"I'm worried. I heard about you, like, attacking Mae Fischer in the hall. Everyone has." Janie drops to the floor on her knees. "Look, I get it. Amelia's always been a little weird. We all know it wasn't your fault that she was standing in the middle of the road in a thunderstorm. It's like that time I stepped on Rusty Linthicum when he was lying on the ground blocking the doorway in third grade. Remember?"

My stomach knots because I do.

Rusty was one of those kids who was always the worst. He'd never listen, always disrupted class. Everyone said he was gifted, but we knew the truth—he was just a huge pain in the ass. One day he stretched his body on the ground, blocking the doorway of our classroom because he didn't want anyone to go to gym class. When I went to step over him, he kicked up his foot and I face-planted in the hallway. Janie was right behind me and instead of hopping over him like the rest of the class, she planted a foot right in his stomach. I remember her grabbing my hand and helping me up while I wiped the tears from my cheeks.

And before I even have time to wonder what memory I lost at the expense of having remembered that moment, Janie grabs my hand and picks me up off the floor again.

"Let's blow this pop stand."

For a second I think about saying no. I think about trying to talk to Mae again. Or heading back to the hospital to try to figure everything out. But somehow I just can't see the point, so I let Janie drag me through the empty halls of the school. I give up control, I stop fighting against the current, and I let myself be pulled along by the human tidal wave that is Janie McLaughlin.

Walking out of the school is just as easy as walking in. Apparently being Sophie Graham really does have its perks. Janie doesn't say much but keeps shooting worried looks back at me as we weave through the cars in the parking lot. Knowing what to do with your best friend when she's having a mental breakdown in school after she almost killed her tennis teammate with a car isn't exactly something that's covered in etiquette class. And that's when I see it.

The Crimson Wave. My Crimson Wave. Mae must have

driven her to school today. I walk toward the car without thinking, ignoring Janie calling out after me. Autopilot takes over and I can already smell the pine-scented air freshener, can feel my fingers wrap around the keys hidden beneath the front seat because Mae and I always joke that if someone actually wanted Crimson, they shouldn't have to break a window to take her.

Learning to drive a stick shift was one of our mom's "things." Self-defense classes, knowing how to change a spare tire, and learning to drive a manual car were mandatory rites of passage for the Fischer girls. Besides, driving a stick shift is kind of badass.

It's not until my fingers slide under the door handle that I see it. A necklace hanging from the driver-side mirror, swaying ever so slightly back and forth like a talisman. Something about the way the metal catches the light brings with it the smell of rain, and I feel like I might be sick. Silver. I'd ripped a silver necklace from around the shadow man's neck.

I gently lift the chain from the mirror, my heart thrumming as I run my fingers over a clasp that is not broken. *It's not the same necklace*, I try to convince myself. Someone gave it to Mae at the hospital. Someone added us to a prayer group. But something about the silver circle at the end, an engraving of an angel holding a small child, makes my head spin.

When I flip it over, I see the words *St. Anthony, Pray for us* inscribed on the back. A saint. Religion has never been a part of my life. We moved too much to ever join a church and most Sundays my mom had to work. Instead of grace before dinner, we thanked our exhausted mom, and instead of prayers before bed, Mae and I whispered to each other through the dark, our limbs practically entangled. I guess it never occurred to us to worship anything else.

Of course I picked up bits and pieces along the way, but for me religion felt like a fairy tale that would never come true for me. After all, where was God when we had to move for the third time in one year? Or more importantly, where was he when I got mowed down by Sophie Graham's car?

And suddenly, the necklace doesn't feel like hope, like some gift of faith from a well-meaning, kind, religious person. It feels like a warning, the same kind of dissonant chord evoked by a random shoe on the side of the road or a child's bike dumped over near woods.

"Sophie? What the hell?" Janie grabs my upper arm and scares the living shit out of me. I drop the necklace and practically jump out of this stranger's body. "If they catch you creeping around Amelia's car . . ."

Lurking around this car is the least of my worries. My eyes dart around the parking lot looking for his black truck, seeking the man in the hooded sweatshirt who destroyed my life. Fear pounds through my temples, and for a second I feel like I might scream. Or worse, tell Janie everything. My mouth opens, but when I process the horrified look on her face, I snap it back shut. Instead, I bend to retrieve the necklace and slip it into the pocket of my jeans. I'm not sure what it means or where it came from, but somehow it feels important.

"What is that?" Janie's face is creased with worry.

"My necklace broke," I lie. "I just don't want to lose it. I'm fine, okay? Let's just get out of here." I need to leave. Now.

Janie's eyes search mine, and I let them this time. "Everything is going to be okay," she whispers quietly. It's easy to let her familiar words wrap around me like a blanket. If only it were just as easy to believe her.

sixteen

"REJUICINATION?" THE QUESTION MARK THAT JANIE INTONES AT the end of the ridiculous word feels like a formality. Based on the endless stream of artfully arranged smoothie bowls and avocado toast that I've seen on Sophie's Instagram from the trendy juice bar on Main Street, I know it's a favorite spot of theirs. I should make it easy. I should agree. But I've never once set foot inside the picture-perfect, polished doors of Rejuicination, and I'm craving something familiar right now. The medallion I lifted off Crimson Wave feels heavy in my pocket. Could it be the same necklace? Did someone have it fixed? Is it his? It was on my car, the car Mae is driving. Is he watching her? Waiting?

Everything is so jumbled in my head, the memories are so murky, that it's impossible to know either way. My mom always told Mae and me to rely on our instincts.

Listen to your gut. Your gut doesn't lie and if it's telling you someone is dangerous or bad, you don't stop and think. You don't try to be polite. You run.

My gut is telling me that this medallion is a warning. A mark. But my brain is reminding me that I'm currently trapped in someone else's body and not really in a position to be jumping to conclusions. Either way I need to figure out a way to warn my sister and there's no way I can do it while sipping some organic, fresh-pressed bullshit.

I need caffeine. I need sugar. I need somewhere I can actually think.

Before I can stop myself I reply, "How about Pete's Donuts?"

There's an awkward pause while Janie's face silently communicates her disgust of the hole-in-the-wall donut shop on the outskirts of town where Mae and I have spent endless hours consuming our weight in fried dough and tar-like coffee. The thing about Pete's is that they don't fuck around. They make these amazing, giant donuts fresh every single morning. The second the last donut is sold, they close. They don't make cappuccinos and they don't give a shit about sustainable ingredients or non-GMO certified flour. They just fry amazing deliciousness and brew terrible coffee. End of story.

"Um, sure? I mean, yeah, definitely, it's good to try something new every once in a while, right?" Janie's voice holds the same false encouragement that people usually reserve for really bad haircuts or tortuous physical therapy. Part of me can't believe that in all the years they've lived in Morristown, these girls have never once had a Pete's donut. But the other part of me, the Sophie part, presumably, understands now that flaky, dough-melting circles of heaven don't exist in this life. It's not on Main Street. It doesn't have a cute sign or minimalist décor. The reality is that there are two very different Morristowns—Amelia's and Sophie's.

Janie stops at a red light and immediately starts stabbing at the radio the way I now understand that she always does. Her arm brushes against mine as some pop song fills the car and words I have no business knowing find their way to my lips. As Amelia, the only radio I ever deemed acceptable was the local college station with its eclectic collection of new bands no one had ever heard of, amazing classics, and liberal news stories.

"This would be on my soundtrack," Janie yells over the music with complete seriousness. "If my life had a soundtrack, this would be track number one." It's some ridiculous pop anthem belted out by a singer with one of those nonsense names like Madame Drama, but the lyrics are so Janie. All passion and pure fun. I laugh because that's what I always do when Janie tries to get all deep. But I spend the rest of the ride trying to decide what number I'd make the song on my own soundtrack.

The light turns green, the song ends, and I'm overwhelmed by the natural mixture of friendship and bad music. "Thanks, Janie." My voice cracks a little on her name. Maybe it's because I see the sign for Pete's and all I can think about is Mae. Maybe it's because the donuts we're about to eat are so fucking good and everything else is just so fucking bad. Maybe it's because Sophie has a best friend who knows when to say yes. I always assumed that they were fake, the kind of faux friends who pose for Instagrams together but couldn't possibly really care about each other. But it's different on the inside. Janie would do anything for Sophie, and by default for me, while I'm stuck in this body anyway. At the end of the day, I've only ever had Mae and she was my sister—biologically compelled to love me and circumstantially destined to be there for me when I needed her because we didn't really have anyone else. Friends are just different.

Janie carefully steers her car into the lot and slides into one of the last open parking spots. She pushes her baby-blond hair behind her ears and throws me a gigantic smile. "You're just lucky I love you." And I don't need to remember anything else to know she does.

Ironically, Pete's sits next to a twenty-four-hour gym, a fact that always made Mae and me giggle. Eat a donut, work it off. The windows of the shop are foggy, but I can still see the "Open" sign flashing red above the door. Thank God. It's barely ten, but there were multiple mornings when Mae and I rolled up at eight thirty only to find it closed. Most of the customers are old men and the occasional hipster foodie who happened to see the little shop featured on Top 100 Hole-in-the-Wall Donuts on BuzzFeed a few years ago.

Janie hangs back a little, taking in the ragged décor and the grimy glass cases that hold only the most basic of donut flavors. Glazed, chocolate frosted, jelly filled and Boston cream. Occasionally, Pete goes crazy and will add sprinkles to the chocolate frosted, but I always sense a little judgment in his eyes if Mae and I order one.

"Hey, Pete!" I greet the old man at the counter cheerfully, forgetting for a moment that he has no idea who Sophie Graham is. He returns with the standard mumbled hello he reserves for well-dressed strangers.

"I'll take two glazed donuts and a large coffee with extra cream and sugar." I hear an audible gasp from behind me and see Janie gaping at me from where she's hovering awkwardly near the door. "Oh, right. Sorry. You want anything?" I forgot about the hundred dollars burning a hole in Sophie's wallet. Mae was always on her own.

"Um, what about your gluten sensitivity?" Janie's eyes are wide and shocked.

"Oh, yeah . . . I, um, well, I'm trying something new. I ate a bagel in the hospital and it was totally fine." Which is one hundred percent true, but she doesn't look like she's buying it. "Let me buy you a donut, okay? I promise you won't regret it."

"I'm good. Thanks anyway." Janie is still staring at me like I landed from another planet and for a split second I think maybe we should leave, but then Pete hands me two perfect donuts and a hot cup of milky, sugar-laced coffee and the smell is so familiar, so Amelia that there's no way I can walk away from it.

I steer us to a small table in the corner and take a huge bite of a donut before I even settle into the cracked vinyl chair. The taste is familiar yet somehow different than I remember in Sophie's mouth. The glaze is a little sweeter, the dough lighter, but the bite washed down with the sugary coffee is still perfect. I close my eyes and for a second I'm Amelia again. The smell of frying donuts, the quiet din of old men arguing about local politics, the sticky chair. When I open my eyes again I almost expect to see Mae sitting across from me, stuffing a chocolate-covered donut in her mouth. But instead Janie is staring at me like a deer blinking in the headlights.

"You have to try a bite. Seriously. So good." I push the remaining donut toward her, but she just keeps staring.

"You know those have more calories than a Big Mac, right?" Janie's tone conveys her complete and utter disbelief.

"That's an old wives' tale. I read something about it on Snopes once," I reply, my mouth full.

"Snopes?" Janie clears her throat and I sense a lecture coming. "I'm worried about you, Soph." Her voice cracks and she gestures with her hand around the room. "This just isn't you. I know you're still getting your bearings and everything and you know I love you no matter what, but it's like you're suddenly this different person."

She's so painfully close to the truth. My hand

subconsciously reaches for the necklace buried in my pocket. This is it. This is my chance. If Janie loves Sophie as much as she seems to, maybe she'll be able to help me after all.

"I saw someone else on the road. Someone else was there when I hit Amelia."

She visibly jerks her head back in shock. "What do you mean, you saw someone?"

"I mean there was a man there. And I think he was chasing her." I need to keep my story simple. Stick to the facts. Get her to believe me and then get her to help me figure out a way to warn Mae. It's not the best plan in the world, but it's the only one I've got.

"I, um, I left something in my car. I'll be right back." I think I see tears in her eyes, but she is up and out of the restaurant before I can say for sure.

Hope explodes in my chest. Janie knows something. She believes me and she'll help me fix this. I don't have to be alone anymore. She'll save me. Janie doesn't take long at the car and is back in the restaurant. My hope is punctured by the haunted look on her face. She looks so sad and so confused and she's holding her phone. My mind immediately races with the possibilities. Is Amelia dead? Has my old body taken a turn for the worse? I hadn't considered the possibility that my situation could get any worse. I stand, the chair almost falling back beneath me.

"What is it?" My heart is hammering so hard it feels like it might burst. Am I ready for this? Whatever *this* is? I stretch my neck to see what's on the screen of her phone, ready or not. A text message appears from— I squint to read upside down. I see an *S*. I think of the stranger, the monster. I think of the name I gave him, the only name that fits. Shadow man. The letters on Janie's phone are all jumbled together but I can only see one word. It doesn't have to make any sense at all in order for the panic to move in. I struggle to blink away darkness curling in along the edges, pull in a ragged breath through a straw because my throat is closing and it's happening and I don't know how to stop it in this body. The florescent lights magnify the dinginess of the restaurant and voices mingle to a constant hum. The donut sits like a brick in my stomach and I'm afraid I might be sick. I fall back into my seat.

"Sophie?" Janie's voice is far away as she repeats the name on a loop. I focus on the sound, let it buoy me like some sort of life preserver, which is odd because the name, her name, is what got me into this mess in the first place. "Sophie, you're scaring me." *You're seeing things*, I think. *Janie is not talking to someone called the shadow man. You are safe right now.* The room comes back into focus, the lights aren't nearly as bright, and the volume returns to normal. I can breathe. Janie is leaning over her phone, which rests on the table between us. The name Sir Graham continues to pop up on her phone. Sir Graham?

Janie follows my eyes to her screen. "I'm sorry, Soph. I had to tell him. Your dad told us how disoriented you were when you woke up at the hospital—that this happens with head injuries." She continues talking but I don't hear anything besides "your dad." Mr. Graham. Sir Graham. Of course Janie programmed in a nickname. I'm so stupid. So stupid for so many different reasons. Words keep pouring out of Janie's mouth, her eyes glassy at the betrayal. "I promised I would tell him if you acted different. We're all so worried about you."

"I'm fine. Really . . ." But even to my ears it sounds like a lie. Because I'm not fine. I'm trapped in the wrong body, in the wrong life. And if Janie's phone, which is currently blowing up with texts from Sophie's dad, is any indication of how little time I have to get the hell out of here before I'm shipped back to the hospital, I have to go.

"Wait! Where are you going?" Janie tries to grab my arm, but I shake her off.

"The bathroom. I'll be right back." I give her my fakest, most reassuring smile and head toward the bathroom but walk right past the ancient wood door with its chipping sign and straight through to the kitchen.

"Hey, you're not supposed to be . . ."

I'm out the back door before an employee can even finish his sentence. I'm moving so fast and I'm so focused on trying to figure out what to do next that I don't notice him until I've walked straight into his chest.

I look right up into the raised eyebrows of Landon Crane.

seventeen

"SOPHIE? WHAT ARE *YOU* DOING HERE?" THE WAY HE SAYS THE word *you* instantly annoys me and briefly makes me forget about the fact that my best friend is currently planning an intervention that I best avoid.

"I happen to love Pete's Donuts, thank you very much. I come here all the time and I've never once seen *you*." I can't help the defensive note that creeps into my voice. Something about the way Landon thinks he knows everything about Sophie bothers me even though he's dead-on and his assumptions are pretty much the exact same as mine.

"Yeah, well, shows what you know. I come here every day during my free period. Pete gives me donut holes and lets me read in the back room if I take out the trash for him. Your turn."

Sure enough, there's a beat-up paperback sticking out of his back pocket and it all kind of makes sense. I mean, of course grumpy Pete approves of Landon Crane with his sarcastic quips and willingness to haul trash in exchange for leftover donuts. Hell, I was sold based on his eyelashes alone.

I clear my throat. "Yeah, well, I happen to come here every Saturday and I actually pay for my donuts." It's a lie but a calculated one. Mae and I really are here almost every Saturday and I'm pretty sure I'd remember if I saw Landon, so for all he knows Sophie is a closet donut aficionado.

"Please. You'd probably get *Sugar Is the Devil* tattooed on your ass if you weren't so terrified of needles."

Touché. So much for my aficionado status. "I'm not terrified of needles." But as soon as I speak the words, I know they're wrong.

"Ma'am, if you can't get your daughter under control, I'll have to call another nurse in to pin her down." The woman's words are clipped.

Panic blooms in my chest at the anger twisting my beautiful mother's features. There's no more room for nice. Her eyes flick away from mine as she grabs my arms and pins them over my head. I scream, not because I'm trying to be bad, but because fear has wrapped itself around my neck like a vise.

The nurse holds a syringe. "This is medicine for kindergarten, Sophie. Don't you want to be a big girl?"

I try to move away from the needle, try to move away from my mom, but she's too strong and she's too mad.

"See? That wasn't so bad?"

I think for a second that the nurse is tricking me, that they haven't given me the shot yet, but my mom's fingers have released my upper arms and I'm free. Shame washes over me because she was right. I didn't feel a thing.

Heads turn discreetly to catch a glimpse of the screamer on our walk of shame through the waiting room. A boy with thick glasses offers me a thumbs-up and I give him a little wave before I'm yanked out the door. His mom pretends not to notice how my mom won't even look at me, but I know she sees.

"We were babies." I breathe the words more than say them. There's not the same softness in his eyes for me now, no adorable thumbs-up. I wonder when things changed between Landon and Sophie. I wonder what caused it. Something tells me it was more than just a stolen scone.

"You're forgetting the time when we were ten and I warned you about the vaccines for your checkup and you tried to run away and live in my attic."

Part of me wants to remember, but I know that every piece of Sophie comes with a price. At least I think I know. It's like I can feel myself slipping away when pieces of Sophie return to me and I can't help but wonder what I lost to gain this memory? What piece of my own fuzzy history disappeared?

I try to remember a moment where Mae and I were at the doctor together. I try to remember if I was scared of shots too. But there's nothing there except Sophie and Landon and the sound of Mrs. Graham's tired voice. The crazy thing about memories is that you never remember losing them and there's no way of knowing if they were ever there in the first place.

Voices float out from inside the donut shop and I remember that I'm supposed to be escaping. There's no doubt that Mr. Graham will be here soon, ready to make good on his promise of rehabilitation, and I'm guessing he's not going to be too happy about it.

"I gotta go." I start to push past him but he pulls me back. The touch of his fingers sends waves of heat up my arms.

"Wait." His eyes aren't quite as flinty now. He's protective, ten years old again and warning me about another round of shots. "Let me drive you."

I'm caught at an unfamiliar intersection of relief, excitement, and fear of what might happen if we don't get out of here before Mr. Graham arrives. As if Landon could get any cuter, he leads me to a faded red Volkswagen Bug parked behind the donut shop and opens the passenger-side door.

"Sophie, you remember Murray? Oh wait, I don't think you've officially met. I got her after you decided it was super uncool to be friends with someone who, and I quote, 'would rather read Stephen King fan fiction than have an actual life.'"

"Did you just make air quotes? Because I'm pretty sure the only people who make air quotes are at least sixty-four years old and frequent bingo nights."

His face clouds for a second, and I worry that I crossed some sort of invisible line that he and Sophie must have drawn up after she chose the Zach Batemans over the Landon Cranes of the world. But then he grins, shakes his head, and actually laughs.

"Just so happens B-sixteen is my lucky number." He leans into the car and tosses a few empty coffee cups into the tiny back seat. "Sorry, we weren't expecting company."

I half expect there to be some sort of adorable puppy named Murray in the front seat, but as Landon pats the roof of the beat-up red beetle lovingly, it's confirmed that I've finally met another person nerdy enough to give their car a name.

In another life, I'm pretty sure Crimson and Murray would be fast friends. I appreciate every dent, every tear in the leather, every spot of rust. The car is rough around the edges, has traveled far and wide. I toss Sophie's bag on the floor and tuck myself into this tiny car that smells like a huge blueberry muffin and feel a little less like a stranger in this body. Much more comfortable than all that supersized, new-car-smell ridiculousness I've been experiencing of late.

Landon folds himself into the car, his head almost touching the roof. "So where to?"

I think of Janie waiting out front at the table where I left her. I think of Mr. Graham pulling into the strip mall parking lot and rushing into the donut shop to pluck his daughter away before any further damage can be done. All I know for sure is that I need to get out of here.

"The hospital," I say. It's the only place I can think to go. If no one will help me in this life, I need to get back to my other one. There must be some way I can switch back. Some trick that I haven't yet thought of to will myself back into the right body. And if it's too late for that, if the doctors and percentages are right and I've been asleep for too long, there at least has to be some way to protect my family.

"They won't let you see her."

"How do you know? And how do you even know who I want to see?"

"You're forgetting I used to know you better than anyone, Sophie. You might have convinced everyone else that you're some perfect, hollow Barbie, but I know you. And the Sophie I know would feel terrible about what happened. She'd want to do whatever she could to help."

I narrow my eyes and consider his words, wishing for a second that despite the risk, I could understand their entire history in all level of detail instead of through disjointed flashes. He's clearly lost respect for Sophie along the way, but he still believes in her.

"I talked to her," he confesses. Before I can remind him that we really should get going, I hear my name and stop. "Amelia, I mean. I've wanted to talk to her for a while and then I finally did it, after the match. The night she . . ." He looks down at his hands. "She was . . ." He shakes his head. "And now, she's gone. I mean, not gone, but . . ." He's scrambling, trying to relay these words without making things worse for Sophie. It makes my breath catch. "And I can't stop thinking about her. I tried to see her in the hospital, but the nurses wouldn't let me anywhere near her. Does that sound crazy? Shit, don't answer that."

My heart is breaking. He's thinking about me. He's thinking about Amelia.

"You're not crazy," I say. "This is all my fault."

And it's the truth. If I hadn't wanted to stay in Morristown, if I hadn't wanted to win so badly, if I hadn't thrown a hissy fit after the match, served all those extra balls, talked to Landon, if I hadn't climbed into Crimson at that exact moment, driven down that rain-soaked road, maybe everything would be different.

And then, without warning, Mrs. Graham explodes out of the back door of the restaurant.

Shit. I think it and Landon actually says it. My entire body sags in defeat.

It's just my luck to get busted by Mrs. Graham the exact moment Landon is confessing that he likes me. Well, I guess technically he's confessing he likes a girl who's currently in a coma to his former best friend turned perpetrator of vehicular manslaughter whose body is being occupied by said crush.

Timing is a real bitch.

eighteen

THERE'S A BATTLE PLAYING OUT ON MRS. GRAHAM'S TAUT FACE that I'm sure she'll regret later. Concern for her daughter in the midst of a mental breakdown versus anger versus a highly cultivated appearance of perfection. Landon is really throwing her for a loop. After all, she just wants everyone to be okay.

She shakes her head, jogging now toward Landon's car. "Sophie, sweet girl." It's not the tears gathering in her eyes or her brows knitting together or her shaking hands that cause a slow burn to spread up the back of my throat. It's not the Sophie in me, it's not her reflex. This time, they're not her tears. They're mine. I hadn't given Mrs. Graham enough credit. Yes, her reputation, their appearance as the perfect family, is vital. But she chose her daughter. In that simple moment as she closed the space between us, everything else fell away, and she said my name. She chose me.

Facing Mrs. Graham, I whisper to Landon, "Thanks anyway," so he can't see the tears that have gathered in my eyes for someone else's mom. And then I open the car door and let Sophie's mother take over. We walk back through the busy restaurant just as Pete turns the last few stragglers away after selling his last Boston cream. Janie is gone, newspapers are folded up, and a woman wipes down tables. It's time to go home.

I watch Morristown slip by outside my window as we head back through town. There isn't a bombardment of memories this time probably because they're all tucked safely inside, woven into a new pattern, not so obvious anymore. I hope I'm not forgetting to panic.

Mrs. Graham stops the car at a red light and takes a deep breath. "Sophie, your father has found a facility that specializes in the brain. They see your kinds of injuries all the time. The doctors can help us."

A facility. Rehab. Reprogram. Forget. The piece of me that had softened toward Mrs. Graham hardens instantly. I can't go to that hospital. I can't risk losing the last of Amelia. The Grahams need me to be fine, so I'm going to be fine.

"Mom." I swear I can see a physical manifestation of that simple word fly off my tongue and strike my target. Such a basic, one-syllable sound, such a powerful, immediate response. "I'm sorry I scared you and . . . Dad. All the questions at school got to me and I felt weird and I just wanted there to be a reason everything happened. But I'm done. No more stories. No more excuses. I'm sorry." I need to take the path of least resistance, the road well traveled. If I keep trying to convince the Grahams of anything other than that I'm better, I'll be put back away, silenced. It's a dead end.

She closes her eyes for a long time. "No, I'm sorry. I thought getting back into your old routine would be good for you. But it was too fast. Too much. We just want what's best for you, honey. This is no one's fault. You need to know this is not your fault." She squeezes my hands between hers and it hurts a little, but I don't pull away. I can't. I just want this conversation to be over. A horn rips through the moment. "Let's get you home, sweet girl. You can take a long rest for the afternoon." There. *That's better*, she seems to say. *No more of this crazy talk. Sleep it off.* And I have to agree. If I'm not more careful, I'll end up right back where I started, connected to some hospital bed, sedated. I don't need anyone to tell me that the second time around would be my last.

The house is quiet when we enter, and I escape to Sophie's room. The second I shut the door, I pull the notebook from her bag and the necklace from my pocket to examine it more closely.

Words trickle into my brain as soon as I run my fingers over the engraving, and I write them on a fresh page of the notebook.

Medallion

*Tony, Tony, please come down, something's lost that can't be
found*

The silver feels cold in my palms and a chill crawls up
my arm, leaving a trail of goose bumps in its wake. My head
aches.

I pull out Sophie's phone and type *St. Anthony* into the
search box. A Wikipedia page comes up first.

*Saint Anthony of Padua was born Fernando Martins de
Bulhões and became a Catholic priest and friar of the Franciscan
Order. He was born and raised by a wealthy family in Lisbon,
Portugal, and died in Padua, Italy. Known for forceful preaching,
expert knowledge of scripture, and undying love and devotion to
the poor and the sick, he was the second-most-quickly canonized
saint after Peter of Verona. On January 16, 1946, he was named
Doctor of the Church. He is also the patron saint of lost things.*

Patron saint of lost things. The irony is not lost on me,
trapped inside this body without a map.

"Tony, Tony, please come down. Something's lost that
can't be found." I whisper the words out loud when something catches my eye on one of Sophie's shelves.

It's our house angel. Only it's not *our* house angel—it's
Sophie's. I stand and approach the beautifully styled white
built-in shelves above Sophie's window seat, eyes narrowed.

It's resting on top of a pile of vintage hardcover books way at the top. I step on one of the shelves and carefully reach up on my tippy toes, hesitating for a second before I pull the tiny house from its spot.

Whether it was on top of a built-in bookcase in Iowa or in a chipped glass cabinet in the kitchen in Indiana or resting on a top corner of the tiny shelf beside the front door in Kentucky, the house angel was always there, watching over us. And now it's here, resting on top of beautifully designed books in Sophie Graham's room.

I pick it up with trembling fingers. I have to feel it in my hands to be sure that it's real. What are the chances of Sophie having the exact same house angel that we have? Could I be dreaming? Hallucinating? This tiny piece of my history in Sophie's room feels wrong, like a false note in a symphony.

Touching the house angel makes me feel like I'm holding a piece of myself that I've never been able to reach before and I'm terrified I'm going to lose it. I run my fingers over the carved wood. There are details I never could have noticed from my view from the floor. Or maybe it's just that I've gotten so used to looking at it over the years that I stopped truly seeing it. It's like staring at your own face in the mirror, impossible to tell if you're pretty or plain because it's just *you*.

The figurine is small and delicate. Flower boxes painted under the windows overflowing with yellow blooms, intricately painted shingles on the roof, a front door with a plaque above it that reads *Morristown*.

Wait, Morristown? We've had our house angel for as long

as I can remember, but we've only lived in Morristown for the past three years. Suddenly it makes more sense for Sophie to have her own house angel. She'd grown up here and now that I think about it it's just the kind of knickknack they'd sell in one of the tiny shops that line Main Street. There are probably hundreds of house angels in hundreds of houses across town.

But how did my mom come by our house angel? Had she visited here before? Did she somehow know that we'd end up living here? Maybe it wasn't so random after all that we ended up in Morristown after all those moves. Maybe she wanted us to make a home here too. The thought makes me even more sad when I remember that she was transferred yet again and that we were going to leave this place behind.

I lower my body into the window seat. Morristown. There's a sliver of space separating the roof from the frame, top from the bottom. I had no idea it opened.

I press on the carved roof to open the box and find a slip of paper inside, four numbers written in a slanted script.

2683

"Sophie?" I startle at the sound of Mrs. Graham's whispered voice, nearly dropping the carving as she taps on the closed door. Slipping the paper between the pages of my notebook, I rush to put the small house back in its rightful place on top of the books. I have no idea why the Grahams have the same tiny house that's followed me all throughout my childhood, and I have no idea what the code inside means. I've never believed in signs, or at least not until I somehow ended up in someone else's body. Now this feels like the universe or someone is trying to tell me something. If only I could figure out how to decode the message.

But there's no time to think about it now. No time to unravel and digest. There's only time for Sophie Graham.

nineteen

IN THE QUIETEST FLURRY I CAN MANAGE, I CLOSE THE WINDOW ON Sophie's phone, shove it under her pillow with the notebook and necklace, and bury myself beneath her overstuffed duvet. "Yeah?" I say groggily.

The door opens a crack and Mrs. Graham peeks her head into the room. "I thought maybe you'd be hungry." She carries a tray with a bowl of soup, a cup of fresh fruit, and a glass of milk on it and places it on the desk. I never thought moms like Mrs. Graham actually existed outside of movies, but here she is, carrying a tray of food upstairs and into my room. She sits on the edge of the bed and brushes the hair off my forehead. I blink lazily hoping to remind her that I'm supposed to be sleeping off my latest meltdown, not participating in an intimate mother-daughter moment. "Daddy's working late tonight, sweet girl, so you can take all the time you need."

Thank the lord. If there's one thing I'm not up for, it's a Graham family dinner. "Oh, good." I yawn the words, stretching them out like taffy. "I guess I didn't realize how tired I was."

"You know I'm here, right? We're all here for you. Me, your father, your friends. Nothing has changed, Sophie. We'll get through all this together."

The way she looks at me makes me realize I've probably been acting all wrong. I know nothing about the intricacies of their relationship. I can only nod because I don't know any of the words Sophie would have used. Mrs. Graham kisses my forehead lightly like that mom from the movies and starts to walk toward the door.

"Oh, I almost forgot—let me just grab your phone." She spins around and cranes her neck toward my bedside table. Panic crashes into me hard and fast the way it might if I were actually Sophie and I actually cared about whatever personal messages my mom might be intercepting all night. I don't care about those messages, but had I closed out my last search? Was there history she might stumble upon? "My phone?" I reply weakly.

"You know the rule, Sophie. Your phone, but we pay the bills. It charges in our room. Your accident hasn't changed that. Besides, you need your rest." After she's unsuccessful at locating the phone on my table, she holds her hand out expectantly. Apparently Sophie is in the business of handing it over. I reach under the pillow and Mrs. Graham raises her eyebrows probably expecting to unearth naked pictures or something. Maybe St. Anthony won't raise any flags.

"Get some sleep, baby. I love you."

I mumble in response and manage to wait until she softly closes the door behind her before I begin to sob. I have no idea where the tears come from, have no idea whose they even are. I don't know if I'm crying because I'm failing everyone in Sophie's life, or because I'm failing everyone in mine, but once I start, it's hard to stop. I cry for her and me and this whole messed-up situation. I cry because I know Mrs. Graham is doing the same and Mae and my mom and maybe even Sophie's friends and it only feels right to join them. The tears fall hot on my cheeks and my pillow is damp by the time I'm exhausted enough to sleep.

I startle awake to an excruciating headache in a dim room, completely disoriented. The clock reads 2:08 a.m.

A light tapping sound comes from the direction of the window and I know immediately that this is exactly what woke me out of a dead sleep seconds ago. I hold my breath because I can make out the outline of a body in the dark, standing on the landing outside. I'm sure my heart has stopped beating, that this will all be over now because I'm going to have an actual, fear-induced heart attack in this borrowed body. It's him. I have no idea how or why, but the kidnapper is back for me. I don't move a muscle, my eyes trained on the window. I do not breathe, I do not shift, I do not blink.

Taptaptap. The sound comes again, this time followed by cupped hands and a face pressed to the glass that does not belong to a shadowed stranger. Instead, I see Jake Radcliff.

He makes an upward motion with his hands, indicating for me to come open the window already, smiling like scaling the side of my house and knocking on my window in the middle of the night is commonplace. I manage to swing my shaky legs over the side of the bed and unlock the latch, opening the window out of curiosity more than anything else. Why the hell is Jake Radcliff acting like it's the most natural thing in the world for him to be appearing at Sophie Graham's window in the dead of the night?

"Hey." The word is stretched a little in the middle, carried on a warm gush of air mixed with Jake's cologne, his soap, and his minty breath.

Laughter rumbles low in my throat, his stubble on the soft skin of my palm as I cover his mouth to quiet him. I feel the weight of his body, the smooth skin of his lips on my lips and my neck and my . . .

"Holy. Shit. You?" I stab my finger into his chest, my eyes bugged out. "And Sophie Graham are . . . are . . . ?" The revelation is too much for this mixed-up brain to process.

"Um, yeah?" Now it's his turn to be confused, his forehead all wrinkled up. "Since when do you talk about yourself in the third person?"

"Holy shit, you know what the third person is?" My laughter sounds borderline hysterical, but this is just too much. Jake Radcliff, known man whore, the only guy who ever asked me out in Morristown, is hooking up with pure-as-snow Sophie Graham, who's supposedly madly in love with football god Zach Bateman. This is brain-melting material.

"Are you okay? You're not really acting like yourself. Why don't you let me in and we can talk . . . or something."

Jake reaches through the window to kiss my neck and it's clear that he's way more focused on the *or something* than he is on the actual talking. I push him back out the window, careful not to push him off the small balcony entirely, although I'm tempted. If only to pay him back for all the hours I spent digging for the perfect dress at consignment stores.

"Yeah, it's over. Sorry." I start to close the window and then pause when I see the words twist up his face even more. "Actually, you know what? I'm not sorry. You know that thing you do with your tongue? It totally makes me want to gag. And since we're being honest, you're kind of like . . . hmmm . . . how do I say this? Small. Like way smaller than what would be considered average. Anyway, just thought you should hear it from me first."

He actually looks like he might start crying. Oh man, this is so much better than pushing him off the balcony. I snap the window shut with a satisfying thud and slip the lock back into place. He stands there for a moment, completely still, and then finally slinks back to where he came from. Payback is a real bitch.

Adrenaline is coursing through my veins. No chance of sleep now. I open up Sophie's notebook to write this latest development. It's definitely not information that will help me find my way back to myself, but since I can't gossip about Jake and Sophie with Mae, I'll have to settle for writing all the salacious details in my sad excuse for a diary.

When I open up Sophie's notebook the folded paper from inside the house angel flutters to the floor. *2683*. A code. It must unlock something. I flip the paper over and notice something has been written on the back.

> *Sophie, if you're reading this, you deserve the truth and I'm no longer here to tell it to you. Unlock the safe in our closet. And remember, we did this all for you.*

The note is written in Mrs. Graham's perfect cursive handwriting. I recognize it from the grocery list she left laying on the counter downstairs. But why hide this note in her daughter's room? What truth could she possibly be hiding? There's only one way to find out.

Since Sophie's phone was confiscated, I'll have to find something else to light my way. Her desk drawer looks like the place where school supplies go to die with its random assortment of pens, unsharpened pencils, some sticky notes, and old notebooks. On the bookshelf I find a collection of textbooks, a huge selection of Nicholas Sparks novels, naturally, a couple of jewelry boxes, a music box, and a ton of tennis trophies. On the bottom, though, beneath a stack of wrinkled *Vogue* magazines, I see a pink metal box.

Inside, there's a set of tools, all with diamond-bedazzled

handles. Jesus. Sophie Graham has a blinged-out tool set. There's a greeting card inside that says, *Congratulations to my dear, sweet daughter* . . . on the front with a bouquet of red roses beneath. Inside the card's script reads, . . . *on getting your period. Welcome to the wonderful world of beautiful, powerful women!* And below that in cursive, *Love, Mom.* Oh. My. God. They make first-period cards. Sophie's mom bought one for her. With a bedazzled tool set.

But thanks to Mrs. Graham's consideration, I find exactly what I'm looking for.

I press the small button on the flashlight on and off. Bingo.

As soon as I open Sophie's bedroom door, I'm assaulted by the sound of someone snoring. Actually, *snoring* isn't even the word for it. This sounds more like a chainsaw attempting to slice through steel. No wonder Jake was able to sneak in through her window all these nights; Mr. Graham's snores create a thunderous white noise in the hallway and would provide plenty of warning if they suddenly stopped. It's a wonder that anyone can sleep in the same house let alone the same room as this man.

The roaring grumble increases in volume as I walk closer to the master bedroom and then just as suddenly, the sound stops. I freeze, sure Mr. Graham has either been suffocated by phlegm or is going to come barreling out the door in striped manjamas complete with a cap, holding a rifle. I'm not sure any man truly wears pajamas with a cap or keeps a rifle under his bed, but given my limited experience with dads and my interactions with Mr. Graham so far, somehow it doesn't strike me as outside the realm of possibility.

But then there's a rattled gasp-snort combination that takes my breath away. Still sleeping, slowly dying? Either way, I continue.

When I reach the master bedroom doors, I peek through the crack, angling my head to get a view of the bed. I see Mrs. Graham's blond hair splayed out across a silk pillowcase. Apparently the woman does sleep. Mr. Graham is as far away from her as their king-sized bed allows, asleep in a tense-looking lump beneath the duvet. Porter or Wells or Gary or whatever the hell that dog's name is is sprawled in the middle. I hope he's a deep sleeper because he really didn't seem to take to me.

I get down on all fours and push open the door to their room. Thank God nothing squeaks or creaks in this house. I hang close to the perimeter, my eyes trained on Mrs. Graham's rising and falling chest with each crawl forward, Mr. Graham's snoring a rhythmic accompaniment. The closet door is ajar and I only need to open it another inch before I can slip through. The dog lets out a breathy sigh, too tired or too comfortable in his cloud-like paradise to care about a crawling intruder.

The closet has to be the size of my old bedroom, but I can't quite remember. The left side is full of gauzy, silky fabric, noticeably lighter and brighter than the dark jackets and pants on the right side. But there's no metal box, nothing that looks like a safe. I push through clothes, shuffle around shoe boxes, but still nothing. Finally my eyes rest on a beautiful abstract painting hanging on the wall in the center. The lines dance across the canvas in perfect shades of ballet pink and bold black strokes. Who the hell hangs art in their closet?

And then, like one of those ridiculous light bulbs appearing in clouds over animated characters in cartoons, I make the connection. I carefully lift the canvas and sure enough there's a metal safe built into the wall behind it. These people probably have a panic room hidden behind a linen closet. The paper with the code written on it is crinkled between my fingers, but I've already memorized the numbers. I train the light on the keypad and press the 2 and then the 6 and then the 8 and then the 3 to a satisfying click I hope is dulled by the sound of Mr. Graham's consistent snores.

I'm not sure what I expect to find inside. A human head? Guns? Evidence that the Grahams are actually Russian spies? A bedazzled handgun? But I can't help but feel disappointed when I see a stack of papers and folders.

I carefully pull out a folder from the bottom of the stack, comforted by the sound of Mr. Graham's rattled wheezing because it means I'm still safe. *Johns Hopkins* is printed on the front, and inside I find printed transcripts for Hillary Vanderplume from 1999–2000. Embryology. Immunology. Microbiology. There are residency papers for Saint Agnes Hospital, Baltimore City. Mrs. Graham was training to be a doctor? It never occurred to me that someone who wakes before dawn to put her "face" on, lives in yoga pants that cost more than a week's worth of groceries, and cooks breakfast for a man who reads the newspaper at the breakfast table would have an MD after her name. Somewhere Gloria Steinem weeps.

Sheets rustle outside the door and I shove the flashlight up my shirt, holding my breath. There's a pause in the snoring, thick silence hanging in the air like a noose. But a long sigh follows the rustle and Mr. Graham sputters to life once again.

I page through the papers and find a Maryland birth certificate for Sophie. May 23, 2001. Hillary Vanderplume and Robert Graham listed as the parents. 2001. Vanderplume and Graham. No wonder Mrs. Graham's last transcript was for 1999–2000. She must have gotten pregnant and dropped out. Oops. And interesting. Can't imagine that would have gone over well with Sophie's grandparents if they were anything like the Grahams.

There's another piece of paper underneath with *Child: Sophie Graham* written on one side and then *Alleged Father: Robert Graham* written on the other. I skim over paragraphs of confusing sentences to the bottom where it says *Probable Paternity: 0%.*

I look up from the paper. Paternity? The word brings to mind trashy daytime television. Women pulling hair and men yelling a string of bleeped-out profanities to the amusement of seemingly shocked audience members and kids taking sick days on couches across America.

Holy shit. Mr. Graham isn't Sophie's real dad.

I think of Mr. and Mrs. Graham just a few feet away, sleeping with a wall of cool sheets between them in this house full of flawless captured moments. They don't look very much like those sad, raging people on TV and yet it all somehow makes sense.

I lift the folder to straighten the papers back inside when something falls to the wood floor with a clink. It's a necklace. As soon as my fingers graze the broken metal clasp, I know. I don't need to feel the delicate etchings on the medallion, the inscription, the swaddled baby. It's not *a* necklace. It's *the* necklace.

Mr. Graham is not Sophie's real father. He knew our names. He tried to take me. He's hiding evidence, covering everything up. He won't let his daughter remember. He wants to send me away. He's afraid I know the truth. Mr. Graham is the shadow man.

I should be listening. I should be focusing. I should be running.

Instead, I feel thick fingers wrap around my upper arm. Again.

twenty

TRAPPED IN SOPHIE'S BODY, I'M NO LONGER EQUIPPED WITH THE strength I need to protect myself. It's like my survival instinct has been dulled by those intricate nuances of Sophie bleeding into Amelia like a stain. Did I once know how to twist my body in a certain way so my attacker released his grip? If I did, it's lost now. Mr. Graham yanks me off the ground, pinning me under a strong arm, knocking the wind out of my lungs and the scream from between my lips. He drags me out of the room, my bare feet grazing the hardwood, the safety of Mrs. Graham's deep breathing retreating behind us.

In those split seconds it takes Mr. Graham to enter the hallway with his daughter in his arms, I cannot make any predictions as to where we might be going or what he might do to me . . . her . . . us. Anger radiates off him, heavy in the silence between us. He pushes me into the guest room and quietly shuts the door.

My entire body is shaking with fear when he turns to face me with his bloodshot eyes.

"You." He points at me and takes a step closer. "Need." He grits his teeth. "To." He closes those scary eyes. "Stop."

This time I fight the urge to give up. Whether it's Sophie's urge or my own, I have no idea, but I swallow it back. I will not nod and back up shaking. If he's going to hurt me, he's going to hurt me. I might as well go down fighting.

"You don't want me to remember, but I remember. You tried to take her. You tried to take her the night of the accident and she pulled off your necklace and you knew it was evidence, so you hid it away. I can prove it all. I've written everything down and I'm going to help her. You can't stop me. You aren't even my dad. You're just a liar and a monster and . . ."

The words spill out and over the course of my diatribe, Mr. Graham's face transforms from anger to shock to hurt back to anger and finally . . . softens into acceptance. He backs away from me and sits down on the bed, his head bent into his hands.

"You're right." He doesn't lift his head when he says the words and if the house weren't cloaked in this dark silence, I never would have heard him. It feels like the kind of moment where I should blink and wake up in the hospital room, his words triggering the monumental shift back. Mystery solved. But even after I shut my eyes for a beat longer than natural,

I'm still standing in front of a broken man and my arm is sore and my heart is pounding.

I shake my head. That's it? I'm right? I don't feel so much threatened by this man as I am horrified. I open my mouth before I can even organize the slew of profanities appropriate for the level of anger coursing through Sophie's tiny body. But her dad speaks before I can.

"I never thought it would come to this. I honestly never considered the fact that you might find out. Your mom and I made an agreement."

Suddenly the safety of Mrs. Graham tucked into a bed down the hall evaporates. I can't trust either of them. "I'm going to the police," I blurt.

Mr. Graham pulls his eyebrows together in confusion. "The police?"

I stand up and wish so badly for my height right now. "I don't know why you wanted to hurt me . . . er . . . Amelia. Did she come too close to winning? Did she threaten your perfect family? Was she inconvenient? Did she know something she shouldn't? See something? Or—"

Mr. Graham stands up now, his eyes narrowed to slits, interrupting me. "Excuse me?" For the first time since I woke up as Sophie, Mr. Graham appears genuinely confused. "Amelia Fischer?"

I shrink back just a little from the question. My eyes are fixed on his, searching for some sort of tell that never comes. "I," I begin, but have no idea how to finish.

"You said you saw someone." He shakes his head as

though the pieces are clicking into place. "Did you think it was me?" Tears gather in his eyes as he releases a short bark of laughter that's all heartbreak and no humor. "Oh, Sophie."

It's not him.

Tears slip from my own eyes and I don't even try to stop them, couldn't if I wanted to. "But the necklace," I whisper.

He reaches out to grab my hands between his shaking ones. "I found it at the hospital. The police had put it with your things and I didn't want it lying around causing more questions. Honey, there was no one else there. It was a terrible accident, but you were driving that car and it's my job to protect you. I've already spoken with Mrs. Fischer and she's not going to press charges. It's time to let this go. It's no one's fault. Not yours or Amelia's. You're going to be okay. You're going to get better."

"But . . ."

"Sophie, we can't help you if you don't let us." He guides me to sit on the bed, patting the mattress beside him.

"Tell me again, Daddy!" My father glances at his watch, but I know when I see him smile that he'll make the time. He sits on the bed and pats the mattress, but I crawl into his lap instead, laying my head down on his chest and breathing in his cologne.

"Once upon a time, there was a beautiful princess." He brushes back my hair and I snuggle in closer. "All she ever wanted to do was help people. She made everyone smile with her kindness. In another land there was a handsome prince who didn't know how to be happy. He liked storms instead of sunshine."

"I like sunshine," I whisper, looking up.

"I know you do, sweet pea. When the beautiful princess and the evil prince met he wanted to take her happiness for himself. And because the beautiful princess was so kind, she let him. A great darkness fell over the land because the princess lost her happiness."

"But then I came!"

"But then you came."

Maybe I crawl into his lap now because I'm more Sophie than Amelia. Or maybe because I uncovered the wrong kind of secrets and they aren't mine to uncover. I think of the choices my mom made, the moving and working and stress. Mae and I always felt like she was purposefully ruining our lives. But maybe everyone is trying the best they can.

Mr. Graham's arms relax a little and he kisses the top of my head. I still fit perfectly within the safety of his arms. At least for tonight.

twenty-one

AN ALARM I DON'T REMEMBER SETTING RIPS ME OUT OF A DEAD sleep. Sophie's phone is on her bedside table with a sticky note attached.

> This was beeping and pinging all night long.
> Don't avoid your friends—they want what's best
> for you. We all do. Love, Mom

Mrs. Graham must have returned it early this morning, but the thought of her creeping into Sophie's room while I'm asleep and completely unaware totally freaks me out. Especially since Mr. Graham caught me sneaking around their room last night. Did he tell her what happened? Is she pretending not to know or did she really not sense the seismic shift that occurred between us? Is this how other families work? Somehow the undercurrent of secrets and half truths that runs beneath the Grahams' day-to-day lives makes me wonder if I was too busy treading water in my old life to see all the murkiness below.

I toss aside Sophie's pillow and breathe a sigh of relief when I find her notebook and the necklace from Mae's car. I lift the silver necklace and clasp it around my neck as a reminder, a warning, a clue. Is the other necklace still on the floor of their closet? Did Mrs. Graham find it? Did Mr. Graham return it to the safe? I can't think about any of that right now. Mr. Graham might think his daughter is suffering from post-traumatic stress disorder, but I need to remember the truth. My sister and I are in danger. Someone is out there. Hunting us. I am Amelia Fischer and I am not safe. I tuck the medallion under my shirt and it's cold and wrong against my skin. I won't forget.

Considering how easy it was to slip into Sophie last night, to crawl into a dad's lap, I can't trust my memories anymore. I'm too scared they'll grow hazy or disappear altogether. Writing everything down and obsessively reading it is the only thing keeping me sane. I start with the most recent entries, the St. Anthony necklace, Sophie's house angel, Jake's late-night visit, the discoveries in the safe. Reading the line . . .

Mr. Graham not shadow man

. . . brings with it a fresh wave of shame. I thought I had

it all figured out, but of course, nothing is ever that easy. I think of Mr. Graham, how he's not really Sophie's dad. It must have killed him when I didn't recognize him that day in the hospital, must have tapped into his darkest fears. Perhaps that's why it's so important for the Grahams to look like the perfect family. Because they're not. What you see is almost never what you get.

Sophie's phone pings and buzzes at the same time pulling me back to reality. Her notification list is extraordinary. There are hundreds of missed texts, Instagram tags, Face-Times, and calls. From yesterday. Janie is sorry, but she's worried about me and loves me and knows I'll forgive her and she has something super important to talk to me about so I need to call her right away. Brooke wants to know if the rumors are true that I ate donuts and tried to run away with Landon Crane. There are messages from girls on the tennis team, from classes, even random followers from God only knows where asking if everything is okay because Sophie hasn't posted in a while.

What does my phone look like right now? Have I missed any calls, gotten any messages? I can barely remember me. Does anyone else? The questions make my throat hurt, so I push them aside, continuing through Sophie's impressive list instead.

Jake wants to know if I have my period or if I'm suffering from permanent brain damage after the accident. Charming. Zach is coming to pick me up for school despite the fact that

I completely blew him off yesterday. Sweet. And then one from a number Sophie's phone doesn't recognize.

It's Landon. Pick you up at 7:30. We should talk.

Super. So my friends are worried, my followers are panicked, and Landon and Zach are both coming to pick me up in roughly twenty minutes.

As I rush around the room, I try not to consider why it feels so natural to select an outfit and put on makeup in this body today. Sophie's preferred life palette of millennial pink, dove gray, and milky white must be the opposite to my . . . what? What color was my favorite shirt, what shade of eye shadow looked best on my still-tan summer skin? I'm clutching onto the broader sense of my old life like a fuzzy dream where if I look a little bit away I can see the big picture more clearly. The general is still there. It's the details that are going. Those insignificant and yet essential intricacies that made me *me*. It makes me want to scream to lose them.

I shoot Zach a quick text telling him not to pick me up and that I'll see him later. I then tell Landon that I'll meet him at the corner. There's no way in hell Mrs. Graham's going to let me get in a car with him after the Pete's incident yesterday.

When I walk into the kitchen it's so silent I almost expect it to be empty. But Mr. Graham is sitting at the table, lost in his phone as it vibrates and swooshes with every click and swipe. Mrs. Graham stares off into space while stirring something on the stove.

Her face falls when her eyes land on me, and relief washes over me because maybe her disappointment means I'm not somehow morphing into her daughter with every second. Maybe I'm still me and she can sense that.

"Oh, sweetheart, I thought you'd still be sleeping." She's panicky and I understand that this isn't about who I am or who I am not. This is about yesterday. I should be sleeping off the crazy. "I thought maybe you'd want to stay home today?" she continues, desperate. "You seemed so tired yesterday."

Without thinking, I place my hand over my heart, over the saint, a twisted pledge to save a girl I have no idea how to save. But today is a new day. I think about Landon and Murray coming to rescue me and quickly shake my head. I paste on a smile and try to find the words I know they desperately want to hear.

"I feel like a new person, actually. I just needed to sleep, that's all. The sooner I get back into my routine, the better."

Mr. Graham looks up and offers me a smile. And I know immediately that we'll never talk about last night. He'll never tell Mrs. Graham. He'll tuck it away, move along, and get back to the business of being okay.

Mrs. Graham is a little trickier. She must not want another Pete's incident. Her mouth opens and closes and then opens again as though she too is trying to find words. She finally smiles back and nods, unconvinced but outnumbered, more questions, more concerns swept under the vintage oriental rug beneath her expensive flats. Their cleaning lady must have a field day over here.

The Grahams have the kind of house I would have driven by in the evening and stretched my neck to peek inside, all glowy and inviting. I'd see Sophie's family at the dining room table, imagine I saw people laughing, joking, talking about their day. I guess that's part of the reason why I used to spend so much time obsessing over Sophie online. Scrolling through the posts about her perfect life made me feel like I was getting a glimpse of what it was like to actually be Sophie Graham. But the reality isn't anything like what I imagined.

When I was eleven and living in Fremont, Indiana, a house in our town caught fire in the middle of the night, killing the entire family. They brought counselors into the elementary school because one of the kids who died, Dave, was in the grade below me. I remember becoming oddly obsessed with the tragedy, riveted by the boarded-up windows and charred edges before they knocked the house down. It kind of set the bar for tragedy for me. Sure, we were poor and constantly moving, but it could always be worse.

I could never properly express with words how or why the Grahams give me the same feeling, but they do. Just in an entirely opposite way. Before, Sophie Graham was a constant reminder of how bad my life sucked—how much I wanted the things she had. Now it feels like there's no better, no worse, no bar set in either direction.

Life went on all around that burned-up house, people still laughed, birds still sang. Life goes on all around the Grahams' house as well. People still get dressed and eat breakfast no matter who's unraveling or what secrets sit locked away in safes.

My thoughts are interrupted by the doorbell ringing shrilly at 7:20. So much for sneaking out with Landon. Guess I'm not the only person who's behind on texts. I try to jump up to intercept but, of course, both Mr. and Mrs. Graham beat me to it.

Voices rise to the fourteen-foot ceilings, hellos and deep laughter and some chirpy sounds coming from Mrs. Graham. Shit. It must be Zach. Why the hell did he ignore my text? And sure enough, instead of Landon's unintentionally shaggy hair, I see a meticulously styled version with identical results. The only difference between Landon and Zach's morning routine is approximately forty-five minutes of extra sleep and a hair dryer.

Zach suffers from a bad case of unintentionally lame. Firm handshakes and perfect white smiles are exchanged between the men, which makes me feel like I'm watching some weird sort of mating ritual. Zach looks like an extra from a Disney movie in his letter jacket and ridiculous pink T-shirt with a navy fish on it. No wonder Mrs. Graham is always pushing neon tropical print. Sophie's preferred muted hues aren't nearly as complementary.

"It's so nice to see you. You're so sweet to pick up Sophie for school." Mrs. Graham gives one of Zach's broad shoulders a squeeze, her smile wide and proud.

And when he looks up and smiles at me I feel this crazy sense of relief wash over me, like that moment when you find your favorite stuffed animal as a kid and squeeze it hard against your chest. Wait. I stop, blink hard to avoid Sophie's feelings bleeding into my own.

Sophie's boyfriend is some kind of walking, talking security blanket. Even Mr. Graham looks happy to see Zach. Apparently, in Graham-land the first step to healing is having your perfect boyfriend pick you up for school despite the fact that you completely blew him off yesterday and the asshole you're hooking up with on the side snuck through your window last night. Fake it till you make it, baby.

"So sweet." The sarcastic edge to my voice is actually a relief, proof that there's still some Amelia rattling around in here after all. I tuck my notebook safely inside Sophie's bag, sling it over my shoulder, and scoot through the door, the lesser of two evils at this point. Or three if I consider the fact that Landon is probably pulling out of his driveway as we speak. "Well, we don't want to be late."

I can't help but notice how Mr. Graham has slipped his arm around Mrs. Graham as they both stand beaming at us from the doorway. It's like they're actors putting on a show, only their smiles are a little shakier and the curtain only rises when there's an audience around to appreciate them. I'm struck by a strange sadness for Sophie and her life. Did she feel like she was acting as well? Is that why she dated Zach but hooked up on the side? Did she know that Mr. Graham wasn't her biological father? Was that part of the performance too?

Once the car doors close, Zach gives my hand a little squeeze, and it occurs to me that there will be no discussion about how I treated him yesterday. "Babe, I've missed you." Ugh, he sounds like a cartoon boyfriend, saying the stuff that he thinks he's supposed to say to his perfect girlfriend. Did Sophie really fall for this crap?

"Didn't you get my text? I don't need a ride. I'm just going to jump out at the corner." I don't even bother buckling my seat belt. Zach drives a brand-new Jeep, checking yet another box in the guide to being the perfect high school prom king. But with the apple-scented air freshener come other feelings powerful enough to make me want to gag.

The glow from the drive-in movie screen illuminates Zach's chiseled angles and reminds me how lucky I am to be sitting next to him. And then I remind myself that I'm supposed to be more confident than that, but that's harder to remember. It just feels right. He and I. Zach and Sophie. My post of us sharing popcorn from five minutes ago already has almost one hundred likes. It's happening.

Channeling the confidence I'm supposed to have, I let my fingers wander a little bit toward the gearshift that separates us, seeking out his hand. I breathe through butterflies and focus on what I want, leaning into my new boyfriend for what is, without a doubt, going to be the most amazing kiss of my entire life.

But when Zach finally leans over, our noses hit and one of his front teeth knocks into mine, sending shivers up my spine for all the wrong reasons. My eyes water and I pretend it's from where his tooth hit my lip, but as usual, it's a lie.

The disappointment of that first terrible kiss comes rushing back as though we're back at that movie and not on our way to school. I've seen the two of them kiss a million times on every social media platform, after tennis matches if Zach doesn't have football, in the hallways. They practically invented PDA. It's the reason they're always voted cutest couple, the reason girls sigh when they look at them, wishing that they had a boyfriend that perfect, a life that perfect, a love that perfect. Because #relationshipgoals. I'm just as guilty, zooming in on every photo, wondering what it might be like to not be me for once, to be someone a little bit like her. To have someone a little like him.

Zach pops his car into reverse and as he waits for the gate to open at the end of our driveway, I can't help myself. I'm going to take one for the team here. I lean over the seat, grab his cheeks, and turn his face toward mine. The moment our lips touch, I know.

When he pulls away, his face is bright red. "Whoa, take it easy, killer," he jokes, but neither of us laugh. "Sophie, are you feeling okay?"

I shake my head. "I can't do this."

Sophie is such a liar. All the endless couple shots, the hashtags, the handholding and kissing and snaps of the perfect couple midlaugh. It's all just a bunch of bullshit. These two people might as well be complete strangers. They have absolutely zero chemistry whatsoever. No wonder Sophie hooks up with Jake on the side. It's just shocking that she's willing to go through the motions. For what? A pretty picture?

"I don't know what your deal is, but you're kind of pissing me off," he says, pulling into the street. I'm pissing him off because I can see right through them?

I see Murray idling next to the stop sign at the corner. I have no idea what *their* deal is, but at this point I don't have time to care. "Actually, I think I'll just get out here," I say, shifting toward the door.

"You can't . . . I mean, if you get out now, it's over. I mean it, Sophie. No Homecoming Queen and King. No Cutest Couple. We're done." Zach's yelling but his eyes look a little like Mrs. Graham's in front of the stove this morning. Desperate.

He's presented me with the opposite of an ultimatum. Yes, please. "Then I guess we're done." I get out of the car and slam the door. Screw Zach Bateman. Screw Sophie and her stupid, fake life. I'm done with it. It's time to get real.

twenty-two

LANDON HANDS ME A STILL-WARM SCONE WRAPPED IN PARCHMENT paper, topped with a thin layer of white icing and speckled with fresh lemon zest. No wonder his car smells like a bakery.

"Trouble in paradise?"

Instead of answering I take a huge bite of the scone. It's like nothing I've ever tasted, all butter and sugar and citrusy deliciousness melting on my tongue.

"Rosemary?" I ask.

He nods. "My mom was skeptical but I couldn't resist. You know how she hates it when I mess with her recipes."

"You made these?" He nods and gives me a weird look, like I shouldn't be surprised. I lean my head back against the seat, resisting the urge to lick every finger. "Oh. My. God." The memory of Sophie stuffing that scone in her mouth has nothing on actually tasting it. I promise to never forget no matter where I end up.

I hear the roar of Zach pulling away and keep my eyes carefully trained on the scone. "I don't want to talk about it."

"That's cool. I totally get it. But something tells me she's not going to take no for an answer."

He gestures out the window and I see Janie running at his car, waving her arms in the air.

"Wait! Wait! Please! It's important!"

Landon rolls down his window without consulting with me, probably because he's worried I'd force him to blow right past her. Even he can sense I'm in full-on destruction mode. Destroying Sophie's friendship with Janie would just be the icing on the proverbial scone. Besides, she sold me out yesterday when she texted Sir Graham. How could I possibly trust her again?

But before I can say a word she's thrusting a wrinkled piece of paper through Landon's window, washed out and bleached by the sun.

"I found it on the side of the road. I couldn't stop thinking about what you said yesterday, about the man trying to hurt Amelia Fischer. So I pulled over to see if I could find anything, any evidence of a kidnapper or whatever. I don't really know what I was looking for but . . . I did find this. I think maybe you're right." Janie's face is tight and there are tears in her eyes. "I'm sorry, Sophie. I believe you."

I recognize the article from the *Haven Times* right away, only it wasn't snipped from the newspaper but rather printed off the internet. My blurry face is circled in black ink, my name below the image highlighted. In the margin of the page all of our names are written in blocky print.

Carol Fischer

Amelia Fischer

Mae Fischer

Below that, *Morristown, Ohio,* is handwritten and under-lined three times.

I feel like I'm going to be sick.

"I'm sorry I didn't believe you, Soph. So sorry. It's just that you've been acting so weird since the accident and your parents made me promise to tell them if I noticed anything out of the ordinary. I was scared."

"Okay, why do I feel like I'm missing something kind of critical here?" Landon is looking back and forth between Janie and me like he's trying to figure out how he got sucked into our vortex of crazy.

"Ugh, keep up, newspaper boy. Sophie saw someone try to take Amelia the night of the accident. And I found proof. And now we've got to figure out what to do about it." Janie locks her car that she's parked on the side of the road, opens the driver-side door, and gestures for Landon to let her in. He climbs out without a word because no one argues with Janie McLaughlin. Not even Landon Crane.

"I need to warn them," I say, the paper shaking between

my fingers. "No one believes me, but I have to show them. This is proof."

Before I can even ask him to, Landon slams on his brakes and takes a left in the opposite direction of our school. I glance at the clock, not for me but for him. "What about first period?" Missing AP chem is no big deal for me, I've already got an A in the class and Mr. Oster loves me. "Janie, you have calc." As soon as I complete the thought, my stomach feels tight. Yet another piece of Sophie has somehow clicked into place in my mind.

"Relax, relax, Ms. I've-Never-Made-a-Mistake-in-My-Life. I've already got it covered," he says, misunderstanding my anxiety. "Also, I'd say this situation kind of trumps first period."

"Holy shit, these are amazing," Janie says around a mouthful of scone that she helped herself to in the back seat. I raise my eyebrows at the girl who wouldn't touch a donut with a ten-foot pole. She shrugs her shoulders. "What? Stress burns calories, right?"

The entire situation is surreal. I'm sitting in Landon Crane's car with Janie McLaughlin, trapped inside Sophie Graham's body, trying to figure out a way to save my family from a crazed, saint-obsessed kidnapper. But what I can't figure out is why. Why would this guy be targeting us? How did he know our names? What could he possibly want with us? We've never been anywhere long enough to piss anyone off.

And then I remember the secrets I'm uncovering in

Sophie's life, all the stuff hidden under that veneer of perfection. If Sophie's flawless family had this much to hide, what skeletons were in the Fischers' closets? And how the hell did I miss them?

The thing is, it's so easy to blow up Sophie's life. To destroy her fake boyfriend, send off the guy she's hooking up with, avoid her worried friends, rekindle old relationships. In Sophie's life this defiance feels possible, natural even. The consequences don't feel quite as real. I can't help but wonder if I was playing it too safe in my old life, always too focused on the one foot we had out the door instead of focusing on the one we had inside. Maybe I missed the skeletons because I was too focused on all the cracks in our foundation. The barely missed evictions, the constant worrying about money, the knowledge that we could have to move again at a moment's notice.

Maybe if I'd been a little more grounded, a little more invested, my life would have had more of *this*. More boys in cars, more friends who text, just . . . more. And maybe I would have seen more too. Maybe then I'd know who hated my family enough to try to destroy it. I need to figure all this out, I need to protect my mom and Mae. I need to understand why someone would want to take us. I know the skeletons are there now, I just have to find them.

But maybe I'm here for Sophie a little bit too. Maybe you don't really notice your skeletons when they're right there hanging in your closet every morning. They blend in with the hangers and you don't want to look too close because if you actually see them it would be a hell of a lot harder to sleep at night.

Maybe I'm here to help us both. Maybe we need to see our lives for what they are instead of for how they feel when we're trapped inside them. Maybe it's time to look at those skeletons in the broad light of day and face them head-on.

twenty-three

THE WINDOW IS COOL AGAINST MY FOREHEAD AS I WATCH MORRIS-town fly by. There's the park where every Thursday in kindergarten Sophie would go up and down the twirly slide fifteen million times to the tune of "Again! Again!" before her mom dragged her away. There's Morristown Country Club where Sophie watched fireworks blooming in the night sky, the bursts of color reflecting in Zach's wide eyes, her chest tight with longing. And the baseball fields where if you drive your car far enough, you can park in a spot where no one will catch you making out with the guy who is definitely not your boyfriend because your real boyfriend definitely doesn't want to make out with you. Did these moments lock into place overnight when Sophie was busy dreaming away Amelia?

I see the blue and yellow carnations first, the colors of the Morristown Knights on a wreath stand like you'd see at a funeral. Only I haven't died. Yet. There are weary-looking stuffed animals, bunches of flowers, a big cross that says *Amelia* that looks way too much like a headstone, and even an old racquet and a can of tennis balls. I can't imagine who would have thought to leave these things in my honor. I didn't really have any close friends. I guess maybe Mae might have left some of it. Or my mom. But when I see a soggy box identical to the one sitting in the back seat next to Janie I realize that maybe there were more people who cared about me than even I realized.

Landon slows down respectfully and the speed of his car, the slow creep, brings back the memory of rain pounding on Crimson's roof. I hold the memory tight even though it's terrible. I refuse to tear my eyes away from the colorful collection along the patchy side of the road.

"Wait. Wait! Pull over." I'm out the door before Landon comes to a complete stop and make a beeline for the cross.

"What is it? What do you see?" Janie sticks her head out the window.

The metal glints in the sun again, the circular coin dangling from a piece of string hanging from the wreath. I lift it and let it rest in my palm, a third St. Anthony winking at me in the sun. I can't help but wonder if he's still here. Watching. Waiting. For Mae? For my mother? Clutching the coin inside my fist, I shiver through a chill despite the blazing sun.

"It was nothing," I lie. I'm not quite ready to tell them

about St. Anthony yet, about the breadcrumbs the stranger seems to be leaving. Janie just ratted me out to the Grahams yesterday and I can't imagine trying to explain the strange necklaces to cynical Landon. My gut tells me to keep the unbelievable to a minimum if I want Landon and Janie to help me get to Mae and I desperately need them to do just that.

"Let's go to Amelia's house, she lives right down here," I say, indicating that Landon should turn right at the stop sign. "Their driveway is easy to miss, so go slow." Where those hidden gems of Morristown shone so brightly through Sophie's eyes on our way back from the hospital and through town today, the street my family has called home for the longest stretch of continuous years feels dull and somehow less familiar. "Right . . . here," I say, pointing to the left where the trees open enough to let a car down the winding gravel driveway.

"I never even knew there was a house back here," Landon says, leaning down a little to make sure he doesn't hit the low branches.

"Seems like that's kind of the point," Janie says.

It's only after I hear her say the words that I wonder if it's true.

All of the different places we've lived have had one thing in common. They were remote, almost hidden, tiny shacks barely seen from the road, shitty apartment complexes in the middle of nowhere. It's like the house angel, right in front of me so long that I never really bothered to look at it. And all of a sudden, I'm back on that road. Sheets of rain pouring around me. Fingers reaching, pulling, fighting to loosen his grip. I'm back in the middle of that road, headlights rushing toward me.

And then it hits me. We were hiding. From someone. From something. All these years, we've been hiding. And now we've been found. And for the first time ever, we can't run. Or else I'll be left behind.

Landon is carefully navigating Murray to the top of our driveway, and it's all I can do not to jump out of the car. I need to get in there. I need to see my mom and Mae. I need answers.

"Actually, stop here. If you go too far up, you won't be able to back out." Landon looks over at me, surprised. "We had a tennis dinner here once and parking was a nightmare." The lie doesn't even sound remotely believable to my ears. "I'll walk the rest of the way. But give me a few minutes. I'm sure this is all going to come as a shock and they're, um . . . super private. So . . . yeah, I'll be back in a sec."

"Um, there's no way in hell you're going in there alone." Janie unbuckles her seat belt and tries to follow me out of the car.

"Stop!" The word comes out too loud, too desperate, and Janie freezes in place. "I mean, I need to do this on my own, okay? We can't ambush them. I need you to trust me this time."

The reminder of her betrayal yesterday has its intended effect, and Janie sags back into the car.

"Fine. But you have ten minutes. After that we're coming in after you."

I take a deep breath, the weight of the bag on my shoulder a comfort because it holds the notebook, the flimsy pieces of paper that tether me to my old life. I walk the rest of the way up our long driveway, turning to see how much of Landon's car I can make out through the thick trees. Just a few spots of red. They won't be able to see or hear me.

The rush of everything hits me at once. Seeing my old house through Sophie's eyes gives me the strangest sense of vertigo or maybe it's more like whiplash: worlds colliding, familiar and unfamiliar all at the same time. I don't have a plan, but maybe that's okay. Maybe it's time to stop over-thinking everything. I have proof in my hands. Proof that my family is being hunted. Proof that we've been found.

But what I don't understand is: Why? Who would want to hurt my family? Why would they want to take me away? What secrets has my mother been hiding from us all these years? I have no answers, but I sure as hell intend to find out.

My stomach sinks when I see the garage door shut tight. I guess part of me had some sort of fantasy where I walked in as Sophie and shared my incredible story and everyone believed me. I'd prove my identity through details only we would know. The year we lived near Dairy Queen in Iowa and Mae and I ate so much ice cream we still, to this day, find rogue sprinkles between the seats of Mom's car. Or how in Indiana, we begged for days for Mom to take us to the

Blueberry Festival. The rides were dinky and the fairgrounds smelled like spilled beer and pee, but the fried dough was so light it melted in your mouth and we were sweaty and tired and happy.

If they were home I could warn them about the shadow man and this time they'd actually listen. And then whatever strange magic landed me here would bring me back.

I stand in front of the keypad for way too long, trying to figure out the combination of numbers that will open the door. But there are too many other numbers rattling around in my head—2683, from Mrs. Graham's slip of paper; 908125, Sophie's iPhone passcode; 8654, her address; 0523, her birthday. Just when I think I have it, I punch in the numbers and nothing happens. It takes me a minute to realize that I punched in the Grahams' garage code. Shit.

I take a step back and force myself to look at the keypad like one of those weird optical illusions that looks like a dog's face, but really is a woman in a dress. I try to squint to convince whatever muscle memory the Amelia in me has left to shut down Sophie's brain and allow the numbers to float through the murk, but it's gone. For good. What will go next? How many other known quantities have slipped away without me realizing it?

I walk around to the front of the house. One of the shutters fell off the dining room window, and it still hasn't been replaced. Two of the outside lanterns are broken because I convinced Mae to hit with me in the driveway last summer.

Remembering all these useless facts makes me want to scream. How can I remember how the lanterns were broken but forget our freaking garage code?

The yard is overgrown and the paint is peeling. There's no doormat. No wreath hanging on the door, no sign that anyone actually lives here. As usual my mom had one foot out the door the whole time. We all did.

I cup my fingers around my eyes and look through the dirty glass windows that flank the front door. There's no movement, no footsteps, no distant murmur of voices. The house looks the same and yet altogether different now that I'm seeing it through Sophie's eyes. It's like returning to a house I haven't been in since I was a toddler. Everything looks smaller, shabbier, and somehow tired, like the house itself has given up.

I see dishes piled beside the sink and papers strewn across the rickety dining room table, and one of the cupboard doors is hanging crooked on its hinge in the kitchen. I can't remember if it looked this way before the accident. When I walk around to the other window, I get a view of the fireplace, of the dusty candles a previous renter left behind, of the miniature painted house identical to Mrs. Graham's placed right in the center.

Seeing the strange connection between Sophie and Amelia gives me courage. I know what I have to do. I ring the doorbell first to be absolutely sure that there's no one home. I can't get caught. When no one answers after a minute, I walk over to the window in the family room. It never latched properly; a tiny sliver of space exists between the bottom and the frame. I push up just enough to get my fingers in and then lift hard, the heavy frame resisting against years of neglect. The window opens just enough for Sophie to slip through, and for once I'm grateful to be trapped in a body the size of an overgrown doll.

The laundry-detergent scent that follows us from state to state, house to house washes over me and, for a second, I'm fully Amelia. So Amelia that I swear even my reflection in the mirror would prove it. But there's no time for that. Instead, I break every rule ever created around the folklore of our house angel, and I pick it up from its spot on the mantle where it's sat for three years since our last move. A tiny house-shaped mark remains on the wood where no dust has settled. With Sophie's heart thrumming a rhythmic beat through my ears, I press on the back to lift a roof I never knew opened.

Inside, there isn't a code. There's a key.

Outside, a car door slams.

twenty-four

I'VE GOT TO GET OUT OF HERE. I DUMP THE KEY INTO MY HAND AND press it into my pocket beside the St. Anthony coin from the accident site. Carefully placing the house back on the mantle, I adjust it ever so slightly to the left so it sits in its rightful spot.

I look at the evidence Janie discovered, the printed article, the list of names. I can make notes in my notebook, but I have to leave this for my mom. Somehow I think she'll know what it means. She kept us hidden for this long, so she must know who we've been hiding from. I have to warn her. I place the paper on the floor in front of the door as though it's been slipped into the old mail slot no one uses anymore. And then I'm out the way I came, with barely enough time to close the window behind me.

Gravel crunches beneath two sets of footsteps as Janie and Landon emerge around the bend in the driveway. "We were getting worried," Landon calls out. I jump away from the window.

"What did Mrs. Fischer say?" Janie asks.

"She wasn't home and I couldn't get the mail slot to open. Finally got it though, so we're good." I avoid their eyes and start walking back toward the car.

Once we've pulled back onto the empty street, Landon asks, "You think the article will help?"

I lean my head against the glass again and hope because it's all I've got. "I guess we'll find out."

As we pull closer to the high school, I start to feel a little panicky at the thought of being trapped in the building with Sophie's memories bombarding me all day. I want to go back to being Amelia again. I want to get back to my old life so I can figure out what's really going on. I have to find out what the key is for. After seeing the contents of the Grahams' safe, I can only imagine what's hiding behind my mom's locked door or drawer or whatever it is the key unlocks.

After we pull into the school parking lot, Landon parks his car and shuts off the engine, twisting around in the seat to grab his book bag and the box of scones from Janie. "One for the road?" he asks. His hair is perfectly disheveled, his dimples out in full force, and he's holding a box of heaven.

Janie stares hard at the box, waging that silent battle between girl and carb. She finally shrugs her shoulders. "I guess I've earned it." I feel a little triumphant when I think of how far we've come since yesterday.

Landon shakes his head and laughs, the sound filling me with an overwhelming sense of gratitude. For everything. Before he can open the door, I reach over and touch his arm. This time he doesn't pull away.

"Thank you," I say and mean it with every piece of Sophie and Amelia combined. I look at Janie in the back seat. "Thank you for believing me." I could go on, explain that their presence beside me brings a level of comfort I'm not sure I've experienced before. Ever. I could tell them that they make me feel less alone, that they make me smile, that they make me wonder, and maybe even regret. I could even tell Landon that if things were different I might be kind of falling for him. Instead I look at him and say, "And your scones are to die for."

"True that," Janie says with a mouthful.

As we walk toward the school office, Landon says, "Let me handle this."

Landon raises a finger into the air as we breeze through the glass office door, the box of scones hidden behind his back, approaching the school secretary at her desk. "Pam, Pam, Pam, not a word. We are late and it's all my fault."

Mrs. Keller, the secretary, leans back in her chair a little, unable to mask the smile that pulls at her lips. She gives him the evil eye for using her first name because she has to, but it's clear she appreciates Landon's antics. "Well, this ought to be good."

Landon turns around and raises his eyebrows at me this time.

Then he places the box of scones on her desk with a flourish. "Boom." He's so pleased with himself that Mrs. Keller can't stop herself from laughing a little. "Happy Secretaries' Day."

"Mr. Crane, I would like to remind you that Secretaries' Day is in April. It's September. And Sophie Graham and Janie McLaughlin. How on earth did you two get dragged into all of this?"

"I blame everything on the scones. We're powerless to resist them." And him, I think. Mrs. Keller winks at me like she knows, so she's either psychic or I'm completely transparent. For one horrible moment I'm sure she's going to tease me about my painfully obvious crush, but instead she grabs a pen and her pass pad. "We're so happy to have you back, sweetheart. And you, Ms. McLaughlin. Keep an eye on him and take care of your friend," she says as she writes out the passes with a smile.

"Thank you," we chorus, accepting the gift.

"Mr. Crane, do not make a habit out of bribing me with baked goods. I will not stand for it." But it's pretty much impossible to take her seriously because she's already taking her first bite of scone, eyes closed with pleasure.

Landon holds open the door as the bell rings, and Janie and I slip under his arm. The hall floods with kids and already I can feel the burn of eyes, can hear murmurs, and then, "Sophie!" from across the way. The safety of our little trio dissipates with the crowd. I'd like to be in the car with them again, puttering through town. I'd like to be anywhere but here.

"I guess I'll see you guys around," he says, a little awkward now that we're in our natural habitat.

"Um, yeah, definitely," I answer. His eyes flick back and forth between mine for what feels like an eternity but is probably only a second. The army-green T-shirt he's wearing has turned them green instead of their usual hazel color.

"All right you two, we've got to get to class." Janie tugs on my arm and drags me away from Landon. "And maybe you should think about apologizing to Zach?"

"Not going to happen."

"But you love him, right? I mean, I totally get that you have a lot going on right now, but are you sure you're ready to just ditch everything with Zach? He's all you've talked about for the past three years."

"It wasn't how it looked, Janie. We weren't this perfect couple or anything. All that shit I posted, it wasn't really real. And I'm done pretending."

She stops in the middle of the hallway and looks at me carefully, almost like she's seeing me for the first time. Then her face breaks into a smile. "You know what? Good for you."

And it feels so good to tell the truth, the real, unvarnished, brutal truth, and to have Janie McLaughlin accept me for exactly who I am. Maybe that's what this is all about.

Maybe it's about seeing things through someone else's eyes and for the first time ever, seeing them as they actually are instead of for what you always wanted them to be.

Without another thought, I walk to my locker, twist the combination, and grab my books for AP English.

It's not until I'm sitting in class ten minutes later that I realize I didn't even have to think about the code to open Sophie's locker.

twenty-five

I SPEND THE REST OF THE MORNING ADDING PAGES OF NOTES TO MY notebook and figuring out how I'm going to get back to my house to find whatever that key opens. There is absolutely no reason for me to be at school right now unless you count adding fuel to the gossip firestorm swirling around me and Sophie and Zach and Janie and Landon and the whole tangled web I've managed to trap us all in. I'm officially the girl who almost killed someone, broke up with her boyfriend, and started worshipping a spiral notebook in less than a week.

By fifth period, I'm about done. If I head through the woods, I can be back at my house in ten minutes. With any luck, the house will still be empty with my mom at the hospital and Mae suffering through sixth period. So I do what any girl stuck in the wrong body would do if she found a key inside the only precious artifact that's survived seven moves.

I cut school.

It takes me twelve minutes to jog home, and I blame the awkward slap of Sophie's bag, her short legs, and her impractical shoes for the extra two-minute lag. The house is exactly the same as Landon, Janie, and I left it this morning. The garage is shut tight, the exterior foreboding, the front window slightly cracked. I hoist up the window and climb back inside.

The key is so small that it can't belong to anything bigger than a diary or a small box or something. Luckily, we don't have all that much stuff, so if there's a secret box or diary within these walls, I think I'll be able to find it. Preferably in the next ten minutes. Something tells me if Sophie Graham is caught breaking and entering, shit would go down. Hard.

I do a cursory glance around the family room and kitchen. If my mom were hiding something from us, I really don't think she'd hide it in the rooms that Mae and I spend 90 percent of our time in. Basement or bedroom are probably my best bet. I start downstairs because it's closer. I'm sweating now, tiny beads above Sophie's lip, delicate like everything else about her. Every minute that I'm here feels like ten; it's like being trapped in one of those nightmares where you're being chased but your body feels like it's running against a tidal wave. But I have to keep searching, keep pushing against the waves of panic because otherwise I'll drown in the terror of getting caught.

In the last three years we've been here I can't remember

anyone ever voluntarily going down to the basement. Even when funnel clouds churned in the sky above Morristown two springs ago, we all hesitated before opening the door and taking cover. Was it because my mom was hiding something down here? Or was it because it feels like a grave? It smells musty, it's at least twenty degrees cooler than the rest of the house, and the floors are made of packed dirt. In the last hundred or so years that this house has been standing, nothing good could ever have happened down here.

I pull the chain at the bottom of the stairs to shed some weak light on the space. I see a few mousetraps, some stacked plastic patio chairs, an old coal-burning furnace I manage to find the courage to open, and the water heater. The corners are bare, there aren't any boxes, and nothing is tucked into the cobwebby wooden rafters above me. I'm out.

I take the steps two at a time on my way back up the stairs, the key sweaty in my palm. There has to be something in one of the bedrooms. As I move through the hallway I pause in front of the doorway to my mom's room. I smell her. I have no idea what the scent is—her shampoo or perfume or maybe some primitive scent shared between mothers and daughters. But it's her. All the tension slips from my body and for a moment I feel completely at home. And it's such a relief because it means Amelia is still in here somewhere. Still somehow able to feel whatever it is that makes me *me*. A car alarm wailing in the distance jerks me out of my spell. There's no time to waste.

The door creaks. I head for my mom's closet as though I'm being pulled.

"Mom?"

I hear a sniffle and rustling behind the closet door and wonder if she's changing. I don't want to get snapped at, reminded that she needs her privacy, so I close the door again.

I drop Sophie's book bag in the entry to get down on my hands and knees, running fingers over the warped wood below me. In the corner of the closet there's a gap where the wood has pulled away from the wall. Scrambling over, I put my fingers in and pull up on the plank and pray that it's more than just damaged flooring. There, between the joists and the floor above, is a rusty, locked box. I lift it out of the floor with shaky fingers. Now or never. And just like that, the key clicks into its rightful place and turns with satisfying ease.

My fingers shake as I start flipping through old photographs bound together with a rubber band. Gummy smiles, first steps and skinned knees, awkward middle years where we're all legs and arms, my senior picture. I guess we have family pictures after all, but for some reason we keep our memories locked up and hidden in the darkest reaches of our lives. I could spend hours poring over each one, drinking in pictures I've never seen. But I have to pull myself away; there's no time.

There's a huge roll of cash and I can't help but wonder

why my mom would have that much cash laying around and how the hell she came by it. When I flip through the bills I notice they're all hundreds and a hard knot of anger begins to form in my chest. How dare she hold out on us like this? How could she hide money that we could have used for school clothes or groceries, gas, or, I don't know, rent to get me through my senior year of high school? There aren't neat folders with our names typed on the tabs, but in the stack of papers are social security cards and birth certificates, proof that I exist. At least on paper.

November 14, 2000. Live birth. Jenna Elizabeth Dowling.

An electric current stabs at my right temple and my fingers jerk to the spot to cradle the pain somehow even though it makes no difference.

Wrong name. Wrong name.

I pull Sophie's notebook from her bag and scribble *Jenna Elizabeth Dowling* on the page.

The next certificate says Haylee Morgan Dowling. May 10, 2002.

This time the floor seems to shift under me. It's like the bottom just dropped out of my life, of my reality, and I'm falling, falling, falling. I whisper the words, focus on each syllable.

I grip the pen between Sophie's fingers again, feel the weight of it there. I can barely read the shaky script of Haylee's name after I add it to the list. *Breathe, Amelia, breathe through it.* I can't lose time now.

Saint Agnes Hospital, Baltimore City. I whisper out loud, trying the words on because they're so familiar. We were born in Maryland? *Saint Agnes*, I scratch on the page. For a second time. I reread the words *Mrs. Graham resident at Saint Agnes in Baltimore?* that I'd written just hours before. Two girls with Mae's and my exact birthday were born in the same hospital where Mrs. Graham, the mother of the girl I'm stuck inside, was doing her residency. And the entire mess is locked away between the hundred-year-old floorboards of the farmhouse where I've spent the last three years of my life.

Suddenly it feels like the ground beneath me is vibrating, humming with the certainty that what I'm feeling is real. I'm not panicking or imagining or dreaming.

Until I realize it's not just a strange sense at all. It's the actual garage door groaning beneath me. I'm no longer alone.

twenty-six

FEAR EXPLODES IN MY CHEST. SOMEONE IS HOME, AND I'M SITTING IN my mom's closet with an unlocked box of our family's secrets, trapped inside Sophie Graham's body. They'll call the police. I'll be arrested, sent to juvie or back to the hospital. I'll never find my way home.

I stuff the birth certificate into the notebook and cram the rest of the papers and the money back into the metal box, lock it up, and hide it back between the floorboards. The corner of the closet that is blocked by the open door is the only place to hide.

I make Sophie's body as small as possible and think of Landon's scones. I read somewhere that negative energy attracts attention and considered it total bullshit at the time, but I'm not about to take any chances. The footsteps pound in quick succession—someone is running. I'm completely screwed. It's over.

But instead of following me into the closet, they stop a bedroom short. A door slams and a girl begins to cry. Her sobs have the power to make me lose all remaining hope in an instant. It's Mae, it has to be, but the heartbroken wails sound like they're coming from a stranger. Is it because I've run out of time? Am I gone? Would I know if I died? Would my soul or spirit or whatever is rattling around inside Sophie's body die right along with me? More questions. No answers.

Grabbing my book bag, I push to my feet and creep out of the bedroom, hoping the squeaky floorboards beneath my feet don't give me away. I know this is my only chance to escape and every part of me wants to run, but I force myself to move down the hallway carefully, like a stupidly slow ninja.

But when I approach my sister's closed door I can't move past it. No matter what's happened to me, there's still time for her. I need to warn her about the kidnapper, but I have no idea how. I want to tell her about what I found in our mom's closet, but if she sees me she'll call the police.

Instead I tear out a sheet of notebook paper from Sophie's notebook and start writing.

There was someone else there the night of the accident. He was chasing Amelia and he said he was looking for you too. Please be careful.

I need her to understand the danger, I need to warn her. So I tuck a corner of the note under her door and hope that she'll take it seriously. I did my best to disguise Sophie's handwriting by using all caps, but it's not like there were any other witnesses to the accident. She'll blame me for this. If she's pissed, I'll deny writing it. But maybe she won't be angry. Maybe she'll somehow sense the truth. Maybe she'll finally be ready to listen. Maybe she'll at least be a little more careful.

I linger in front of Mae's door, letting her cries wash over me, wishing for the ability to absorb all of her pain. Why can't whatever magic is at play here work that way? Why can't I fix anything? The night Jake stood me up I was so humiliated, so devastated that I locked myself in my room. Mae stood outside banging on the door, begging me to let her in. But I ignored her. I was too pissed off, too embarrassed. All I wanted to do was blast angry music and ugly cry alone. After a few minutes the banging on the door stopped and I figured Mae had given up on me, which of course just made me cry harder. Hours later after the tears dried and my iPod ran out of batteries, I opened my door. And there was Mae. Curled into a ball at the foot of my door, fast asleep with one hand on her heart and her other hand on the doorframe. Later she told me that she sat out there forever trying to absorb my pain so I wouldn't have to feel it alone. When I rest my hand on her door I close my eyes and take a deep breath, willing her heartbreak toward me, trying to save her from the despair and the pain. It's the best I can do.

I tiptoe down the stairs because I have no other choice. As I slip out the front door, I notice the newspaper article I'd placed by the door this morning has blown into the corner. I move it back into place and hope they'll see it.

My feet hurt, my eyes burn, and my throat aches. The tears start without warning. I can't do this anymore. I can't handle not understanding anything that's happening to me. I have nowhere to go.

I should be used to this feeling, the constant isolation that comes with moving around so much etched into my personality, but nothing feels familiar right now. It's like driving around the day after the first snow of the year. You miss turns because the world is now sparkling white and new. Instead of taking the scenic route and marveling at the beauty of a world I don't recognize, I'm muddying the waters with secrets. I'm a stranger in this body and I'm a stranger in that other world, that other life. I picture the birth certificates with strangers' names on them. How can I continue to fight for my life, for Amelia, without really knowing who or what I'm fighting for?

I wipe my tears but more follow, running under my nose and along my chin. And all I want is another scone. I have to laugh at the ridiculousness of it, at the ridiculousness of laughing out loud by myself in this stupid outfit, with these stupid shoes, with this world-altering information in this stranger's life.

So I turn back to school even though the day is all but over. I go back because I have nowhere else to go and I can't walk another step farther and there's a boy whose car smells like a bakery who can give me a ride home.

The doors are unlocked now that the last bell has rung and as everyone's fighting to come out, I'm fighting to get in. The whispers are the same and I imagine a girl like Sophie Graham is accustomed to being talked about. Preferably without mascara tracked down her cheeks.

Scones. Landon Crane. His vintage red VW. The thoughts propel me forward with more confidence and I lift my delicate chin a bit through the crowd. I finally find Landon lingering by the senior lockers and I wonder if my new social standing will impact the way he treats me, for better or worse.

When he sees me coming, he smiles. For better. "Well, look who it is! Did you see that someone created a meme of you eating a donut?" He laughs as I near. His friends raise their eyebrows and clap him on the back before slamming lockers and heading out like everyone else. "You must have hit your head harder than everyone thought."

Under different circumstances, I'd curtsy and take full credit for the implosion of Sophie Graham. But everything's come to a head and I feel all those tears bubble up again because I'm not even sure of my own name anymore. Everything is completely out of my control right about now. I'm exhausted.

Landon's eyes widen, and when he blinks they're softer somehow. "Oh, I didn't mean. . . ."

I shake my head and sniffle. "I was just hoping you could give me a ride again."

When he reaches for my hand, I lace my fingers in between his. And for a second my world stops spinning so wildly around me. For a second I feel safe.

twenty-seven

LANDON RUBS HIS HANDS OVER THE STUBBLE ALONG HIS CHIN AND looks over at me as we wait at a red light. "Do you want to talk about it?"

I think of everything I have to say, think of the notebook and all the information I've gathered and haven't shared. I think of the fight to get out of this body, the impossibility of everything, the absolute powerlessness of it all. Do I want to talk? It's the only thing I want to do. Spill everything. Have him believe.

But the real truth is just too impossible to say out loud. In words. Even to Landon. How do you tell someone you're trapped in the wrong body? How do you tell him that the person you thought you were might not even exist?

"I'm just really overwhelmed." Truth.

He makes the turn onto our street and I see the Grahams' house looming at the end and I just can't do it. I can't go back there yet. I've barely digested everything that's happened today and I can't process with Sophie's mom breathing down my neck.

"Would it be okay if I came over for a little while?" I scramble to think of a reason, an excuse, because I've just invited myself over to the house of the cutest boy I've ever met. "Our internet has been super spotty and I really need to look some stuff up." It is such a stupid excuse, but I just can't bring myself to care anymore.

"I've been used for a lot of things, Sophie Graham. My mad baking abilities, my kickass Photoshop skills, and even this guy." He pats Murray's steering wheel lovingly. "But I can safely say no one's ever used me for my internet. Lucky for you the Cranes take wifi *very* seriously."

I laugh. In another life, butterflies would flutter through my stomach. In another life, this would feel like the beginning of something. But all I can think is that the girl he's starting to like is Sophie Graham, not Amelia Fischer. And it feels more like an end than a beginning.

What if that's the whole point. What if I'm supposed to forget about Amelia and her twisted life and try to be Sophie Graham? Try to be okay with letting go?

"Have you ever felt like maybe you're in the wrong body?" I spit the question out of my mouth before I can bring myself to worry about his answer.

"You mean, like, do I ever wish I was a girl? Because honestly . . ."

I cut him off. "No, I mean like the wrong life."

"Like reincarnation? Because I totally believe in that. My mom had this friend whose kid remembered all this weird stuff about a village in Thailand and when they finally brought him there on a vacation he recognized people and called them by name. When he got older, he started to forget, but my mom totally believes that he lived another life before this one."

I stop and absorb what he's saying. Reincarnation. Is that what this is? Some kind of weird next life since my current body is on life support? Does that mean I'm going to forget all about Mae and Amelia and my mom? Does that mean that I'll never know the real truth behind everything locked inside that box? So many questions and still no answers. Maybe this is it. Maybe it's time to give up.

But I think about Mae. I think about the girl I used to be. The prickly little thing who loved her mom and her sister with ferocity. She wasn't perfect, but she wasn't a quitter. And even if my life as Amelia is over that doesn't mean I can't save my mom and sister from the shadow man. Because maybe once I've saved them it'll be okay to let everything else go.

We pull into his driveway. The Cranes' house is an anomaly in Morristown. It's tiny and painted a deep, moody blue with white trim, with window boxes overflowing with late-summer blooms and a tarnished brass plaque next to the front door that identifies it as a "Century Home Built in 1901." It's one of the few historical houses that butt up to the sprawling estates developed a few years back. And it looks weirdly familiar. It takes me a minute to recognize it but the moment I do I gasp loud enough to make Landon slam on the brakes.

"The house angel!"

Landon looks panicked. "Oh shit. Did I run it over?" He slams the car in first and jerks up the parking brake then looks at me. "Wait, what the hell is a house angel?"

"Your house. It looks exactly like this little figurine my mom has on our mantle."

Landon looks relieved. "Oh, those. Some old couple makes them in Baltimore—the wife grew up here. They do a new historic house every year and come up for Art Fest. Ours was one of the first ones they ever did, before I was even born. My mom's never been able to snag one. I'm surprised she hasn't stolen yours yet."

"Oh yeah. Right." I'm processing the information, trying to figure out how my mom ended up with a carving of Landon's house years before we moved to Morristown. My brain catches on something. Sophie grew up with that house on her mantle too. She's lived here her whole life. I'm somehow trapped in her body after a man tried to take me. And then I find birth certificates with the wrong names unlocked by a key that was hidden in a wooden house from a town where we'd never actually lived. My mind tries to string all

these details together, tries to pick up the thread and understand how they're connected, but the whole story is a knotty
mess.

I'm snapped back to reality when Landon opens my car
door.

"Coming?"

As soon as we walk into Landon's house, I hear his mom
call, "Hi there, sweetheart!" and Sophie's six again.

*There are moving boxes stacked in every room and my parents
are yelling at each other. The doorbell rings and they stop. They
never fight when other people are around.*

*I open the door, happy to meet someone else. Happy that the
yelling is over for now.*

*"Hi there, sweetheart!" a woman says, smiling widely. My mom
comes up behind me and squeezes my shoulders just a little too hard.
"We just wanted to welcome you to the neighborhood!" she continues, holding out a basket of fresh bread, muffins, scones, and cookies.
They smell so good, but I'm distracted by the boy in glasses standing
behind her, stretching his neck to see inside the house. He probably
heard my parents arguing. The thought makes me blush.*

*My mom takes the basket from her. "We're just getting all set-
tled in, you know how it is to move. Even if it's only across town!"*

*"Oh, just the worst," Mrs. Crane replies. "I know I've seen you
around, but we haven't had a chance to officially meet. I'm Emily."
She reaches out her hand and looks so pretty when she smiles.*

*"Hillary," my mom replies coolly. She smiles, but I can still see
the tears in her eyes.*

*Mrs. Crane probably sees them too, because she turns to me.
"This is Landon!" she says, nudging the little boy forward. "You'll
be going to kindergarten together! What's your name, honey?"*

*I open my mouth to answer, but my mom beats me to it. "This
is Sophie. And yes, she's six, but she'll be in the gifted class. Is
Landon in the gifted program?"*

*Mrs. Crane flushes and pats Landon on the head awkwardly.
"Afraid not. We're aggressively average over here."*

*I feel my mom's fingers tighten on my shoulders again as my
dad comes to meet the new neighbors. I already know they won't be
friends.*

"Sophie Graham!" The memory disintegrates, and I see
a slightly older version of the same small woman with her
son's golden eyes. Her arms wrap me in a hug tight enough
to knock the wind out of me and elicit protests from Landon
who rolls his eyes. For someone so small, she's strong as hell.

The house is cozy in the best way possible, at least fifteen
degrees warmer than outside, and smells like something that
would have a flaky crust and melt in your mouth. There
are window seats and original moldings and a dusty piano
tucked into an alcove with sheet music stacked in piles on
top. The floors creak and the ceilings are low, but it's somehow still bright and airy. The kitchen is a disaster of dirty
dishes and spilled flour, and when she sees me looking, Mrs.
Crane apologizes.

"Oh, please ignore the mess. I have scones ready to come
out of the oven and cookies about to go in."

"It's fine, Mom. It's just Sophie. All I promised was a fast internet connection and the pleasure of my company." He looks oversized in this tiny kitchen, kind of hunching over like his head might graze the ceiling. So incredibly different from the boy in Sophie's memory. Is it because she was the one doing the remembering? Would I have seen him differently as a six-year-old?

"Follow me." Landon grabs a plate of scones and leads me down a narrow hallway toward the back of the house.

He opens a pair of glass French doors and I notice his laptop all set up in the corner, a few cameras, lenses, and a tangle of cords beside it. Landon places the plate on a table and if it weren't for the view out the wall of windows, I'd have already stuffed a scone in my mouth. But even the smell of buttery deliciousness is no rival for the Cranes' backyard. It's literally a graveyard. Well, I guess technically the graveyard is behind them, but beyond their postage-stamp-sized backyard there are rows and rows of ancient headstones lining the green grass. I stare at them in shock, if not for the buried dead then for the memory that follows.

Candy sits like a brick in my stomach and I'm afraid I might be sick. I blame my mom because we never have it around, but it was still stupid for me to blow through half my bag before the night is even over.

"You're up, Sophie!" Janie singsongs. Half our class is here, circled around the creepy tombstones that border Landon's backyard. We still end up here every Halloween even though Brooke calls him

220

*a dork behind his back. We've never done this before though, and my
stomach does a little twist again, nerves mixed with way too much
sugar.*

*I lean forward and spin the bottle, the glass cool on my fingertips.
It doesn't spin well on the grass and before I even look up to see his
amber eyes magnified by those stupid, thick lenses, I know it's him
because everyone laughs.*

*"I get a redo," I snap. Maybe it's the candy, my churning stom-
ach, everyone else. But the words come out just as nasty as my
nausea and I can't take them back.*

*He rolls his eyes like he knows something I don't, but still sits
there like a lump while our classmates begin to chant the word* kiss.

*Now I know I'll be sick. I break away from the circle, laughter
lifting into the chilly night air behind me, with an acute understanding of an age-old set of rules. It doesn't matter what I want anymore.
It's not worth the stomachache.*

Landon reads my shock wrong, and I wonder if he
remembers the Halloween where everything changed. "I
guess it's been a while, right?" His golden eyes follow mine
to the graves. "You get used to it."

The Amelia in me has so many questions. "Aren't you
scared? Like, at night?" I can't help but ask the obvious one
that I'm sure has been covered in the past.

Landon looks at me like I have two heads. "No, Sophie,
they're friendly ghosts, remember?" He shakes his head and
laughs.

I don't. I'm transfixed by the neat rows. I don't think I've ever believed in ghosts but suddenly I'm sure they're real. I can imagine their spirits weaving and wandering, calling out to one another and pressing themselves into the historic walls of Landon's home. The stones feel alive in a way that they shouldn't, and I realize with a sick certainty how much has changed. Maybe I do believe in ghosts. Or maybe it's Sophie, yet another piece of Amelia gone. Or maybe it's just that I can feel them more acutely now that I'm a wandering spirit too. Trapped in the wrong body instead of my own. Or instead of a casket. The thought feels like sharp fingernails trailing down the back of my neck.

"No one's been buried here for pretty much a hundred years anyway," he says, watching me closely. I pull my eyes away from the stones, giving myself permission to take in the sight of him. His shaggy hair shines gold in the sun and I see those blond tips on his eyelashes again. It must make him a little uncomfortable, because he pushes his computer toward me in an attempt to break the moment. "Are you ready?"

Am I ready? I don't know if it's the smell of those incredible scones or the warmth of the room or his perfect lips or his terrifying backyard full of memories and ghosts. Maybe it's the image of Landon soaking wet, grinning at the real me behind the chain-link fence after my tennis match, or it's Sophie's six-year-old version of Landon with glasses and rosy cheeks. Or maybe I don't want to follow the rules anymore. Maybe Sophie doesn't either. Maybe it doesn't really matter.

I raise myself up on tiptoes and press my lips to his. His mouth parts without hesitation and he tastes like ChapStick and breath mints and possibility. I want to move closer to him, I want to feel his body against mine. I want to forget all about who I am and who I'm trying to find. I just want to be a girl, falling for a boy.

And for a second it doesn't matter who I am. The only thing that matters is the way his lips feel, the way his hands hold my face, the way my fingers curl easily around his hair when they wind around his neck. For one magic second it's nothing but that stomach-liquefying feeling of mouth against mouth, body against body.

When I finally pull away to catch my breath, I look straight up into his golden eyes, power surging through me. I'm not Amelia, I'm not Sophie. I'm someone new— someone who kisses boys in light-filled rooms with ghosts as witnesses.

He shakes his head and sits next to me. "Right, well, I'm gonna go ahead and take that as a yes."

"Wait, what was the question?" I can't help but mess with him a little.

His face reddens and he flips open the screen of his laptop. I take a deep breath and prepare myself for whatever comes next.

Ready or not, here I come.

twenty-eight

WHEN I PLOP DOWN NEXT TO LANDON ON THE COUCH MY HAND brushes his arm, sending a shiver of longing through my body. Focus. I need to focus.

"I found something this morning at the house. Birth certificates for Amelia and Mae. Amelia's birthday was right, but the names on the certificates were different."

He wrinkles his forehead a little. "Wait, you found birth certificates? How?"

"Let's just focus on the facts, okay. Birth certificates. Wrong names. Scary guy trying to kidnap Amelia. Something is going on."

"Uh, yeah. Have you told your parents? Gone to the police? I mean, you said you saw someone try to take this girl. And now you have birth certificates? Sophie . . ."

"I tried to do all that," I say, even though I haven't gone to the police. Not sure my story would hold up there especially with all the breaking and entering of late. "But I'm one 'episode' away from another hospital stay. My parents are convinced that something is seriously wrong with me. I have to do this on my own."

He opens his mouth like he's going to say something, but our eyes lock. I meet his gaze, unblinking, willing him to see the truth behind Sophie's mismatched eyes. And then he nods and I know I've passed some sort of test.

I open a new tab on his computer. My hand shakes, screwing up a few letters as I type the unfamiliar name.

Jenna Elizabeth Dowling

The first result is a Google image. Jenna Elizabeth Dowling looks about two years old. She smiles back at me on the computer screen, parallel to a picture of Haylee Morgan Dowling, who looks a little younger. *HAVE YOU SEEN ME?* headlines the top in big bold letters and the girls' birthdays, heights, weights, eye colors, and hair colors are listed below. A paragraph explains that the children were last seen with their mother, April Nicole Dowling, fifteen years ago on September 4 in Baltimore, Maryland.

Next to it is a blurry picture of a much younger version of my mom.

I scribble April's name down in my notebook without tearing my eyes off the pictures of the little girls. Identical sprays of freckles across their noses, those baby-fine curls you only ever see on little kids.

Jenna and Haylee.

Me and Mae.

Same girls. Same faces.

New names. New truth.

"Holy shit," Landon whispers.

twenty-nine

MY ENTIRE LIFE IS UNRAVELING RIGHT BEFORE MY EYES. I GUESS I
always knew there were loose threads, things about my family that were strange, the stuff that made us different. The
constant moving, my mom's refusal to talk about my dad.
It's like your oldest, warmest sweater that's itchy and tight
and threadbare, but you never pull those threads because
even though it's uncomfortable sometimes, it's still your
sweater. And now the thread has been pulled and my entire
life is unspooling before me. My trust for my mom, the
endless stories Mae and I concocted about our dead father,
the moving.

On one hand, I hate myself for being dumb or dismis-
sive or naïve enough to ignore all of it or think that it was
normal. On the other hand, I want to go back to being that

dumb, naïve girl. Because that girl isn't sitting in a sunroom next to the cutest boy she's ever kissed feeling like she might vomit all over his charming whitewashed floors.

With shaking fingers I click on the link to read the story about our disappearance in the *Baltimore Sun*.

Girls, 1 & 2, Abducted by Mother Wanted for Questioning in Stepfather's Death

According to investigators, April Nicole Dowling is suspected of abducting her two-year-old daughter, Jenna Elizabeth Dowling, and one-year-old daughter, Haylee Morgan Dowling, at three a.m. from their home in Deerfield while their father, Dr. Edward Dowling, was on call at Johns Hopkins Hospital.

Dowling's car was found abandoned near the harbor with the car seats still installed.

"She was not of sound mind. I am worried for her safety and more importantly the safety of our children," Dr. Edward Dowling said in a recent statement to the press asking for any information on the whereabouts of his children.

Police say April Dowling, twenty-six, is also wanted for questioning in connection to her stepfather's death six years ago.

Anyone with information is asked to contact Baltimore police.

The picture that runs next to the story is of my mom, Mae, and me. There's no question that it's us. No possible mistake. This is my mother. This is my sister. This is my life. My stomach heaves and as much as I want to rush to the bathroom and be sick, I need to know more.

"This is crazy, Sophie. Like we need to call the police and tell them immediately." Landon's voice sounds like it's coming from a million miles away. I can't even begin to formulate a response, I'm too focused on trying to process "not of sound mind" and "wanted for questioning in connection to her stepfather's death."

With trembling fingers I type *April Dowling* into the search bar and hit enter. The hits are fast and furious. A stepfather who died in a house fire. His death was originally ruled an accident, but when April's daughters went missing, Edward Dowling said she had confessed to killing her stepfather and threatened to take his daughters. He kicked her out of the house, but she took the children from a babysitter when he was at work one night.

My mother stole me and Mae. She's a kidnapper. A liar. A murderer.

And that man. The man who tried to take me was my father. And he was actually here to save me. To save us. From our mother. The woman who stole us from our beds and moved from tiny town to tiny town, burying us in middle America like stolen treasure.

A surreal sense of detachment washes over me, like I'm watching this from my coma in the hospital instead of living it in Landon Crane's sunroom. I click and read and scroll. Memorizing every detail. Trying to connect this story, this woman, this man, to my actual life.

It's the quotes from my father that my eyes end up skimming for in every story.

Devastating loss.

Pray for my girls.

I will not rest until I find my family.

My fingers automatically reach for the coin in my pocket. *Tony, Tony, please come down. Something's lost that can't be found.*

Up until Sophie and Mr. Graham and this moment, dads were like dinosaurs or unicorns—fascinating to view from a distance, disappointing in reality, but in my life, my real life, completely extinct. Mythical.

But suddenly my dad is real. His name exists on a computer screen and he's talking about me and Mae and how much he loves us. I can hardly look away from the screen long enough to write his name down beside April's.

When we were little, Mae and I learned about dads from TV shows. They were always around, wearing suits, eating breakfasts, teaching their kids how to play sports, and telling them to listen to their mothers. We were living outside Dallas when I started kindergarten and we finally stayed in one place long enough for me to wonder about our dad. I remember watching kids walk into school, hands gripped between two parents, fathers and mothers dressed for work. Not pretend dads. Real dads. Present. Alive. With their kids every single day.

When I got home one afternoon, I asked my mom the obvious question.

"Can we get a dad?" I said, like he was a puppy or something you opened on your birthday.

She dropped a plate of cookies she was holding. I remember the white shards dancing across the floor, tiny painted blue-and-yellow flowers skirting the edges.

She walked right over the broken plate, the thick-soled shoes she wore to her job crunching across the glass. Bending down to my level, she gripped both of my hands into her larger, warm ones and looked me right in the eye. "Your dad is in heaven."

We never talked about heaven, never went to church or prayed, but I'd seen it in movies and TV shows too and there were clouds and angels and singing. I remember wondering if we could visit him there, jump from cloud to cloud and watch life continue below like I always imagined.

As we got older, the heaven story wasn't enough anymore. We'd ask questions. But my mom seemed to curl into herself and hide for days whenever we mentioned our dad. Eventually Mae and I stopped asking because it wasn't worth it to lose our mom too.

But now he's here, alive on the computer screen, and I can't stop poring over every word. Every time I click on a link, my stomach clenches, hoping for a picture of the man who is my dad and who has not died in some sort of mysterious accident that traumatized our mom, but there are only pictures of Mom and Mae and me. My eyes drink in every snapshot, every smile, every piece of the life that my mom destroyed when she stole us.

Dr. Edward Dowling. I whisper the name as I type, and I brace myself when I hit enter. There's a litany of websites listing doctors, but they don't provide much information beyond the fact that he's located in Baltimore, Maryland.

I think about the man who tried to grab me. The sweatshirt hiding his face. The rain. The urgency in his voice. If I'm Jenna Dowling, the man who tried to take me (save me?) had to be Dr. Edward Dowling. He wore a necklace of St. Anthony, the patron saint of lost things. Finally, the pieces snap into place.

My hand is shaking when I click on the link to view images, but there are so many different faces and random pictures that come up in the search, I have no real way of knowing which face belongs to my dad. I'd like to think that some primal part of me would recognize his eyes or the set of his jaw, that I would see a ghost of myself hovering in front of my dad's features, but all the photos I page through look like strangers.

"They have a father. He's not dead. I wonder if that's the man . . ." My voice trails off because I can't bring myself to say it out loud. Not yet.

"We have to tell someone. . . ." Landon's voice shakes a little. This is too much for him.

"No!" The word comes out too fast, too loud. I'm not even sure why I'm saying it, but I know we can't tell anyone about this. Despite the fact that I'm completely falling for this guy, I wish he wasn't next to me. I need time to think. Time to process.

A doorbell rings, but the sound is distant, like it's at

another house in another world. I lean in closer to the computer as though the words will make sense if I can only see them clearer. My mom hasn't ever seemed crazy or unstable. She's never tried to hurt us. The facts are all here in black and white, but somehow, as angry as I am with her, I can't imagine turning her into the police. Not without an explanation for all she's done. Anger pounds through my skull to the beat of clicking high heels, the death march of time slipping between my fingers once again. Voices drift beneath the paned glass doors of the sun-filled room.

Landon's mom asks someone if they'd like tea. I hear a clipped voice answer, "No, no. I've just been trying to get a hold of Sophie and we were worried, so . . ."

Shit. Mrs. Graham.

I'm the girl who kisses boys just because she feels like it, the not-Sophie, not-Amelia girl who does whatever the hell she wants and finds the truth at all costs, I remind myself. But when I see Mrs. Graham's face through the glass doors, I want to scream. I need more time.

"Sophie? Oh, thank God."

"Oh, hi, Mrs. Graham," Landon says, closing the laptop with a click. I want to reach over and yank it out from under his fingers. I need more time with those names. I need to know more about April Dowling and her daughters. "We were just working on a government project. Sophie tried to call you, but the reception in here sucks."

Mrs. Graham is distracted by the graveyard out back for

a second, but it doesn't last long.

"Okay, well, time to go." Like I'm four and this is a play date and she's exhausted by the number of warnings she's had to give me.

"Oh, Hillary, I wish you'd have some tea and a scone. I just made them, the kids can—" Mrs. Crane is silenced.

"Sophie?" The word is made of sharp edges, and I realize that this is how Sophie's parents must control her, all these tiny little humiliations. Landon is uncomfortable and embarrassed for me, but I hardly notice. My eyes are still trained on the closed laptop sitting on the coffee table, full of truths that I can't quite process.

Mrs. Graham turns to Mrs. Crane now with a wide smile as though she's not about to lose her shit over her missing daughter who keeps having these inconvenient lapses. "Emily, thank you so much for your hospitality. I keep meaning to run that basket back over!"

Mrs. Crane shakes her head. "Keep it," she says with a strained smile.

"See you later, I guess," Landon mumbles.

The entire day swirls in front of me. The light streaming into this magical space, our kiss, all the secrets, all the lies. I shake my head to clear it, and his face falls. None of this is real. It's not fair to keep going, not fair for Landon or for Sophie. I'm not who he thinks I am. I'm not who I think I am. I shouldn't have let it get this far.

I let Mrs. Graham guide me toward the door without another word. I shouldn't have come. This was a mistake.

As much as I want to look back, want to thank Mrs. Crane for baking scones that taste like heaven, thank Landon for giving me the hope that maybe I don't have to do this alone, that maybe I don't have to do anything alone—I can't. Because I know that the hurt in Landon's eyes will kill me. Because this is what he expected of Sophie Graham all along. And I hate that he was right.

thirty

MRS. GRAHAM PULLS HER CAR UP THEIR LONG DRIVEWAY AND PUTS it into park, keeping her hands fixed on the steering wheel, her eyes trained forward. When I shift to unbuckle my seat belt, focused on rushing up the stairs two at a time, locking the door to Sophie's room, alone with her phone, the note-book, Google, she puts her hand on my arm and stops me.

There are fine lines etched into the thin skin around her eyes, unshed tears trembling over mascaraed lashes. It's hard to look at her because I want to see a stranger, someone else's mom, someone else's problem, but instead I hear muffled cries behind closed bedroom doors, I see folded clothes in neat piles, I taste thoughtfully prepared meals, and I hear her supportive cheers. With every passing second she's becoming less and less someone else's mom, and more and more mine. "I'm worried about you," she whispers.

Her tears swirl with my reflection, my dark hair always such a shock to people when she'd take me out as a child. "She must look like her father!" Strangers just couldn't help themselves. And if they bent down closer and saw my eyes—one green, one blue—they'd grow quiet because they'd already wasted a comment on my hair. Missed opportunity. Sophie's memories no longer come as a shock. They're just there.

"I'm fine," I whisper back. And maybe I really will be fine. Maybe Sophie's life is easier. Maybe their secrets aren't as toxic. Why am I fighting so hard to get back to a life that wasn't even real in the first place?

But then I remember Mae. I remember my sister. I remember my dad, the man I thought was trying to abduct me. And I remember my mom, the woman who actually did.

Mrs. Graham swipes away the tears and shakes her head. "I know. I know." She tries to convince herself. "I just want everyone to be okay."

She presses a button on her rearview mirror to open one of the garage doors and pulls forward. I see Sophie's black BMW SUV parked in the garage as though it didn't just mow an innocent girl down during a thunderstorm. Mrs. Graham slams on the brakes, just as shocked as I am. We idle for a second and then she reverses and repositions to pull in beside it. "Oh. Your car's back," she says finally. "Daddy must have picked it up today." She turns to me and smiles. I guess this is

Mr. Graham's way of wanting everyone to be okay too. Moving right along. But Sophie's fancy car looks way too much like freedom for me to do anything but return her smile. If Mr. and Mrs. Graham want everyone to be okay, then I have to be okay. I lean over and kiss her cheek. "Thanks, Mom." And then I unbuckle, hold on tight to my book bag, and head for the house.

I could read the same articles all night. I could switch search terms to dig for pictures, obsess over details, and reread my notes until the words are carved into my vision and I see them hovering even when I look away. I could.

But this isn't only about Amelia. It's about Mae, it's about Haylee, that smiling one-year-old face on the missing children's poster. She needs to know the truth.

So I smile through dinner, linger over dessert, and suffer through the latest episode of some reality show that has celebrities competing to build furniture because I'm hoping that's what Sophie would do. Lights out at ten and phone turned over to charge in your parents' room in the Graham house, to ensure eight hours of uninterrupted sleep. If my plan works, I won't even get a power nap.

Instead, I focus on the ticking clock in the upstairs hallway, the leaves rustling outside the open window. I let the soft percussion of this household become a soundtrack. Sophie's bedazzled flashlight is aimed at a new page of the notebook as I write, the words trailing across the page as if by magic.

My eyes are heavy, the pen bobbing along with my head, sharp lines cutting through every couple words. I sit up in bed, rub away the heaviness, and swing my legs over to get a drink of water. As soon as my bare feet touch the cool wood, I hear a tiny scratch, ping, bounce on my window. I freeze. Silence. And then it comes again, this time, ping, scratch, ping, ping. My heart pumps furiously inside my chest and I don't move or even breathe because I need to hear. One last time. Tap, tap, ping.

And then I hear him say my name.

"Sophie? Are you up?" The threat dissipates as fast as it appeared. I rush to the window, and there he is—Landon, partially illuminated by the dim streetlight.

"I swear throwing rocks at your window was my last resort," he says. I think of Jake scaling the house and know it could be worse.

"I'm sorry about today, Landon." As I say the words, I try to channel so much more into the apology. "But—"

He cuts me off and shakes his head. "Don't." He looks away for a second and then back up, his jaw set. "I can't stop thinking about that newspaper article, the birth certificates, these people. We need to go to the police."

His words send flares of panic shooting through my brain. "I'm not ready. . . . I mean, my dad made me promise not to do this. He doesn't want me to get involved."

"We can't just pretend like this isn't happening. They could be in danger. Amelia's already in a coma and you think you saw someone try to take her. This isn't a game, Sophie. This is her life."

I want to cry because I know he wants me to do the right

thing and we both know I'm not going to.

"Please, Landon. Please don't go to them. Not yet. Just give me some time to talk to my dad first, okay?"

"Fine. I'll give you twenty-four hours. But after that I'm calling the police with or without you. Got it?"

He doesn't wait for me to respond, he just turns on his heel and walks across the street, over to his house with the permanent bakery smell and whatever ghosts might be lingering in his backyard. I watch him glance up to my window one last time, but I've already stepped back into the shadows.

I feel like I've burned two lives to the ground. Everything I touch turns to ash and now it's all slipping between my fingers—pieces of Sophie, pieces of me, lifted by the wind before they even hit the ground.

When I sink into Sophie's bed later, I curl up into her blankets and lose myself in her pillows. I let the tears fall then, let them soak her million-thread-count, Egyptian-cotton sheets. And in the darkness with my eyes open but seeing nothing, I give myself permission to feel every loss, every regret, every missed opportunity as I wait for morning.

thirty-one

THE SUN IS JUST RISING AS I APPLY A FINAL COAT OF LIP GLOSS AND smack my lips together. Hair done, makeup applied, dressed, brushed, and ready to go. Today I'll wear Sophie's perfection like a suit of armor. I check my bag to be sure the letter is inside, throw it over my shoulder, and head for the stairs. All the doors that line the hall are still shut tight, the sound of running water traveling through the walls as the Grahams get ready to face the day.

I have more than enough time to make breakfast as planned, so I pull eggs, almond milk, and gluten-free bread from the fridge and get started on French toast. Mrs. Graham walks in first. Her eyes widen when she sees what I've been up to. I put two pieces on her plate and push the bottle of organic maple syrup across the table with a smile.

"Oh, Sophie . . . how nice." She glances back toward the hallway, sharing a long look with Mr. Graham. "Look, Robert, Sophie made us breakfast, isn't that just lovely?"

Mr. Graham nods distractedly. "Oh thanks, Sophie. Smells great, but I have a meeting I can't miss." Ever since our confrontation in the guest room the other night, he hasn't so much as looked at me. But I don't have time to worry about Sophie and her not-real dad's tenuous relationship. He offers his wife a quick kiss and is out the door in seconds. I look over at Mrs. Graham and see her close her eyes for a second, her lips stretched into a thin, tight line. The memory of the Grahams yelling and the hidden papers that proclaim Sophie to be someone else's daughter are such a stark contrast to the world Sophie has painted for herself online. There are secrets here too. But they're not mine, at least not yet.

"I just had a huge craving for French toast and didn't want to bother you . . . Mom." That word still sounds all wrong and I wonder if she notices. The way she looks at me like I'm a complete stranger in this kitchen makes me feel like maybe she does. Is it my hair? Or maybe my makeup? I knew I put on too much eyeliner. My smoky-eye attempts tend to leave me looking more like someone who accidentally slept in her eye makeup than a doe-eyed model. Sophie's strange eyes somehow just make it worse.

"Okay, well, I don't want to be late for school." I'm fifteen minutes early, but anxious to get out of here. It's been real, Grahams, but I'm ready. It took the darkest, most silent time of the night for me to realize that Landon was right. He gave me twenty-four hours, but I only needed a pen, paper, and the morning. "I'm picking up Janie and she has to meet a teacher for some extra help before first period."

Mrs. Graham opens her mouth to say something but throws me a tired-looking smile instead. And I'm free.

Sophie's car is iridescent black with rich tan leather seats. It's the kind of car Mae and I roll our eyes at in the school parking lot. As soon as I tuck myself into the spacious interior, the memory comes.

"Thank you, Daddy!" It took me three tries to pass my driver's test and I finally managed to score that thin piece of plastic by the skin of my teeth. The shiny black car has been mocking me in the garage since that first failed test. Climbing in feels more like a right than a privilege.

As soon as I press the start button like some sort of video game, the seat automatically adjusts to the perfect height for me to reach the steering wheel and gas pedal. The engine purrs to life, and I try not to think about what part of the car hit me and where.

Before pulling out, I wonder if I should throw open the door and run back up the steps, say good-bye again, appreciate something that might be missing when I switch back. But it's too late for that. It might even be too late for me. I need to get to Mae.

When I press the button for the radio, I'm assaulted by the loudest, most aggressive heavy metal I've ever heard in my entire life. Even after I stab at the button again to silence the blast, it feels like my ears are bleeding, the bass still reverberating within my rib cage. Oh. My. God. That cannot be a real thing that just happened. And yet when I look down at Sophie's iPod, I see a playlist entitled Morning Metal with an unassuming smiley face beside it.

In another life, I'd have time to appreciate Sophie's surprises.

The Morristown Police Station doesn't see very much action. In fact, the running joke in this town is the *Morristown Gazette*'s weekly police blotter. *Police were called to a Larkspur Way residence after a suspicious package was found on the front porch. The package was cleared of all suspicion after the officer asked the resident if she had ordered anything from Amazon recently.* I imagine that's why my mom chose Morristown. No one does anything wrong here. You can go to sleep with your doors unlocked and your windows cracked, leave your purse in the car, your keys in the ignition. You can fly under the radar. You can disappear.

I imagine who might read my letter. Who will pull up our names in their database? Who will start a file? Who will finish what I started? Before I lose my nerve, I pull Sophie's beast of a car as close to the Morristown Police Station's mailbox as I can, open her car door so I can reach, and slip the envelope inside. I pull away and don't look back. This is for Mae now. This is all for Mae.

I'm relieved to see Crimson Wave parked in front of Pete's Donuts when I pull into the lot. So many things have changed, but at least Pete's is still the place you can find Mae on any given morning. The lot is spotty; it's late. But I'm not here for a donut. The familiar bells jingle their welcome and I turn toward our usual booth tucked into the back corner. Sure enough, Mae is there, sitting alone, nursing her coffee.

But before I can navigate around the maze of half-filled chairs toward my sister, I hear another voice that I'm confident will remain etched into my soul like a fingerprint despite whoever's genetic code wins in the end. They say a baby can recognize her mother's voice even before birth. I imagine that whooshing darkness, the muffled vibrations connecting my mom and me together despite all the ugliness of this life. I recognize my mother's voice even after my apparent rebirth. The sound grounds me like gravity and I'm pulled toward the back room where Pete's office door is slightly ajar.

"I won't take your charity. That's not why I'm here. I know you're short staffed and I just need a little bit to tide us over while Amelia . . ."

Dies? She can't bring herself to finish the sentence.

I can't make out Pete's reply, but knowing him he's trying to throw money at her. He's well known for his generosity toward regular customers. He once paid a preschool tuition for one of his employee's kids after her husband was laid off from his job. It was supposed to be anonymous, but the preschool totally gave him away. Pete still grumbles about the local newspaper article that ran featuring his random act of kindness one February.

"No, no, no. I insist. Just one shift under the table. I can't do this any other way," she pleads. I need to hate her. But the desperation in her voice makes it hard.

Pete tugs my mom in for one of his gruff hugs and pats her back. "You need anything . . . anything, Carol, you know who to ask. Got that?"

My mom nods, her head bent into him. She looks so defeated. But I know she'll manage to put on the "I Donut Care" T-shirt he's handed her and paste a smile on her face. She could pass for exhausted, maybe a little sad as she hands a customer his change. If only everyone knew. As Pete moves toward the office door, I bend in front of the drinking fountain long enough for him to head back into the kitchen to tackle the morning mess, and then I return to the door like a magnet. I can't not watch her. I might never see her again no matter where I end up. And it's so sad. So fucking sad. Even in this body, with Sophie's heart and this mixed-up sense of self, it feels like someone has yanked out every essential piece of who I am and torn it to shreds. Tears slip down my cheeks and my mom swipes an arm across her own. I'm crying her tears, feeling all her hurt in this moment like those weird stories you hear about twins who feel the pain of the other even miles, worlds away.

I will myself to stay angry. This is the woman who lied to me my entire life. This woman is wanted for murder. When she stole us, she robbed us of a normal childhood. She robbed us of a dad. I can't ever forgive her for that. I won't.

But somehow I can't take my eyes off her. And when

she lifts off her sweatshirt the tank top she has underneath comes with it, leaving her back exposed before she yanks it back down.

And there it is. Right in front of me this whole time. My whole life. I was wrong. So wrong. My pulse quickens and I can't pull enough air into my lungs. The hallway starts to close in on me and I can't help but breathe faster, shorter breaths, which never helps. Sure enough, my vision is burnt along the edges, the black creeping its way in. I fight it, blink it back. Not now. Not now. I have to get back to the police station. I have to get back.

"Sophie? What the hell?" Mae rounds the corner, ripping the panic right out from under me. Her face turns bright red with anger and, worse, embarrassment when she sees what I've been doing. "Are you watching her? Does this get you off? Watching the poor people scrounge around for money after you destroyed our family? What the fuck is wrong with you?"

My mom pushes through the office door, a shell of her old self. "Mae Avery!" she screams, but like everything else, it's too late.

Mae is already out the front door of the restaurant. I run after her, not knowing what else to do. "Wait, Mae! I can explain. There's something you need to know. It's important!" I have to tell her everything. I have to make her believe. The truth has been right in front of us all these years. "Mae, wait. Please!" I chase her into the parking lot, focused on the back of her head, her bobbing ponytail. So focused that I don't notice the red Honda Civic backing out of its parking spot.

So focused I can't even be sure I feel the impact. For a moment I'm suspended midair until I fall hard and skid across the gravel in the parking lot. I'm level with the car's tires, a low whooshing rumbling through my ears, the too-bright sun blocked occasionally by crumpled faces, mouths huge with panic, and then . . . nothing.

Now you see her. Now you don't.

thirty-two

THERE IS AN ODOR IN MY ROOM. I NOTICE IT BEFORE I EVEN OPEN UP my eyes. Like boxed mashed potatoes and the chemicals they sprinkled over Teddy Whitehall's vomit when he got sick in the back of the bus during second grade. When my eyes finally adjust to the light, I don't see the dove-gray walls my mother and I spent weeks debating before painting— French Toile was too purple, Nimbus had blue undertones, but Shaker Gray, it turns out, was the perfect backdrop for my outfit-of-the-day posts because . . . priorities. Instead, I'm in a room with pockmarked walls painted a dirty white.

I wrinkle my nose. I'm stuck in a hospital. I remember slamming on my brakes for something in the road, my head smacking against the dashboard.

I have a killer headache and what feels like some serious

ass bruising, but beyond that my worst symptom seems to be dry mouth.

"Mom?" There's a strange note of desperation in my voice and I feel the same blind panic that suffocates me in a dark room when I wake up from a nightmare. The need for my mom is strong and sharp and almost supernatural in its strength.

She jerks awake in a corner chair, smoothing back her hair from her face. She looks like absolute hell. "Sophie? What's wrong?" She launches her body out of the chair to my side, grabbing my hands as though I'll be ripped away from her if she doesn't hold on tight enough.

For a moment there's nothing but relief. I'm so happy she's here, so grateful for her touch. But then I remember that I'm not nine years old anymore, and I pull my arm away, retreating into a pile of cheap pillows propped up behind me. "How long have I been asleep?"

She looks so much older, and suddenly I'm sure I've woken up from a coma after sleeping away five years of my life. There are memories curling around the edges of my consciousness. Someone singing to me softly. A man whispering, "Anthony, Anthony, look around, what was lost has now been found." Panic rises in my chest.

"I remember the accident, but am I okay? Can I still play tennis?"

She just stares. I realize that she's speechless. My mother. Without words.

"Mom? Hello?" My voice goes up an octave. There must be something wrong with me. Something awful. I either have a brain tumor or I'm pregnant.

"Sophie, honey, just relax. I'm going to call the doctor, okay? I think he can help. . . ." Her eyes are wild, fiercely searching mine. Her forehead wrinkles in a way I never thought possible after thousands and thousands of dollars spent on Botox and chemical peels.

"Relax? I wake up in the hospital and you won't tell me what's wrong with me, and you expect me to relax?" I'm frantic now. Trying to pull memories from the darkness. Cold metal against my chest, a searing pain in my head. And Amelia Fischer, who I beat for first singles. Something happened to her, and the memory of it is infuriatingly close, but completely inaccessible.

"Amelia?" I ask aloud. The name sounds weird, wrong. Like a word I've said so many times that it's lost all meaning.

My mother's reaction is instantaneous. She's up and jabbing her finger into the call button above my bed before the last syllable leaves my mouth.

A doctor strides purposefully into the room and I fire questions at her. "What happened to me? Why am I here? When can I play tennis? How long do I have to stay? What the hell is wrong with my mother?"

The doctor talks to me like I'm a kindergartner who walked into the wrong classroom on the first day of school. She starts talking about accidents, about side effects, concussions and confusion, that they're being extra careful since I've suffered two head injuries in such a close period of time.

She keeps talking, but I'm not listening anymore, because I'm pretty sure she said something about two accidents, about the days following the first. Days that I was apparently awake and doing things that somehow negated the effects of my mother's monthly Botox.

"Wait, what day is it?"

"What day do you think it is?" The doctor's voice is so condescending that I feel like rattling off March 22, 3014, just to watch her punch furious notes into her little computer. But given the situation, I figure it's best to go with the truth.

"September 20." The day after I won the first singles position. But I know as soon as I say the words that I'm wrong.

"Sophie, it's September 24." The doctor pauses a moment to let me digest her words. "We believe you're suffering from post–traumatic stress disorder. It's not at all unusual for someone who's suffered two accidents this close together."

I let her voice wash over me, not sure whether to feel relieved that I'm not dying or with child or terrified that I have no memory of the past few days of my life. Mostly I just want to go home. I want to be back in my room with its gray walls and comfortable bed. I want to be back on the tennis courts. I even want to be at one of our endless family dinners watching my parents try to out silence each other. Basically, I want to be anywhere but here in this depressing room with those depressing brown watermarks on the ceiling with this depressing woman who is supposedly my mother.

"Well, I feel fine now. Just give me a couple of Tylenol and we'll be on our way." I use my homecoming queen voice and my sweetest smile, which hasn't ever failed me.

Until now.

thirty-three

AS IT TURNS OUT, EVERY RIDICULOUS CLICHÉ ABOUT HEAD INJURIES is true. They wake you up every hour to make sure you haven't slipped into a coma. Doctors actually ask you how many fingers they're holding up and you're supposed to know how to rate your pain using ridiculous cartoon faces. And of course the endless questions about why I was at Pete's Donuts when I should have been at school. A question I'm completely unable to answer because I haven't eaten a donut since I was literally five and my parents decided that a gluten intolerance was holding me back from my true potential. Personally, I think my mother just couldn't risk being around refined carbohydrates while in the throes of a ketogenic hell of her own making.

The thing is, I'm fine. Fine. Fine. Fine. I mean, I don't

have to remember what happened over the past few days to be okay. The doctor said herself that some memory loss isn't at all abnormal with head traumas like mine. I just don't understand why we're not throwing a coming-home party and reveling in our normalcy. There has to be something they can give me to make me remember. I mean, we're Grahams. Better living by pharmaceuticals is practically our family motto. But the nightmares come every night. Filled with wailing sirens and haunting lullabies and when I lay in my bed unable to fall back asleep, I think it's probably better that I've forgotten.

Regardless, I have to put some distance between this hospital and me. No one will talk about it, but I know Amelia is still here, connected to machines. And even though we weren't best friends and even though she almost beat me for first singles, the thought of her broken body, a body that I technically broke, makes me physically ill. I know it was just an accident. I know it wasn't my fault that I hit her, but it doesn't change the fact that I was driving that car. And it definitely doesn't change the fact that she's stuck in a coma while I lie around complaining about hospital food. I have to get out of here. It's time to go home.

I hear a tentative knock on my door and immediately paste on my best I'm-no-longer-concussed smile.

But when Janie walks into the room, I let it slide right off my face so a genuine smile replaces it. "What are you doing here? I've missed you!" My words come out in a rush. I'm just so happy to see my best friend.

Without warning, she crumples.

"Soph, I've been so worried—"

I cut her off. She's scaring me. I don't like this one bit. "I'm fine. Swear. It's my mom who is insane and my dad who can barely look at me. I just need to get the hell out of here. They're still waking me up every hour and I've been here for almost two days."

Janie pulls her eyebrows together in confusion, her eyes frantically searching mine, when my mother swoops back into the room. "Well, you're in luck," she proclaims, like a knight in shining couture. "I'll pack your things. We're going home!"

thirty-four

"JANIE . . ." I COMPLAIN AT HER THE WAY I HAVE A MILLION TIMES before when I'm waiting for her to pick out an outfit or decide between eight hundred identical pictures to Insta. "I'm in, let's go already." I'm sitting in the wheelchair the nurse insisted we use, waiting for her to wheel me as far away from this hospital as humanly possible.

Janie finally grabs the handles and pushes me down the hall. It was my mother's idea to pull the car around and wait for us at the entrance. She said she wanted to give Janie and me some time to catch up. But Janie's been weirdly quiet. I can tell there's something bothering her, and honestly it's kind of pissing me off. I mean, I'm the one who's been in two accidents. What could she possibly be obsessing over?

I'm about to ask Janie if she wants to sleep over as we

weave our way through yet another waiting room, but she suddenly freezes.

"Why are we stopping? I'm dying for some unfiltered, nonrecycled air." I swivel around to see what she's looking at, but she doesn't seem to hear me. She's staring at a nurse and a resident with a clipboard in front of the doors to the ICU. My throat starts to burn. I need to get away from here.

"Amelia Fischer, bed twenty-seven, respiratory distress, condition worsening," the nurse says as the resident writes furiously.

"Janie, come on. This isn't any of our business." I feel like I'm going to be sick. They can't be talking about Amelia. She can't be getting worse. Janie shakes me off and takes a few steps closer to hear exactly what is being said.

"Almost a week? Percentage of full recovery reduced by approximately 67 percent?" The resident looks up as he speaks, recalling the information.

The nurse nods. "If she were breathing on her own, she'd have a fighting chance." She shakes her head.

Janie turns to face me. "Did you hear that? She's getting worse. We have to do something."

I can't do this right now. My head pounds and I really might vomit.

"You don't remember, do you?" Janie's eyes are so serious, so sad.

I shake my head. I should be annoyed. Of course I don't remember; I have no idea what she's talking about. But I'm more focused on not getting sick. I take deep breaths, but still my mouth waters and I feel like I'm losing this particular battle. To make everything worse, I can tell by the way my best friend cocks her head at me, the way she straightens her spine before speaking, that she knows something, something important about me and the lost days after the accident.

"You've been carrying around a notebook. Writing stuff in it. Ring any bells? I found it after . . ."

"Stop. Please." Because I don't want to know. I really don't. Something happened over the past few days. Something awful and strange and unbelievable and I don't want to think about it. I don't want to try to understand it. Because once I ask the question, I might be faced with an impossible truth. And I try to avoid those. The only thing I want right now is to go home and pick up my life exactly where I left off.

So I pretend not to notice how disappointed Janie looks when I interrupt her again and demand that she keep pushing me the hell out of this place. As soon as we exit the front doors of the hospital and I see my parents waiting to take me home, I know it was worth it.

I jump out of the wheelchair and thank God I'm a Graham.

thirty-five

I'M ANTSY IN THE BACK SEAT THE ENTIRE WAY HOME. MY MOM LOVES any excuse for a party and knowing her she's probably planned something ridiculous to welcome me home like when I had my tonsils out in fourth grade. They invited over one hundred kids, and there was an ice-cream truck and pony rides and a ridiculous pink, tonsil-shaped cake that no one ate because it kind of looked like a vagina. Even though I could barely talk, I remember being so proud that my parents loved me enough to prove it.

I hold my breath when we approach our street. My mother types a message into her phone, probably warning the crowd that we're coming. I hope my parents didn't go too crazy this time. They have the tendency to invite the entire world to these things, and today it would be nice to have something a bit more intimate.

I have to admit, I'm a little surprised that Zach didn't come visit me in the hospital. We never miss an opportunity to post something adorable, and what could be better than my boyfriend feeding me ice chips or something? Or wheel-chair races. Or us playing doctor.

But I'm sure he's texted. Maybe he just wants to surprise me once I'm home. My phone was smashed in the accident, and I keep reaching for it like some kind of tic. My mom promised me a new one and I feel twitchy just thinking about all the missed messages that must have piled up over the past couple of days.

I crane my neck to look out the window, checking for cars. I'm sure that's why Janie was acting so strange back at the hospital. It must have been awkward for her to pretend that she knew nothing about my party. But the streets are empty, and when we pull up to our house, the garage is closed. The windows are all dark.

And I have to give my mom credit. She's really going for it this time. It's one thing to throw your daughter a welcome-home party after a short stay in the hospital, but it takes a certain *je ne sais quoi* to pull off a legitimate surprise.

The second the car stops in the garage, I throw open my door and run into the house. I can't wait to see my friends. I feel like it's been months since I've seen them. I need Brooke's stream-of-consciousness catch-up since Janie is acting like a capital *B*. I want every piece of juicy gossip, but also the random, mundane details no one else ever cares about. I want it all. I miss Zach. I miss everyone's easy assumptions, my purpose and place in the pecking order. I need that so badly right now . . . and Jake. I need him too. But for different reasons entirely.

I'm smiling like a freak when I run into the house. So much for the surprise. Whatever. Is anyone ever really surprised at these things? I dash into the dark kitchen and brace myself for the onslaught of voices that no matter how much you prepare yourself for still scare the shit out of you.

My smile wavers.

Because the kitchen is empty. The house is dark. Nobody's jumping out and yelling surprise. In fact, it smells like dead flowers and there are dirty dishes near the sink.

"Hello? We're home. . . ." I still expect someone to throw their arms around me, but when the door slams behind me, it's only my parents.

"Did you need something, honey? I thought I heard you call out." My mom slides the hair back from my forehead, and I lean into her for a minute. My parents either think I'm too traumatized for a welcome-home party or they invited my friends and no one bothered to show up. I'm honestly not sure which scenario is worse.

"Can I have my new phone, please?" I hold my hand out and my parents exchange concerned looks.

"Honey, the doctors suggested we ease back into things. . . ." She cuts herself off as my father inhales sharply.

262

"What your mother is trying to say, honey, is that we'd like you to get acclimated before jumping back into things . . . socially. . . ."

"But Zach . . . ," I start.

"Can wait," my mom says with finality.

Before I can press them any further, the doorbell rings. I dash through the hallway before they have the chance to stop me. Through the glass, I glimpse a gigantic bouquet of sunflowers. I can't quite see his face, but I'm sure it's Zach. Yes, I already feel something.

I fling open the door and the flowers move aside. But I don't see Zach's perfectly styled hair or warm eyes. Instead I see Landon Crane.

"What do you want?" The aggressive words don't quite match the tears gathering in my eyes. What the hell is happening to me?

"I . . . just . . ." I've never seen Landon Crane blush. At least not since he was five or so. It's even less cute now than it was then. "I know how we left things but I'm serious about calling the police. I found her dad. He's here, Sophie. Dr. Edward Dowling . . ."

Without thinking, I slam the door in his face.

As I walk upstairs, I hear Landon ringing the doorbell repeatedly, calling for me, his voice muffled, and I could swear he says something about bringing me another scone. I let out a little snort. Now I know he's crazy.

thirty-six

MY ALARM CLOCK GOES OFF AT FIVE A.M. AND WITHOUT MISSING A beat, I'm up and out of bed. I take my time in the shower. It's so nice to be back in my own bathroom with all of my favorite products. I linger over the rose-scented shampoo and treat myself to my favorite exfoliator. I just want to be perfect today so I can forget all the weird stuff from the hospital. Maybe if I can start looking normal on the outside, I'll start feeling normal on the inside.

It takes me almost an hour to style my hair, pick out the perfect outfit, and apply the kind of minimalist makeup that's supposed to make you worthy of the iwokeuplikethis hashtag. If I'm going to talk my parents into letting me back into my old life, I'm going to have to look exactly like my old self.

My mom loves telling me that you don't get what you wish for, you get what you work for. Well, today, I'm ready to work it.

I know that I'm going to get my way when I sit down at the breakfast table and my mother takes one look at me and dissolves into a puddle of tears. "Oh, honey, I'm sorry. I don't know what's come over me, but it's just such a relief to see you looking like yourself again."

Forty-five minutes later, I'm breezing through the front doors of Morristown High School and I can't wait to see everyone. Janie always teases me for my incurable FOMO and she's totally right. I hate missing stuff. I hate not being in the middle of everything, the girl who everyone loves. The one who's never left behind.

Honestly, the whispers don't surprise me. They're a fact of life. It's the pointing, it's the averted eyes, and more than anything else, it's the silence that terrifies me. Janie and Brooke aren't waiting for me by my locker, no one calls my name from across the hallway, no one even bothers to smile in my direction.

I walk to Zach's locker. If there's anyone I can count on, it's him. It might not feel as perfect as it looks, but now, more than anything, I need him. Sure enough, he's standing with his back to me, and I can't stop myself from wrapping my arms around his waist. In spite of everything that's changed over the last few months, all the growing apart and tense conversations, I want to feel close to him again. We can start over. And maybe this time we can do it right.

When I settle the side of my face in the nook of his back where it fits perfectly, he completely tenses up. Oh my God, I've made a mistake. I've hugged the wrong guy. Did he change lockers? My cheeks are on fire as I pull away, but then he turns around.

"Hey, Sophie. Glad you're okay." Zach slams his locker door shut without even looking me in the eye.

Pain explodes in my chest and for the first time since I woke up, I feel like I might have an actual breakdown. Zach has always been there. Sure, things have been a little weird between us, but that's how relationships go. Everyone has their issues. We can figure them out. What could I have done that was so awful? Did something happen with Jake? Did he find out?

My head is spinning, but more than anything, I'm pissed. "Really? That's it? That's all you have to say to me?"

"Yeah, I guess it is. I mean, you have Landon Crane now, right?"

"Landon? What are you even talking about?" Truthfully, I'm starting to have a pretty good idea, considering Landon showed up at my house with flowers yesterday, but I'm choosing to ignore that minor detail because I firmly believe that if I don't think about it, it never really happened.

"Look, Sophie. What you've been through is awful. I get it. And I cared about you, but I meant what I said in the car. We're done."

Cared. Past tense. Done.

"What you said in the car? I mean, I don't remember any

of this. Can you please just tell me . . . ?" I grab his hand.

And he shakes it off.

"I'm sorry, but I can't. Not now." Zach turns and disappears into the crush of students buzzing around the hallways. My eyes scan the crowd for Janie and Brooke and their endless questions and worries. Or even Jake—my mom is supposed to be at Pilates and it wouldn't be the first time we've snuck back to my house for some extracurricular activity together during school hours.

But there's no one there. Not even a friendly face or a curious acquaintance. I realize all at once that there's nothing here for me. My life as Sophie Graham is over.

I walk right back out the front door.

thirty-seven

WHEN I GET HOME, I DO WHAT ANY MATURE, SEVENTEEN-YEAR-OLD gifted student would do after she finds out that everything she's worked so hard for has suddenly gone up in smoke. I lock myself in my room and refuse to come out for the rest of the day.

My mom stands on the other side of the door for hours, pleading with me to let her in. To talk to her. To explain what happened. But I can't do it.

Eventually she gives up. And the house goes silent and I'm left with nothing but my mixed-up thoughts.

Before the accident, I could tie my life up in a perfect bow. I knew how to loop my parents around, my friends, even Jake. I knew how to twist tennis and tighten school. I needed Zach as the knot. It wasn't always perfect, it never is, but you can't have the bow without the knot. I never meant to hurt him, to have him find out. I never meant for Jake to even happen, if that's what this is all about. I knew we'd figure things out, that one day we'd be on the same page. It kills me to wonder if we'll ever have that chance. I can't even consider how Landon is involved. I haven't thought about him since sixth grade.

Someone knocks so softly that, for a minute, I'm sure I must have imagined it. I open the door more out of curiosity than anything else.

It's Janie.

"Your mom called me. I'm sorry I wasn't there today, I'm just not sure what to do, Soph."

"Whatever." I feel the anger bubbling up in my chest. She should have been there for me. Janie of all people. She's my person and she disappears because of some stupid fight we had while she was pushing me in a wheelchair. Screw that.

She pulls a spiral notebook out of her bag. "I'm sorry. Really. I am. But you need to read this." Janie hands me the notebook, her eyes pleading.

Part of me wants to slam the door in her face, but it's Janie. She's practically my sister. I take the notebook from between her fingers. Somehow I'm not surprised when I flip open the cover to see that almost every single page has been filled with my loopy, familiar script.

There are pages of lists with words that make no sense to me. There are letters. And there are stories. I skim through all the names and memories, words like *Mae* and *St. Anthony* and *house angel* dancing off the page. Unfamiliar people and locations, as out of place as a discordant note in a symphony.

The words begin to blur together, and my head starts to spin. Something is wrong. I'm missing something. Something I once knew, something I still know but can't quite reach.

Until I see it on the last page, written so small that I have to squint to make out the words.

I am Amelia Fischer

thirty-eight

"WHERE DID YOU FIND THIS?" I ASK, GRIPPING THE NOTEBOOK TO MY chest like the words might slip right down the pages, bleeding ink onto my hardwood floors.

Janie hesitates. "You've been writing in it constantly over the last few days and I knew when you were in the hospital the second time, you wouldn't want your parents to see. I found it in your car. Sophie, you told Landon and me that you saw someone there, trying to take Amelia. The night of the accident."

I shake my head. This can't be happening. It's too much. None of it makes sense. "So, I got in an accident, I hit my head and woke up as Amelia?" I realize I'm whispering now, because how could those words ever be truly spoken aloud?

"I think so." There's a note of awe in Janie's voice. "I

mean, how else could you have known this stuff? I read it like a million times and it doesn't even sound like you, Soph. You were different. I can't even explain it, but I think it's true."

Am I losing my mind? Is this all some sort of weird hallucination caused by too much stress and too many hits to the head?

But somehow the notebook between my fingers feels like a lifeline. I sink back to the floor and run my fingers over the words, letting color spread to all the white space in my memory. There's the date of the accident, *September 19*, and I hear pounding rain, feel a hand around my arm, the palpable threat. It's fuzzy and distorted and feels so completely wrong.

There are observations about my life, secrets on the page written out in my perfect script.

Birth control hidden in doll. Respect. Also, not taking them.
Sorry?
Sophie cheating on Zach with JAKE.

And then, in the middle of a crowded page:

Mrs. Graham=DOCTOR Graham. Mr. Graham NOT
HER DAD????

Wait, what? I have to read it again because it can't possibly be true. My father can be distant and awkward, but he's definitely my father. And my mother a doctor? There's absolutely no way. If any of this were true it would mean that my entire life is a lie. These are the ramblings of a crazy person, not facts.

But then the notebook is filled with truths that only I would know and observations about my life that I've always taken for granted. The stilted relationship between my parents, saying good-bye to Grandma Hazel, spin the bottle in Landon's backyard, meeting him for the first time. It's all there and it all somehow adds up to someone who looks like me but doesn't quite feel like me. It's like seeing my life in a fun-house mirror—I know it's mine, but it looks twisted and wrong from this perspective.

And when I read the words again and again and again, the shock of them starts to wear off and I see a strange truth between the lines. My father is so demanding and oddly critical of me. And the dynamic between my parents is off—my mother always seems to be trying to make everything perfect for him, for us. And she is kind of a whiz with medical stuff. I remember her grilling my doctors about tests and treatment options and the pros and cons of surgery when I had to have my tonsils out, if I skinned my knee, twisted my ankle. I guess I never really considered it odd that she used a flashlight to look down my throat if it was sore, that she never panicked if I had a fever. I thought all mothers behaved that way. Suddenly the notebook doesn't seem so crazy.

And then there are the names. *Jenna Elizabeth Dowling. Haylee Morgan Dowling. April Nicole Dowling. Dr. Edward Dowling.*

Amelia Fischer jumps off the page of the notebook and the reality of what has happened to her, to us, hits me in a way I can't possibly begin to explain or understand. But I can't deny the collision.

I look back down to the notebook in my lap. Her mom was lying to her all these years, pretending to be someone she wasn't, moving them around, running from the police. And now it's finally caught up with her. Dr. Dowling came back for his girls and it's my job to reunite them. Maybe that's why all this happened.

But if I'm here—back in my life, in my body—does that mean Amelia is back in hers? Stuck in a coma with no way out? Is that where I spent the time that she was me? I have so many impossible questions and no answers. The words are noise, screeching and ugly, and I press my fingers to my ears to block it out.

"Sophie? Sophie?" Janie's voice softens the cacophony until it's nothing more than a dull hum. "I shouldn't have given you this. It was a bad idea." Her face comes into focus. She's red-cheeked and glassy-eyed, as though she might burst into tears.

I need to pull it together.

"No. No. I'm fine." I clutch the notebook to my chest. "I just need some air. Can you open the window?"

She rushes to a window and pushes up dutifully. I breathe in the fresh air and try to wrap my brain around where to go from here. Janie sits next to me on the edge of the bed.

"What now?" she asks.

"We have to save them." The moment I say the words, I know that's exactly what I need to do.

If only I knew how.

thirty-nine

THE SHADOWY MEMORIES BEGIN TO CRYSTALIZE IN MY BRAIN. I WAS Amelia Fischer. We shared a respirator, IVs, a hospital bed. I heard her mother's whispered pleas for forgiveness. I felt her father's hand on her forehead while he talked endlessly about his lost girls and St. Anthony, who had finally helped him find them.

I was Amelia Fischer. And now we share an unspoken promise to finish what she started.

"How could it possibly be true?" I ask, looking to Janie, grateful that she's here, a witness. I never could have absorbed this information alone without breaking down completely.

"I don't know. But there's no way you could have written some of the stuff that's in that notebook and I'm honestly not sure there's any other explanation."

"But why?" I guess that's the other thing bugging me. If I'm actually going to accept the fact that I switched bodies with Amelia Fischer, I need to understand why it happened. Yes, there was the accident and maybe some weird psychic energy transported us. But there has to be a *reason*.

"Well, you were both born in Baltimore, at the same hospital, it looks like. Maybe there's something there."

"Yeah, maybe, but our birthdays are like months apart. I just feel like there has to be some other reason. Something important."

Janie and I both jump up when we hear the clinks of pebbles against my window. When we get to the window, we see Landon Crane at the bottom, cheeks flushed, pacing.

We watch as he climbs the emergency rope ladder I have hanging off the side of my fake balcony. In fourth grade we had an assembly about fire safety and I couldn't sleep for weeks. I was afraid my fan would fall and start a fire or the furnace would explode or lightning would strike our house. My mom bought rope ladders for every room when I started having recurring nightmares about our house catching on fire. Unfortunately, ladders can't cure anxiety, but Lexapro can and did. Thank God. Once upon a time, Landon used the ladder almost every night so we could read comic books together under a blanket with flashlights, but now it's almost exclusively used by Jake. *Jake.* My stomach twists a little as I remember the way he avoided my eyes at school this morning and I'm pretty sure there's more to the story than what Amelia wrote down in the notebook.

And now Landon Crane, the human barnacle who refused to believe our childhood friendship couldn't survive middle school, is climbing into my bedroom just like he used to in fifth grade. My head might seriously explode.

"Oh look, the gang's all here," he says, folding his long body in half to climb through the open window. Janie and I roll our eyes in unison.

"Look, I'm sorry about yesterday," I begin. "I know things have been different since the accident, and I can't pretend to know exactly what's going on, but I need your help . . . still," I add, thinking about the journal and how much Landon has been involved. "I mean, Amelia needs our help."

He looks away. "Okay, whatever. I want to help her too. That's why I think we need to call the police and I just thought . . ." His voice trails off and for one horrible moment, I'm sure he's going to profess his love for me. And if he goes there, I can't be held accountable for my actions.

Janie must sense impending disaster, because she cuts in.

"Before we go to the police, we have to tell Mae. At least then she'll be prepared for what's next."

Landon gives me a long look and finally nods. "I guess I can live with that. I also found out a bunch of stuff about Amelia's dad, Edward Dowling. He's a doctor. In Baltimore. But it looks like he's been doing some mentoring at Marymount over the past month or so."

"Wait, so he's been working here? At the hospital?" I

think about the whispers I keep remembering and the shadow man Amelia wrote about.

"Yeah, he's a pretty well-known general surgeon, based on a couple of Google searches."

"Honestly, I'm shocked he hasn't gone to the police. Why all of this stalking?" I flip through the papers, looking for something that might explain his motives.

"Well, you said that you saw someone try to take Amelia, right? Maybe it was him."

Right. Where would we possibly be without the powers of Detective Landon's deductive reasoning? "Of course it was him," I say. *Jackass*, I think. "The question is why?"

"Maybe he didn't want to deal with the police until he knew for sure it was them?" Janie says.

"Yeah, maybe," I say. "Whatever his reasons, we have to get to Mae. She deserves to know the truth before her life gets turned upside down. Amelia would want it that way."

Landon gives me a strange look and I'm sure he thinks I'm crazy, but I'm equally certain that I'm past the point of caring. I just want to make good on my promise.

"Now I need to figure out how to get to Mae." Based on the fact that I've apparently been stalking these people, I'm fairly confident they have a restraining order out against me. "I could go back to their house?" It's the best I can do.

"I don't know. Given what we overheard yesterday, it sounds like Amelia isn't doing well. I think the hospital might be our best bet."

"Do you really think that's a good idea . . . ?" Landon's voice trails off.

"I'm open to suggestions, but it doesn't sound like you're willing to give any. Also, you need to leave. My mom will freak if she finds you here and then I'll be right back to square one." The hurt look on Landon's face reminds me of that horrible game of spin the bottle and the sick feeling of regret I tried to ignore after completely ditching him. I mean, it doesn't make sense at all for us to be friends; we move in different circles and we have absolutely nothing in common. "Thanks for all your help," I say to try to soften the blow, but he just rolls his eyes.

Well, at least I tried.

Landon Crane is the least of my worries right now. He can't possibly understand why this is all so important. If I finish what she started, Amelia Fischer might finally wake up.

forty

I THROW MY BOOK BAG ONTO THE EMPTY SEAT BESIDE ME, NOTE-book safely tucked inside. My seat rises and shifts forward until it clicks into the perfect position after I press start. The car is oddly silent and I really don't want to be alone with my thoughts right now. I'm afraid they'll make me lose my nerve. I press a button on my steering wheel and close my eyes for a second as the car floods with screaming guitars and shrieking voices, the only sounds that are ever loud enough to drown out all the self-doubt in my brain.

"Sophie? Where do you think you're going?" My eyes snap open and I see my mother sliding into the passenger seat, looking seriously annoyed and stabbing at random but-tons on the car radio to make the music stop.

For once, I say the first thing that pops into my brain.

"Who is my real father?" It's a dirty way to fight, but I don't have a lot of time. I had the bomb. I dropped it. There are worse things.

Her face goes completely white. "What? Sophie, I'm not sure why you think that, but . . ."

"Save it. I saw the test results. Does Dad even know?"

Her face collapses in defeat. "I . . . well, yes. He found out eventually. It was your eyes, really. You got them from your birth father."

She grabs my hands and pushes my hair out of my face.

"Is that what this is all about? Don't run away from me, Sophie. Let's sit down and talk. People make mistakes. I can explain. . . ."

I think of Zach and Jake and Landon and Amelia and a whole lifetime of mistakes. I've done so many things that I'm not proud of and I'm not even eighteen.

"I'm not going to be able to make you understand what I need to do right now, but I'm doing it. With or without your permission." In a weird way this feels like the first adult decision I've ever made. "Who was he?"

The words are out before I can stop myself from asking. My father is not my father and I know we can't really talk about it. Not now. But I still have to ask.

"No. Not until you're ready to really talk about this. Like adults." And then she reaches across the console and wraps her arms around me. "You underestimate me, Sophie. Go and do what you need to do. But come back home. Come back home and we'll talk."

I think back to what she said about mistakes and being old enough to make them. I've made mistakes. Lots of them. But maybe I can change. Maybe I'm different now. Maybe we all are.

"Okay," I whisper, leaning over to kiss my mother on the cheek. I catch a wave of her delicate perfume, the way it mixes with her tropical-smelling lotion. She makes me feel like it will be okay. And even if it's not, she makes me feel like it could be.

After I park my car in the visitors' lot of the hospital, I'm running with the notebook clutched to my chest. I don't have time to answer any more questions or use my manners or even stop and think.

Once I'm in the hospital, I focus on looking like I know exactly what I'm doing. I make my way up to the ICU where we saw the doctors talking yesterday, and I stop to take a long drink from the water fountain, praying that someone will come so I can get through the doors. Finally, a nurse walks up and uses her badge to open the doors, and I walk on through right behind her. It's a little disappointing how easy it is, but I shake my head to clear it. *Don't be stupid.* I'm in.

I've been here before, or part of me has, anyway. I'm struck by a whisper of déjà vu that under any other circumstances would have made me find the nearest chair to catch my breath. I've walked these tile floors, I've heard the hum and beep of these machines, the low murmur of voices at the desk. I know exactly where to go. The curtain to Amelia's section of the room is closed. Before I can stop myself, I pull back the fabric with authority and see exactly who I came to find. Mae is standing beside Amelia's bed, her eyes wide and confused.

And he's standing next to Mae, between his two daughters. I recognize him immediately somehow. Dr. Edward Dowling. His eyes flash to mine, angry at the interruption. I hold my breath because something is familiar about him, that weird tickle where it feels like you've met someone but you just can't place them. I know him. I must know him. But then I make the connection.

I don't know him. I know his eyes.

Even in the dim light, I notice that they're two different colors. One blue. One green. Just like mine.

forty-one

WHEN I WAS LITTLE I HATED MY MISMATCHED EYES. STRANGERS were always commenting on them and my mom was constantly flustered by their questions about whether they ran in our family. But as I got older I started to enjoy the attention around my eyes. They were so distinct, so *me*. And I guess somewhere along the way, I got used to them. Honestly I forget all about them until someone inevitably comments on their color.

But in all these years, I've never seen two different-colored eyes on another person. Seeing my identical eyes reflected back to me on someone else's face is surreal. I stare, mouth open, my mother's words ringing in my ears. *You have his eyes.* I hear Janie's voice. *You and Amelia were born in the same hospital.*

And I know, somehow, some way, that I'm looking into the eyes of my birth father.

I imagine those ladderlike genetic animations every science teacher talks about with more enthusiasm than I could ever understand. I see missing links and disconnected rungs, the secret code that ties all this together. This man is my father. Mae and Amelia are my half sisters. Nothing makes sense. Everything makes sense.

"Excuse me, the curtain was closed." It's his voice. The one from my dreams about when I was lost in the dark as Amelia. The one who whispered about lost girls and saints.

"Wait, Sophie!" Mae's voice pushes past the memory, shaky with desperation. It's the fear I sense trembling there that gives me the strength to walk into the tiny space.

"I, um, well, I found something that we think might belong to Amelia. I was just going to leave it for her." I hate myself for stuttering, but I hate myself even more for not being fast enough to stop this man, our father, from grabbing the notebook out of my arms.

I can't take my eyes away from his, and not just because of their similarity to my own, but because they're an angry bloodshot red.

"Sophie." Mae repeats my name like a warning, her eyes trying to tell me something. Did Dr. Dowling already tell her the truth about her mom? Is she panicked? Angry? Looking for me to rescue her from an awkward confrontation with a father she's never known?

Amelia's journal looks all wrong in his shaking hands,

and I can't help but notice how his skin is drawn too tightly across his cheeks. Does he know that he has another daughter too? Will he recognize me for who I am? I look down at my toes to be safe.

Mae is examining a silver necklace looped around her fingers. She looks so scared and alone that I reach out to grab her hand and she actually takes it.

"You're here to tell her all this? You're here to tell her the truth?" I don't risk looking at him as he speaks. Instead, I manage a tense nod.

His face breaks into a huge smile and he's completely transformed. "Oh my God. I can't, I mean, I can't thank you enough." His fingers reach for the medallion hanging around his own neck. "Haylee, honey, you have to see this. It's everything I was trying to explain to you. It's all here." He thrusts the book in Mae's direction and she takes it with trembling fingers. "Do you girls know who St. Anthony is?"

We both shake our heads. His intensity, the way he says his daughter's name, the crooked smile, it feels wrong. His eyes might be unnervingly familiar, but I can't find anything else there, no deeper, primal connection, no calming presence. His voice, the poem, the coins, and the desperate whispers that sliced through the darkness of Amelia's coma again and again, it all feels . . . broken.

"He's the patron saint of the lost." He reaches up and unclasps the chain from around his neck, his fingers running across the engraving on the coin. I bring my hand to my own neck. It might be bare now, but I can still feel the links that lay on the smooth skin, the coin that hung down the center.

"Every day, I prayed to him. I prayed for him to return my lost girls. The girls who could not be found." His eyes fill with tears as he walks toward Amelia's bed.

Her chest rises and falls thanks to the work of machines. He places the medallion around her neck, St. Anthony settling between wires.

"And he found them for me. He found my Jenna, my Haylee." He reaches out to grab Mae's hand. "But then . . . this . . ." He can't bring himself to finish the sentence. Instead he breaks down, sobbing over her body.

I look over at Mae, lost, but she looks like she might pass out. "I . . . I . . ." She takes a step back and sinks to the tile floor, cradling her head on her arms. If this moment is intense for me, I can only imagine how it must feel to her.

I am not equipped to deal with this. And while part of me wants to get the hell out of here, another part of me, the part I can't understand, is drawn to him, drawn to Amelia like a magnet.

Dr. Dowling lifts his head and wipes his eyes. "Will you pray with me? Will you pray for her?" He reaches his hand toward me and his voice is so broken, that indescribable force so powerful, that I can't refuse. I walk toward the hospital bed and before I can second-guess myself, I wrap my fingers around his and cradle Amelia's with my other hand.

The moment the three of us touch, my world explodes.

forty-two

SOMETHING'S BURNING. BUT IT'S NOT THE SMELL OF A CAMPFIRE OR blackened toast. It's the wrong kind of burning.

And there's screaming. At first it's piercing, but then it's muffled and stifled. And before I can stop myself, I'm screaming too and suddenly, he's lunging for me. His strange mismatched eyes burning with a fury I can't understand.

The walls crumple in as she tries to protect me, the side of her face an angry red, one eye swollen shut. The medallion he holds in his gloved hand glows fiery red and it burns brighter and brighter as it dances over the flame of a fat candle.

"You think anyone will ever believe you? With your history? Don't forget where you come from. No one else will. I know what you did to your stepfather. I know and once I tell them, you'll rot in jail." His voice leaves a different kind of scar.

Something clink, clink, clinks to the floor, and he swears, fumbling, vulnerable for the second it takes to find an opening. And we're scooped up.

She's running with both of us wrapped in her arms when there's usually only room for one. The sky is dark and there's only the sickeningly sweet smell of burnt flesh.

"Good girls, my good girls, my sweet girls." When we reach the car, she doesn't even buckle us into our car seats.

Fear hovers behind us, not in front of us. Where we've been. Not where we're going.

And I know. I know.

forty-three

IT FEELS LIKE MY SKULL HAS BEEN CRACKED OPEN LIKE AN EGG. THE pain is a lightning strike, a destructive web threatening to incapacitate my entire body. Through a fog of tears and this newly muted world, I watch Dr. Dowling touch his forehead, chest, and shoulders. The action looks all wrong, like he's got his fingers crossed behind his back as he prays to the wrong kind of God. Amelia thrashes on the bed below him, her fingers clawing at her neck as though she can't breathe, her eyes wild like an animal's. She's awake. He lifts his head to the ceiling, a silent celebration, before calmly disconnecting the girl from all the monitors and tubes and cords that have kept her alive against all odds.

First sound, then color returns. I wake up from the blurry nightmare to a crisp one.

Mae is huddled in a corner of the small room, black streaks down her cheeks, eyes wide. She shakes her head back and forth as though, like me, she can't possibly be seeing what she's seeing. My heart roars to life, thrumming in its cage. This cannot be happening again. He is not going to take Amelia. But still the clicks of switches punctuate the silence like gunshots.

I focus on Mae, repeat her name in my mind as though I'm screaming, because if I can switch bodies with one half sister, surely I can direct the other with my eyes.

"Let me help. . . . Dad. I want to get out of here." Her voice trembles with emotion and I hate how nothing works the way I need it to. They can't leave with this man. I can't let this happen.

But Dr. Dowling is already looking up from Amelia's bed, a manic smile pasted on his face.

"Go find a wheelchair for your sister, okay, honey? Let's get you girls home."

Mae rushes off, and I'm left alone with this monster. Every part of my body is screaming for me to run, to escape. The muscles of my legs tense. I'm ready to go when my eyes lock with Amelia's.

I recognize her fear, her helplessness, her panic. She's trapped. And I know I can't let this man take her away. I have to finally do something, anything to save her.

Without thinking, I launch my body toward Dr. Dowling, knocking him off-balance. For one amazing moment, I think I've actually stopped him, but then he laughs, like all five-foot-nothing of me trying to stand in his way is the funniest thing that's ever happened to him. He's still chuckling to himself when his forearm slams into my face. My cheekbone explodes in blinding pain.

A nurse rushes into the room, sees me on the ground, and shrieks in surprise. When she sees a doctor, her face relaxes.

"He's taking her! Help!" I scream.

Dr. Dowling raises his hands. "Karen, please call security. I found this young woman tampering with the equipment in this room, and it is no longer safe for this patient."

And then five words ring out across the ICU. Five words I will never forget. Five words that finally have the power to save Amelia Fischer's life for good.

"Police! Put your hands up."

forty-four

I'VE BEEN AWAKE FOR FOURTEEN HOURS AND THIRTY-TWO MINUTES, according to Mae. She hasn't left my side since they took our father away. The doctors say I'll be fine, but I think we're both worried that I'll slip back into the coma again if I fall asleep. And so we've been sitting here holding hands like we're little, talking and laughing and crying. Trying to make sense of our lives.

For a while it was just the two of us, but then my mom came back from the police station. Exhausted and scared, but somehow lighter than I've ever seen her. And then came Sophie and Mrs. Graham, awkward and reluctant to impose, but somehow unable to stay away. We form a loose circle.

"Once upon a time, there were two women," Sophie Graham eventually whispers, breaking the silence. I'm not sure what's more surreal, the fact that my mom, Mrs. Graham, Mae, and Sophie are all in the same room or the fact that Sophie Graham is telling me a story. I'm pretty sure it's a tie. "Neither of them knew the other, but they were connected. One was a nurse and one was a doctor."

"Studying to be a doctor," Mrs. Graham interrupts.

"Same difference," Sophie continues. "Every story has to have a villain, but ours hid it well. He was handsome and smart and wealthy. Like all villains, he preyed on the weak." Sophie glances at her mom and my mom and shrugs her shoulders. "Sorry, but it's true. Well, at least initially. Right?"

I sit up a little bit in bed because I know this story. It's been haunting us like a ghost with every move, just a little bit out of reach. I look to my mom and Mae, and my mom reaches for Mae's other hand so we're all connected.

My mom clears her voice. "Well, my story starts before this and the end won't make sense unless you hear the beginning." Mrs. Graham hesitates before reaching out to grasp my mom's hand. The contact makes her awkward; her chin lowers, her back hunches. "The police showed me your letter." She looks at me first and then Sophie because I guess it belongs to both of us now. "You were so close. So smart." She takes a breath for courage before continuing. "I hate to think about all the pain I've caused you girls every time we moved. But it couldn't have been any different. Lesser-of-two-evils sort of thing. When I was growing up, it felt more like we were running toward trouble than away from it."

Her eyes glisten as she remembers. "All the men were some form of bad, some worse than others. The longer they stuck around, the worse they got. When I was ten, my mom got remarried. I thought maybe it would be different this time because he wasn't just another boyfriend. I thought maybe getting married meant something more. But for my mom, it just meant she was more stuck. And I didn't have a choice."

Mae squeezes my fingers and I know my mom did the same to her. I think about that word: *choice*. Mae and I never had a choice when it was time to go, and the older I got, the angrier it made me. But there are all different sorts of choices. I know that now.

"The mean started slow. It always did. It was just words at first. And then the manipulation—accusations that started as lies, but somehow began to feel true so that when he finally started hitting us, it felt like our fault. He would drink and smoke and hurt. I would hide, but our house, if you could call it that, was never big enough. I dreamed of running away, but where would I go? My mom had no family I ever knew. It was just her and me. And him."

I'm not sure anyone's breathing while listening to her talk. I've never heard my mom say so many words. She feels like a complete stranger at the core of this circle of women.

"I lived that way until I was seventeen. I'd hidden enough money from my mom to leave and never look back. I remember wondering if I would miss her, if I could ever help her. Save her." Tears fall down my mom's cheeks and land on the sheets, leaving a circle that grows larger as I watch it. "She wasn't home at the time. I didn't leave a note because I didn't want her to try to find me, although it wouldn't have mattered anyway. He was on the couch passed out and I knew he'd kill her one day. I'd hear about it on the news. So I lit one of his cigarettes and I threw it on the floor beside him. The room went up fast, so fast I barely had time to get out. I left that night and started a nursing program. I buried my past and threw myself into work. I let myself forget. And then, almost five years later, I met someone even more broken than me. And I remembered. He felt like a second chance to make up for everything I'd done. But instead, I just ended up right back where I started."

We weren't moving, we were running. Mae and I could have been just like her. She could have been just like her mom. But she hid. She protected us. It was all for us.

Mrs. Graham reaches for Sophie's hand before picking up the story. "You have to understand that he was charming. And even though, at first glance, everything about him seemed perfect, there was something a little dangerous too. Something I thought I could fix. When you're twenty-something, finally away from your parents for the first time, and an older doctor pays attention to you, it matters. But I learned very quickly that he wasn't just another bad boy. He had problems that I couldn't even begin to understand. When I found out I was pregnant, I thought about telling him. I knew he was married and stupidly wondered if he'd choose me. But when I overheard a resident congratulating him on his wife's pregnancy, I knew I had to go. The day I dropped my classes, my advisor pulled me aside. She knew. It was like she sensed it. She gave me a tiny wooden house from her hometown with a slip of paper inside that said, *To help you find your way home.*"

"The house angel," Mae and I whisper in unison.

"Well, I took it as a sign," Mrs. Graham continues. "Instead of letting my parents drag me back to Chicago, I moved to Morristown and met a nice lawyer. I was lucky. I got away. And I got to keep you." She kisses Sophie on the cheek.

"The princess lost her happiness . . . and then came Sophie. . . ." I whisper, smiling a little at Sophie through the dim light. Mr. Graham told her the story as a child. The memory is wrinkled and frayed at the edges, but still there. For now. I consider Mr. Graham and his hollow veneer of perfection. I know he's a lawyer. I know he's Sophie's father. And yet there are other conflicting details and half truths that I've already lost, but still somehow feel, shadows of memories that haven't completely faded.

I reach for Sophie's hand and close the circle. If this were a movie, we'd see sparks or something. Instead, I just feel hope.

"I wish I could have warned you." Mrs. Graham's voice cracks as she looks at my mom with tears in her eyes.

She shakes her head. "I believed him." My mom shrugs her shoulders. "I wanted to believe he could get better, that we could be a family. I was so young. And he knew about my stepfather. He threatened me. And it almost worked. But then I had my girls." She looks between me and Mae, back and forth like it's the first time she's ever looked at us, like we're babies and not gangly teenagers. "I didn't have a choice. It was easier because it wasn't just about me." She smiles sadly. "Plus, I got my own sign. The day before we ran away for good," my mom continues, "someone left me a tiny wooden house at the end of my shift. I didn't recognize the handwriting, but the note said, *Everyone deserves a safe home,* and gave me a number to call day or night when I was ready to leave. I never did call that number, but the house became my talisman, a lifeline. There's an address of the historical home printed on the bottom and I remember running my fingers over the name of the city, promising myself that one day, when it was safe, we'd live there. Happily ever after. So I saved Morristown for last."

epilogue

I'VE LEARNED THAT MEMORY IS A FUNNY THING. WE ALL WALK around so confident in our memories, so sure of our past. But memories are alive. They live and they breathe. They're unpredictable, they burn and bend and break like unstable elements when exposed to hate or love or loss. And the truth is, memories can't be trusted, because memories lie.

The moment I opened my eyes to see my dad praying over my bed, the moment I saw Sophie Graham pale and shaking beside him, the moment I heard the hum of the machines, felt the cords and wires running like veins up my arms, I remembered. From long-buried memories of him hurting my mom, the rows of circular scars of the St. Anthony's medallion lining the creamy skin of her back, to my time spent as Sophie Graham. It was all there, with blistering, brutal honesty.

But it was like waking up from the kind of lifelike dream that you understand with perfect clarity. You think you'll always remember. After all, how could you possibly forget something so real, something so true? Then once you're awake, reality sets in, your day-to-day life is there, demanding to be lived, and slowly but surely, your dream fades into a whisper, a glimmer of something lovely and strange that you can't quite put your finger on.

I remember the gasp when I awoke in that hospital bed. I remember the panic of his hands ripping the cords off my body. I remember the way he lifted me off the bed like I was two years old again. I remember the police storming in with my mom on their heels. I might even remember a boy, skirting the edges and hanging back. And I definitely remember the relief of my mom's arms around me again, sure and strong and real.

But the longer I'm awake, the more my memories as Sophie begin to flutter away, like flower petals on a breeze. I would have gathered them up and held them close if I had known it was coming. But it's too late. Because they're all spread across my past now and as hard as I might try, you can't resurrect a flower from scattered petals.

I catch Janie McLaughlin looking at us sometimes. I know she's wondering if it's all true, if this all possibly could have happened, and I guess I can't really blame her. How?

Why? The questions hover like spirits whenever I'm with Sophie. Questions we'll never ask for fear of breaking their spell because it would be far too easy to explain away everything with car accidents and head trauma. And we know better.

"Amelia, can you come set the table?" my mom calls as she pops her head out the door. "Dinner's almost done."

The physical therapy really helped. You'd never know by looking at me that I survived a horrible accident. The other kind of therapist helps too. I understand now that I can't do this alone.

But I still have the dreams. They're filled with images of dark saints and hooded men.

I remind myself that we're safe now. Thanks to my sisters. The plural word still feels strange on my tongue, but it's true. They saved me. Mae rushed into the nurse's station and called for help and Sophie gave the police all the information they needed to take him in. They have Dr. Dowling in custody now, and they set the bail high enough that he'll have to stay there until his trial. I have to believe that after all this there will be justice. I have to believe we'll somehow get our happily ever after.

"Amelia, come on." Mae drags out every syllable of my name and I can't help but smile. It's crazy how even after everything changes, some things stay the same.

"Okay, okay. I'm coming."

I start to get up, but stop when I hear gravel crunching down our driveway. An old VW Bug rounds the bend slowly.

I don't immediately recognize the driver, but I'm charmed by his choice in cars, and I admire the way his thin T-shirt hugs the outline of his chest when he opens the door and gets out. There's something remarkable about the way his eyes crinkle at the corners when he sees me, and my stomach takes a little dip.

"Amelia?" His voice is shy, hesitant. "You probably don't remember me. . . ."

But then, suddenly, I do. It's him. The guy who was taking pictures for the paper at my tennis match. The one who lost his lens cap and ignored a thunderstorm to ask me about it. Landon. His name comes to me from the depths of my memory, even though I could swear he never introduced himself. Somehow Sophie has neglected to mention him.

"It's you."

He smiles then. "Yeah, I guess it is me." He brushes the hair away from his eyes. "I heard you were home and I . . . was thinking of going to the trail to take some pictures. Do you maybe . . . I mean, if you're not doing anything?"

I hesitate for a minute. I barely know this guy. What if we have nothing to talk about? What if it's awkward or forced or uncomfortable? There is so much uncertainty, so many unknowns. He shrugs his shoulders again when I don't answer right away, and I realize he's probably asking himself the same questions about me.

So I smile at him, because his eyes are still the most beautiful I've ever seen. "Actually, I have a better idea. We're just about to eat dinner, and my mom makes the most disappointing fried chicken you can imagine. There's actually a decent chance it gives you food poisoning. You should totally stay." I hold my breath as he considers my offer. It's kind of random to invite a complete stranger in for a dinner that's pretty much the culinary equivalent of playing Russian roulette, but somehow I can't resist.

"This is so weird, but disappointing fried chicken is like my favorite food." His lip twitches up in a half smile. "I mean, talk about an offer I can't refuse."

"Perfect. I guess I should probably warn you though, we have company."

And as if on cue, Sophie pops her head out of the front door. Her eyes roll automatically. "Ugh, Landon. I should have known you'd show up here at some point." But her smile sucks all the venom out of the words.

"If you guys want to eat," I say, "you better hurry. My mom's trying a gluten-free batch for Sophie and I can say with authority that you do not want this chicken getting cold." Before I can think twice, I grab his hand and pull him toward the door. When our fingers touch for the first time, I feel the glimmer of afternoons spent talking over gravestones and stolen moments in the front seat of his tiny car. My head spins with the rush of it.

"Oh, wait. I forgot something." He drops my hand and jogs back to his car and grabs something out of the front seat. It's a white box tied with a piece of string, and when he hands it to me, I can imagine exactly what he must have looked like as a little kid, right down to his sticky fingers and shy smile.

I can smell them before I see them. Six perfect orange scones.

"No one has ever brought me baked goods before." The truth slips out before I can bite it back. "I mean, usually my suitors try to woo me with expensive jewelry."

He laughs. "Right. I'll remember that for next time."

I open the door and run directly into Mrs. Graham. She takes one look at Landon and the box in his hands.

"Don't even think about bringing those scones in here, Landon Crane. I'm finally back on my cleanse." Even though she winks after she says it, I'm still only half-sure she's kidding.

I can't resist grabbing a scone; it's like biting into a dream. "Guess I'll have to take one for the team." The flaky citrus-flecked pastry brings a flash of a memory. The sun shining through a glass room, all filled up with pure joy. "I take it back. These are better than diamonds."

"Definitely. Besides, those crumbs all over your face are *super* elegant."

He brushes his fingers against my lips, and I should be embarrassed or terrified or probably some horrible combination of both, but I can't feel anything but this heart-pounding sense of anticipation.

Because this feels like something completely different, something special, something a little bit like magic.

acknowledgments

This book began with a very long phone call, as they all do, but would not have been possible without the endless support of our agent, Rebecca Podos, who saw promise from the very beginning. Enter Alex Arnold, whose editorial feedback and vision for *Now You See Her* pushed us to dig deep and then dig even deeper (and then again . . . and again) to uncover the best version of our story. A special shout-out to Katherine Tegen, Tyler Breitfeller, Stephanie Boyar, Katie Fitch, Rebecca Aronson, Kathryn Silsand, and the entire team at KT Books and HarperCollins Publishers. We know it takes a village to build a book and we're honored to have ended up in yours. We would never be where we are today without the guidance of our parents, who thought they were being practical by encouraging Lisa to minor in English lit and Laura to focus on middle childhood education and ended up with daughters who thought it'd be easy to write books. Insert eye roll here. Loretta, we are so appreciative of your generous encouragement through all our early drafts. You're also one of the smartest, strongest women we know. Thank you to our sister, Stacey, for suffering through read alouds of favorite chapters, our husbands for the space to be creative, and our kids for occasionally thinking it's cool that their moms write books. And there's no match for the creative energy harnessed during a wing happy hour in the company of strong women in a small town in the middle of Ohio. Sarah McCall, Sera Mathew, and Caroline VonVille, your invitation to the Perseverance Café inspired us to battle through a particularly grueling round of edits. We'll never forget the look of horror on so many conservative faces when you yelled, "Down with the Patriarchy" in our honor. This one's for you.